KENDRAI MEEKS

ISLE OF AFTER

ENTER THE KINGDOM
BOOK TWO

ISLE OF AFTER
Copyright 2022
Kendrai Meeks
ISBN: 978-1-953073-14-3

Cover: MIBL
Proofer: C.B. Moore Editing

Tulipe Noire Press
USA
tulipenoirepress.com

PRAISE FOR KENDRAI MEEKS

A charming adventure into the digital landscape, full of mystery and political intrigue. Complete with ALL the Cinderella tropes we each know by heart. For the tech savvy, there's plenty of IT-geared explanation to satisfy the reader who wants to know HOW it all works. Made sense to me, and my job is literally waging war in simulated environments.

-ROD A. GALINDO, AUTHOR

An exciting read I did not want to put down. Meeks has created an incredible worlds and explored the ramifications of what technology like this would cause - both in the gritty dystopian real world and the gilded virtual world. Lots of fun Easter eggs throughout. A rich plot with well drawn characters - the kind you love or hate, they might frustrate or infuriate you, but they are never bland.

-VINE VOICE REVIEWER MAJORIE

I absolutely loved this Cinderella retelling! Kendrai's version of this well known story is just brilliant. The way she weaves in parts of the original tale with this new one blows my mind. I was quite impressed that 2 wholly different story lines could have such similar foundations.

-THIS LITERARY LIFE

This book is dedicated fervently to Steve Harold, from whom I learned the value of hard work, the importance of humility, and the grace of forgiveness.

Love you always, Dad.

PROLOGUE

REX DIDN'T BOTHER TRYING TO HIDE. He respected his wife's intuition and intelligence far too much to try to lie. "Hello, dear. I thought I'd sneak down to the lab here while you were napping and look at this—thing you've been working on behind my back for the past few weeks."

He expected scolding. Normally kind Omala had a darker side when it came to protecting her tech. Luckily, he'd caught a break. His wife's mouth curled into a wicked smile, part admonishing mother and part coquettish playmate.

She stepped forward, wrapping soft fingers around the... whatever he was holding. "Are you trying to steal my trade secrets, Mr. Tieg?"

He cleared his throat. "Technically, because we're married and business partners, I'm only trying to steal your half of them."

She curled up on her tiptoes, pressing her lips to his. What might have been taken for the opening address of an invitation, however, quickly revealed its truth. The kiss was a distraction, and when Omala pulled back, the gadget went with her.

"I told you, I'll share anything that shows promise." She paced towards the cabinet with the door still open. "If I presented every fancy and failure to you, you'd see how big of a fraud I really am."

Hardly, and she definitely didn't think of herself that way. Maybe she wanted to be teased? He'd play along and see if luck was on his side.

Rex twined his fingers behind his back. "And which one is that?" His head bobbed to indicate the space on the shelf we're she'd stashed the prototype. "Fancy or failure?"

The corners of her mouth dropped. "Both, sadly."

Concern blew away his tickled libido. "I could reach out to some people in San Francisco, see if any of them could consult on a solution. That is, if you let me know a little about what you were hoping it would do."

"It was..." She turned scrutinous eyes on the gadget. "...an experimental jacking device."

Rex was forced to reexamine the contours of what he'd held just a few minutes ago. Rectangular and only the width of his palm wide, the dimensions were all wrong, not to mention the scale. Jackpods had to enclose their users, not to mention all their wires, chips, motherboards... Even the minimalist ones were the size of prison cots. What he'd seen only make sense if she was trying to jack a mouse into the vreal.

Omala continued. "My first concept called for it to be worn as a necklace or a comque. I even thought it might work in a shoe, embedded into the soles. Securest that way. On the body, but out of sight."

Rex tilted his head to the side. "That's, like, the opposite end of the body from where it needs to be. How would it read and write brain waves from the bottom of your foot?"

"And thus, my shortsightedness." Omala reached out, twisting her fingers in Rex's hair. "Maybe I should have consulted with you earlier and saved myself hours of fruitless research and development."

Rex Tieg was a lot of things, and that included being his wife's intellectual inferior. He was not, however, stupid. There was no way Omala would have gone as far as to build a prototype without a firm foundation in how it could function. The woman didn't doodle, she sculpted. His brain labored to solve the problem himself. It was such a big gulch between design and function he knew she would have had a plan to cross it. How would a jacking device worn under foot communicate with the brain up to two meters away?

A strong enough epsilon signal might do it, but the bandwidth it would have to produce would fry a human brain. It would need interlays with transmitters and translators. Maybe something physical? A wire that ran up the pant leg and back, nesting in a node hidden in the hair? But a wire exposed in that way would be too susceptible to pirating and environmental risk, not to mention damn inconvenient when using the bathroom.

Then, a tug of memory tapped. The man they'd talked to last year in Asia, an older biotech scientist who asked the young couple to just call him Dr. Sri... He'd mentioned something that might do the trick, but he'd also been a crackpot talking about silicone-grafted transponders. A way of connecting and interfacing immersive tech so seamlessly that the user could think his way through an application rather than rely on a complex super processor running some vreal to do it for him.

And Rex had his missing link in her design.

"Omala, please tell me your plan didn't involve using nanites injected into the bloodstream."

Her whole body seized. "If I don't speak, I can tell you nothing."

That was as close to a confession as he was going to get. Or, frankly, wanted. Sometimes the burden of knowledge was the knowledge itself.

"Nanobots are illegal, dear." The word came out bathed in a sarcastic tone. "Not to mention as expensive as hell and highly experimental."

"So was jacking into a vreal the first time. And self-driving cars. And using bio-print organs."

"You're only proving my point. A lot of people died in the development of each of those things."

Omala folded her arms over her chest. "And a lot more people have been saved by the perfection those early sacrifices allowed to develop."

Apparently, she'd made up her mind on the issue, and the gravity of the universe couldn't pull Omala away once that had happened.

He pushed fisted hands into his hips. "The King?"

Omala nodded. "I couldn't pay for them myself."

Of course, she couldn't. Gaia's launch and rapid adaptation had made them the most famous power couple in the world, but oddly, that status didn't come with a salary. Every bit that member nations paid in for access and upgrades rolled back into the startup and expansion costs. At Omala's insistence, she and Rex only drew enough compensation off the top to afford a modest living. Besides, why have a patron if you didn't call on his patronage? Andalusia's sovereign was eager to throw money at whatever Saint Omala wanted, all because Gaia had saved his country when on the brink of war.

"Do you have them here already?"

Omala drew in a deep breath through her nose, closed her eyes, opened them, and crossed to her own work area. From a small drawer, she pulled out a ballpoint pen. The antique-styled writing instruments were crude, but they did allow for a certain tangibility that working on a datapad did not.

Rex shook his head, narrowed his eyes. "What, are you going to draw me a map to where you hid them?"

Omala mastered condescension in her glare. "This is the injection device that was smuggled to me from Dr. Sri."

With equal parts excitement and foreboding, Rex snatched the "pen" and held it up to the light. He wasn't sure what he expected. A tiny, tubal aquarium maybe? Nanobots or nanites by definition were, well, nano. You couldn't see the tiny botics without a microscope. For some reason, Rex thought in a collective, they might be discernable. Instead, the container looked empty.

"It was only enough for two doses, and Dr. Sri had to find a way to package them that wouldn't raise attention." Omala said unprompted. "Customs wouldn't look twice at something as low tech as an ink pen, especially if it was functional." She took the instrument back, demonstrating in time with her explanation. "Do it once, the writing tip lowers. A second time, it goes away. But thrice in quick succession and—"

With a tertiary click, a tiny, metallic tube the length of a fingernail shot out the end of the device.

"Simple, but brilliant." Rex leaned over, his hands on his knees and one eye closed as the other squinted. "And still illegal."

"Not in Andalusia."

He side-eyed his wife and stood up at his full height. "I have a feeling the King would make murder legal to please you."

"No, he wouldn't, but he might issue me a pardon."

All thoughts of nanites forgotten, Rex pulled his wife into his arms and against his chest, her back to his front. He nuzzled into her throat. "I should be jealous, but I'm the one you said yes to."

She cooed and tilted her head to the side, giving his lips more ground for exploration. "I haven't said yes yet tonight, but I might, if you keep doing that."

Playful Omala. That was a side of the living saint not many people saw. Rex himself couldn't remember the last time she'd made an appearance. Omala's work was the third party in their relationship. Given the potential for it to make them god-shamingly rich, he supposed he shouldn't complain. All he had to do was convince his wife that it was okay to save the world and cash in on it, too.

"Something I have operates in a very similar way, Mala. Maybe we should go upstairs so you can click it three times and see what happens." Rex pressed a kiss behind her ear. Then, suddenly, he tensed, as the echo of what Omala had said a few minutes before hit. "You said it was only enough for two doses."

He felt his tension mirrored. Omala's hand, which had been reaching back to lace through his hair, froze. Her head hung forward. "Don't make me tell you this, pyar beti."

The passion that had filled him moments before burned to ash. Rex's hand grasped Omala's arm, swinging her around to face him. "Who?"

"I made certain there would be no harm to either of the—"

"Damn it, Omala!" She winced as his grip threatened to break her little sparrow bones. "Who?"

Even before she said it, even before her mouth began to move, Rex knew. "It was Cindira, wasn't it?"

A quivering lip and tiny inhale were all the confirmation he needed.

Tears were weakness. Crying was for fools. But rage could

be righteous. "You injected nanites into our three-year-old daughter?" He swallowed the cracking in his voice. "Without asking me first? Hell, without even telling me after?"

"I am telling you now."

"Only because I've learned to see around the corners you talk behind." His hands fisted, relaxed. Fisted, relaxed. Violence wouldn't undo what had been done. "You know the risk nanites pose. You've read the studies. Hell, you volunteered in the nursing facilities. It drives some people mad, Omala. The nanites get into the brain, they subvert healthy, normal functioning. How could you do that to our child?"

"I could do that because the research is incomplete." Her tone was as matter-of-fact as if she'd been giving him the current time and temperature. "Nanites form a symbiotic relationship with their host, but only in hospitable, evolving environments. All the test subjects to date have been adults, whose neural pathways were already well established. But a child—"

"Could become some kind of freak of nature!"

Omala cut off with his outburst. "Is that anyway to talk about your own daughter?"

"I wouldn't have to if you hadn't taken steps to make her into some kind of cybernetic guinea pig."

Pacing in place, Rex tried to shake out the consequences. They were as wide as the mountains and as deep as the abyss. Death, of course, though that was unlikely. There was a slight chance that Omala was right and a juvenile brain would grow to embrace the nanites, leading to some kind of specialized genius, but that risked drawing dangerous attention. If anyone back in the Pacific States found out, the consequences could be dire for two up-and-coming tech professionals. Omala was an idealist who presumed the potential of human kindness. The constantly shining spotlight blinded her to those working against her in the shadows below. People already whispered about Gaia's potential to usurp power from the very nations it helped to save. With a nanite-enhanced daughter...

"No one must ever know."

Omala's back went rigid. "But she will be—"

"NO ONE MUST EVER KNOW." He braced her arms, pressing to the point of pain. "Swear to me, Omala, that you won't tell anyone. Not even Cindira. Especially not Cindira."

"But to advance her abilities—"

"Don't you get it? She could be seized by Authority!"

Omala's face bleached of all color.

Finally, Rex reached her. "You probably could get away with murder here, Omala. The King buys into you being some kind of modern-day saint. But back home, she'd be seen as an engineered human. Oh, Authority wouldn't kill her, but even we would wish they had by the time they finished experimenting on her."

Omala turned her eyes to the floor. Slowly, then with greater speed, she nodded in agreement. "You're right. I didn't think that far ahead. I only thought about... It doesn't matter." Admonished, she lifted her gaze to meet his. "I promise, Rex, I'll never tell her. I'm sorry. I was just so inspired by the results I saw with the test subject. If only you could see what Paco's potential has become since the injection, you'd—"

"I don't want to know." Rex held up a hand, arresting her words. "Don't tell me. I want to be able to claim ignorance."

For once, Omala granted his wish the first time.

CINDIRA'S ENTIRE LIFE had been an exercise in invisibility. How had she suddenly become the most famous person in the world?

"Crazy times we live in."

Asla's comment, rhetorical though it was, still begged a response. Cindira drew in a deep breath, though the Public Health Department suggested against it, given the day's environmental conditions. Soon, there wouldn't be much opportunity to be outside, and she was going to take advantage of it now.

"The city's dangerous enough as it is. I've heard stories of what happened in 2109 when Hactiva stormed City Hall. How many innocent bystanders died in that?" Cindira shook her head. "I'm only sending you away in case there's some kind of uprising or military counteract like that again."

"You're only sending me away because you know more about what happened last week than you're letting on."

The young woman turned wide eyes on the nanny, but Asla remained nonplussed.

"Don't worry," she said. "I'm not going to ask. That way, you won't have to answer. Because I know you would answer me, and then what would be the point of me leaving and taking all your secrets with me?"

Cindira's lungs burned, but not from the air. She realized suddenly she'd been holding her breath until the nanny had said her piece. She let it out in a long exhalation while shaking her head.

"If you wanted the truth, Asla, I'm not sure I could tell you. I'm fuzzy on the details myself. There's still a lot that doesn't make sense."

When the coder had returned to the vreal for the first time in fifteen years, saving the life of Gaia's reigning monarch hadn't been on the agenda. Taking on the Kingdom's state-of-the-art security bot and escaping alive? Not in her wildest dreams. No, Cindira's only concern had been investigating her father's disappearance. Sadly, she'd succeeded at preventing regicide but still had no clue about Rex Tiegs's whereabouts, or even if he was alive at all. Inside the Kingdom, she'd discovered his inactive avatar lying comatose, but what did that mean? And now, she was in an even worse position to solve the mystery than when she'd started. On the streams, in the streets, and around Plaxis's corporate office, people were placing bets on the identity of the elusive and daring hacker disguised as Omala Grover. Who could possibly have the kind of skills not only to crack into a Plaxis system, but then to show up at a royal ball, kidnap the prince at knifepoint, and get away with no one able to stop her?

Everyone had a favorite suspect. But without any leads in the investigation, the Authority were referring to her merely as "The Bandit." Possible charges included illegal hacking into a secure system, impersonating a dead avatar, and attempted vreal regicide. Forget the fact that Cindira had saved Prince Francisco Batista de la Reina's life, or that she hadn't been the one threatening him. For better or worse, the larger plot at play that night remained buried beneath the gossip.

That didn't mean she was about to overlook it, though. Sooner or later, someone would figure out who she was. Once that happened, she'd be powerless to help find her father, "fairy godmother" or no.

Asla tapped on her arm, bringing her thoughts back to the present. "You keep your confusions to yourself until they make sense. Don't sell your worries wholesale. Let them unravel only for you, so that nobody can twist and untie them for you, or more importantly, tie you up with them."

"Your metaphors are tying me up."

The old woman slapped her grown charge on the back of the hand. "Don't play smart with me, lass. I've been your nanny for twenty-five years, and I lived in that house with you and your mother for the first ten of them. Don't think I don't know what kind of woman she was, and what kind you are."

"I'm nothing like my mother."

"You're just like your mother."

A declaration, not open to interpretation. Cindira knew when to argue and when to cede a point to her superiors. Whether because they were right, or because convincing them otherwise would be only an exercise in frustration.

Asla continued. "She could have used everything she knew and everything she could do to bring the world the world to its knees or even just to become obscenely rich. But bless Omala's memory, she decided to lift the world instead. You're doing the same thing, in your way."

Cindira guffawed. "Auntie, I clean up dirty code and design fancy environmental skins for the obscenely rich. I'm not trying to save the world. I'm just trying to live in it and stay out of everyone's way."

You say that like a person who didn't just prevent an assassination, a little voice inside of her nagged. A little voice which Cindira dismissed, instead leaning forward to look up the street for the tiktok cab that was supposed to have arrived already.

"That's all you've done so far, but you're capable of so much more." Asla stood in silence for a moment before shrugging to herself. "That's why she taught you everything she knew."

"Not quite everything."

Not a single mention of a pair of silicone slippers that allowed their wearer to toggle between the vreal and the real, for example. No explanation for why she was supposed to keep her mastery of Purusha Prime a secret. Growing up, Cindira hadn't known her mother's lessons would become a burden she'd alone would bear. Surely, she thought, a multi-billion crypto company couldn't function if only one of its founders had complete control over the foundation it was built upon. How many times had Cindira wished she could export her ability to think in code to others? Hell, she'd even grab a pen and paper and open a school, teaching them the old-fashioned way. Let others spend their hours sealing up the cracks in the code. Maybe then she wouldn't have to work such long hours for such little pay. (Being the CEO's daughter had some benefits, but compensation wasn't necessarily one of them.) She pictured for a moment an existence where the vreal had no influence, where every day wasn't lived in the shadow of her mother's legacy and her father's neglect.

Cindira sighed. Then again, without those abilities, could she have any hopes to do what she was about to? Her father had been missing for going on three months, all while his avatar lay comatose in the vreal. Any other coder wouldn't be able to use that truth to do much more than shrug. With any luck, she could use it as a starting point to discover what had really happened to him.

"I'm sorry it's taking the taxi so long to get here." Cindira side-eyed the childhood-nanny-turned-unlikely-auntie's derelict suitcase. "And I wish you'd have let me buy you a new bag."

"Didn't need it." Asla sniffed the air. "The movers took what little I had any interest in keeping yesterday. These are just a few trinkets I wouldn't have trusted to the parish priest."

Behind them, inside the fence perimeter, stood what had once been a pool house (back when outdoor pools were legal), now left nearly bare. Even though they'd lived in the shadow of the Tieg's palatial house since Cindira finished school and returned to the city, they agreed that the tiny two-bedroom structure had never been a home for either of them. Cindira considered it its own kind of pumpkin, a storage facility where they existed as utilitarian droids, called to service when convenient and necessary by the Tiegs. It had taken the movers less than two hours to wrap, pack, and load all their belongings into the cart: Asla's boxes, destined for a cargo transport heading east over land before hitting water on the opposite coast; Cindira's, into a storage unit outside the city limits, to be claimed at a yet undetermined date.

"If they don't hurry, you're going to miss your transport, and there's not another transcontinental one due until tomorrow." Cindira pulled up her comque and manipulated the interface. "I should have found a way to hire a private taxi. Maybe I can find one nearby who'd take a last-minute request."

"At the rates those pirates charge? I wouldn't hear of it. Besides, I know you must have spent most of your crypto already." She turned her head toward the girl, beaming with pride. "I know it was you paying my salary all the years I've been working in this house, cleaning up after your father's family's mess, and I know moving me off grid halfway around the world took even more from your paycheck."

Countryside living required a special permit, and they didn't come cheap. Centralized governments wanted their citizens in cities, where communal resources would be less stretched and where access to services could be streamlined. A country cottage in Asla's native Wales came with a substantial price tag. As did hiring one of the locals to check in on her nanny daily and make sure she had everything she needed.

"Oh, and there must be sheep! We had them when I was young and I used to love watching them, lying under a cloudy sky." Asla had worn a dreamy look on her face when they discussed the plan, followed immediately by a screwed-up expression that her wrinkles highlighted. "Though I can't say I care for the smell. But they'll make up for it with their wool."

Livestock needed food, care, land to graze... Every need, another permit. Not as expensive as a Rural Occupancy Voucher, but still... there were multiple sheep to consider.

"You knew?" Cindira blinked in her surprise. "Auntie, I hope you don't think—"

"Don't go into some kind of long-winded explanation about how you don't want me to think it was charity or pity," the old woman said, cutting her off. "I never have. That's what grace means, child: to accept the kindness of others without letting it belittle you. Besides, I earned every bit of crypto cleaning up Kaylie's bathroom. I'm only sorry I didn't have the courage until now to thank you for what you did."

"I—"

Cindira swallowed her emotions. If she cried now, she didn't know if she could stop. Her needs had always been met: food, clothing, shelter, education. The only desire she'd ever had was a loving family. For years, Asla had been that family. In the tumultuous days after Omala Grover's death, the nanny had been the one to stroke her hair and tell her the hurt would pass in time. When Rex had forced Cindira to move in with him and his new family, the manipulative Johanna and her terrorizing twins, Kaylie and Cade, it had been Asla who comforted her tears. And after the family had shipped Cindira to a boarding school in Andorra for her remaining childhood years, it had been Asla always at the transport dock, waiting to welcome her back during breaks and over the summer.

Finally, a vehicle in the shape of a giant wheel the height of a grown man turned up the drive. In its center, a cabin just big enough for two occupants and their bags. The self-automated vehicle kicked out temporary docking pads as it slowed to a stop before them. Cindira leaned in, pressing her comque to the gray sensory panel, verifying that she was the booking party. Two soft beeps sounded in confirmation before the side of the cab nearest the sidewalk pivoted, allowing access.

The smell that wafted out served as a sampling of city life: smoky air, dirt, and something slightly acidic. As the cheapest form of regional transportation, tiktoks had been the savior to the drunk too plastered to walk or navigate home for decades. Though usually, the transports that served the city during the day were tolerable enough.

Asla looked back over her shoulder at the gate they'd already locked. "Tell me again why you're not staying here after I leave? It is such a nice little place, even if it is in the harpy's backyard."

A tiny laugh escaped before Cindira could stop it. She slapped a hand over her face. "I'm not sure that's true." She hoped her well-rehearsed response would satisfy. "It's simple: because I'm twenty-eight years old and it's time for me to grow up. I have to make a life"—and maybe even someday, a family—"of my own."

"You're not lying to me, but you're also not telling me the truth." Asla used her free hand to take up Cindira's assistance to step into the cab. "How many times have I told you I despise thespians?"

What was she supposed to say, that she could no longer tolerate living on the same property as the woman responsible for her mother's death? Or worse, that to try and save her father, Cindira had agreed to work with Johanna in secret, supposedly to open the source code and deliver it to whomever was keeping her father prisoner? If Asla knew the truth, she'd never leave. Maybe there was a way to say more, though, without saying anything at all.

"Because I'm about to do something that's going to tick off a lot of people, dangerous people, and it's especially going to make Johanna insane. I don't want you anywhere in the vicinity if there are any ramifications."

"Ha! Now, that's something worth leaving for." Asla stopped, and when she looked up, all the humor was gone from her face. "Your father. He's not just gone on a business trip all this time, is he?"

There was no use in towing the company line on this one. Even casual members of the press had begun to wonder why Rex Tieg, world-famous entrepreneur and man-about-town, hadn't been seen in the city—or anywhere else—since his Asian trip two months ago. Plaxis stock sank as the rumor mill geared up, something Johanna had already expressed her frustration over as "reorganizing" several underperforming units.

Jeffrey Mackey hadn't made it back into the line-up when the "Kitchen's" cupboards had been restocked.

Cindira bit her lip, trying not to focus on the loss of an ally, especially when she had so few. It only compounded her father's predicament, not to mention her own. Mack wasn't dead, he was just laid off. He was a talented coder and a hard worker. If Tagentry, Plaxis's primary rival, had any smarts, they'd snap him up in a second.

And if you were smart, you'd follow him there and try to put any connection with Plaxis behind you. People as connected as him don't just disappear in this day and age. Your father is probably dead. Do you want to join him?

The little voice in her head, made bold since daring to kidnap the Prince of Gaia inside the Kingdom, picked up in volume. It had been doing that more and more lately, and Cindira didn't know whether it thrilled her or scared her to hell.

"No, he's not just on a business trip," Cindira admitted. "But I'm going to look for him. Even if we barely spoke, he's still my dad."

Asla chewed on the statement before her jaw squared. Her head gave a speedy nod. "Then I have no fear for Rex's fate. Even if I had wanted to knock that blockhead's hair implants from his skull for years for the way he treated you, I wouldn't want anything truly bad to happen to him."

Cindira put the old woman's bag on the floor of the cab before crawling in beside her. She'd see her off, assure she'd made the flight. "And Johanna?"

Asla's smile sparkled like that of a mischievous child. "Perhaps best if I don't say. At least until I'm safely outside of the city and halfway across the Atlantic."

ONE

CINDIRA'S ENTIRE LIFE had been an exercise in invisibility. How had she suddenly become the most famous person in the world?

"Crazy times we live in."

Asla's comment, rhetorical though it was, still begged a response. Cindira drew in a deep breath, though the Public Health Department suggested against it, given the day's environmental conditions. Soon, there wouldn't be much opportunity to be outside, and she was going to take advantage of it now.

"The city's dangerous enough as it is. I've heard stories of what happened in 2109 when Hactiva stormed City Hall. How many innocent bystanders died in that?" Cindira shook her head. "I'm only sending you away in case there's some kind of uprising or military counteract like that again."

"You're only sending me away because you know more about what happened last week than you're letting on."

The young woman turned wide eyes on the nanny, but Asla remained nonplussed.

"Don't worry," she said. "I'm not going to ask. That way, you won't have to answer. Because I know you would answer me, and then what would be the point of me leaving and taking all your secrets with me?"

Cindira's lungs burned, but not from the air. She realized suddenly she'd been holding her breath until the nanny had said her piece. She let it out in a long exhalation while shaking her head.

"If you wanted the truth, Asla, I'm not sure I could tell you. I'm fuzzy on the details myself. There's still a lot that doesn't make sense."

When the coder had returned to the vreal for the first time in fifteen years, saving the life of Gaia's reigning monarch hadn't been on the agenda. Taking on the Kingdom's state-of-the-art security bot and escaping alive? Not in her wildest dreams. No, Cindira's only concern had been investigating her father's disappearance. Sadly, she'd succeeded at preventing regicide but still had no clue about Rex Tiegs's whereabouts, or even if he was alive at all. Inside the Kingdom, she'd discovered his inactive avatar lying comatose, but what did that mean? And now, she was in an even worse position to solve the mystery than when she'd started. On the streams, in the streets, and around Plaxis's corporate office, people were placing bets on the identity of the elusive and daring hacker disguised as Omala Grover. Who could possibly have the kind of skills not only to crack into a Plaxis system, but then to show up at a royal ball, kidnap the prince at knifepoint, and get away with no one able to stop her?

Everyone had a favorite suspect. But without any leads in the investigation, the Authority were referring to her merely as "The Bandit." Possible charges included illegal hacking into a secure system, impersonating a dead avatar, and attempted vreal regicide. Forget the fact that Cindira had saved Prince Francisco Batista de la Reina's life, or that she hadn't been the one threatening him. For better or worse, the larger plot at play that night remained buried beneath the gossip.

That didn't mean she was about to overlook it, though. Sooner or later, someone would figure out who she was. Once that happened, she'd be powerless to help find her father, "fairy godmother" or no.

Asla tapped on her arm, bringing her thoughts back to the present. "You keep your confusions to yourself until they make sense. Don't sell your worries wholesale. Let them unravel only for you, so that nobody can twist and untie them for you, or more importantly, tie you up with them."

"Your metaphors are tying me up."

The old woman slapped her grown charge on the back of the

hand. "Don't play smart with me, lass. I've been your nanny for twenty-five years, and I lived in that house with you and your mother for the first ten of them. Don't think I don't know what kind of woman she was, and what kind you are."

"I'm nothing like my mother."

"You're just like your mother."

A declaration, not open to interpretation. Cindira knew when to argue and when to cede a point to her superiors. Whether because they were right, or because convincing them otherwise would be only an exercise in frustration.

Asla continued. "She could have used everything she knew and everything she could do to bring the world the world to its knees or even just to become obscenely rich. But bless Omala's memory, she decided to lift the world instead. You're doing the same thing, in your way."

Cindira guffawed. "Auntie, I clean up dirty code and design fancy environmental skins for the obscenely rich. I'm not trying to save the world. I'm just trying to live in it and stay out of everyone's way."

You say that like a person who didn't just prevent an assassination, a little voice inside of her nagged. A little voice which Cindira dismissed, instead leaning forward to look up the street for the tiktok cab that was supposed to have arrived already.

"That's all you've done so far, but you're capable of so much more." Asla stood in silence for a moment before shrugging to herself. "That's why she taught you everything she knew."

"Not quite everything."

Not a single mention of a pair of silicone slippers that allowed their wearer to toggle between the vreal and the real, for example. No explanation for why she was supposed to keep her mastery of Purusha Prime a secret. Growing up, Cindira hadn't known her mother's lessons would become a burden she'd alone would bear. Surely, she thought, a multi-billion crypto company couldn't function if only one of its founders had complete control over the foundation it was built upon. How many times had Cindira wished she could export her ability to think in code to others? Hell, she'd even grab a pen and paper and open a school, teaching them the old-fashioned way. Let others spend their hours sealing up the cracks in the code. Maybe then she wouldn't have to work such long hours for such little pay. (Being the CEO's daughter had some benefits, but compensation wasn't necessarily one of them.) She pictured for a moment an existence where the vreal had no influence, where every day wasn't lived in the shadow of her mother's legacy and her father's neglect.

Cindira sighed. Then again, without those abilities, could she have any hopes to do what she was about to? Her father had been missing for going on three months, all while his avatar lay comatose in the vreal. Any other coder wouldn't be able to use that truth to do much more than shrug. With any luck, she could use it as a starting point to discover what had really happened to him.

"I'm sorry it's taking the taxi so long to get here." Cindira side-eyed the childhood-nanny-turned-unlikely-auntie's derelict suitcase. "And I wish you'd have let me buy you a new bag."

"Didn't need it." Asla sniffed the air. "The movers took what little I had any interest in keeping yesterday. These are just a few trinkets I wouldn't have trusted to the parish priest."

Behind them, inside the fence perimeter, stood what had once been a pool house (back when outdoor pools were legal), now left nearly bare. Even though they'd lived in the shadow of the Tieg's palatial house since Cindira finished school and returned to the city, they agreed that the tiny two-bedroom structure had never been a home for either of them. Cindira considered it its own kind of pumpkin, a storage facility where they existed as utilitarian droids, called to service when convenient and necessary by the Tiegs. It had taken the movers less than two hours to wrap, pack, and load all their belongings into the cart: Asla's boxes, destined for a cargo transport heading east over land before hitting water on the opposite coast; Cindira's, into a storage unit outside the city limits, to be claimed at a yet undetermined date.

"If they don't hurry, you're going to miss your transport, and there's not another transcontinental one due until tomorrow." Cindira pulled up her comque and manipulated the interface. "I should have found a way to hire a private taxi. Maybe I can find one nearby who'd take a last-minute request."

"At the rates those pirates charge? I wouldn't hear of it. Besides, I know you must have spent most of your crypto already." She turned her head toward the girl, beaming with pride. "I know it was you paying my salary all the years I've been working in this house, cleaning up after your father's family's mess, and I know moving me off grid halfway around the world took even more from your paycheck."

Countryside living required a special permit, and they didn't come cheap. Centralized governments wanted their citizens in cities, where communal resources would be less stretched and where access to services could be streamlined. A country cottage in Asla's native Wales came with a substantial price tag. As did hiring one of the locals to check in on her nanny daily and make sure she had everything she needed.

"Oh, and there must be sheep! We had them when I was young and I used to love watching them, lying under a cloudy sky." Asla had worn a dreamy look on her face when they discussed the plan, followed immediately by a screwed-up expression that her wrinkles highlighted. "Though I can't say I care for the smell. But they'll make up for it with their wool."

Livestock needed food, care, land to graze... Every need, another permit. Not as expensive as a Rural Occupancy Voucher, but still... there were multiple sheep to consider.

"You knew?" Cindira blinked in her surprise. "Auntie, I hope you don't think—"

"Don't go into some kind of long-winded explanation about how you don't want me to think it was charity or pity," the old woman said, cutting her off. "I never have. That's what grace means, child: to accept the kindness of others without letting it belittle you. Besides, I earned every bit of crypto cleaning up Kaylie's bathroom. I'm only sorry I didn't have the courage until now to thank you for what you did."

"I—"

Cindira swallowed her emotions. If she cried now, she didn't know if she could stop. Her needs had always been met: food, clothing, shelter, education. The only desire she'd ever had was a loving family. For years, Asla had been that family. In the tumultuous days after Omala Grover's death, the nanny had been the one to stroke her hair and tell her the hurt would pass in time. When Rex had forced Cindira to move in with him and his new family, the manipulative Johanna and her terrorizing twins, Kaylie and Cade, it had been Asla who comforted her tears. And after the family had shipped Cindira to a boarding school in Andorra for her remaining childhood years, it had been Asla always at the transport dock, waiting to welcome her back during breaks and over the summer.

Finally, a vehicle in the shape of a giant wheel the height of a grown man turned up the drive. In its center, a cabin just big enough for two occupants and their bags. The self-automated vehicle kicked out temporary docking pads as it slowed to a stop before them. Cindira leaned in, pressing her comque to the gray sensory panel, verifying that she was the booking party. Two soft beeps sounded in confirmation before the side of the cab nearest the sidewalk pivoted, allowing access.

The smell that wafted out served as a sampling of city life: smoky air, dirt, and something slightly acidic. As the cheapest form of regional transportation, tiktoks had been the savior to the drunk too plastered to walk or navigate home for decades. Though usually, the transports that served the city during the day were tolerable enough.

Asla looked back over her shoulder at the gate they'd already locked. "Tell me again why you're not staying here after I leave? It is such a nice little place, even if it is in the harpy's backyard."

A tiny laugh escaped before Cindira could stop it. She slapped a hand over her face. "I'm not sure that's true." She hoped her well-rehearsed response would satisfy. "It's simple: because I'm twenty-eight years old and it's time for me to grow up. I have to make a life"—and maybe even someday, a family—"of my own."

"You're not lying to me, but you're also not telling me the truth." Asla used her free hand to take up Cindira's assistance to step into the cab. "How many times have I told you I despise thespians?"

What was she supposed to say, that she could no longer tolerate living on the same property as the woman responsible for her mother's death? Or worse, that to try and save her father, Cindira had agreed to work with Johanna in secret, supposedly to open the source code and deliver it to whomever was keeping her father prisoner? If Asla knew the truth, she'd never leave. Maybe there was a way to say more, though, without saying anything at all.

"Because I'm about to do something that's going to tick off a lot of people, dangerous people, and it's especially going to make Johanna insane. I don't want you anywhere in the vicinity if there are any ramifications."

"Ha! Now, that's something worth leaving for." Asla stopped, and when she looked up, all the humor was gone from her face. "Your father. He's not just gone on a business trip all this time, is he?"

There was no use in towing the company line on this one. Even casual members of the press had begun to wonder why Rex Tieg, world-famous entrepreneur and man-about-town, hadn't been seen in the city—or anywhere else—since his Asian trip two months ago. Plaxis stock sank as the rumor mill geared up, something Johanna had already expressed her frustration over as "reorganizing" several underperforming units.

Jeffrey Mackey hadn't made it back into the line-up when the "Kitchen's" cupboards had been restocked.

Cindira bit her lip, trying not to focus on the loss of an ally, especially when she had so few. It only compounded her father's predicament, not to mention her own. Mack wasn't dead, he was just laid off. He was a talented coder and a hard worker. If Tagentry, Plaxis's primary rival, had any smarts, they'd snap him up in a second.

And if you were smart, you'd follow him there and try to put any connection with Plaxis behind you. People as connected as him don't just disappear in this day and age. Your father is probably dead. Do you want to join him?

The little voice in her head, made bold since daring to kidnap the Prince of Gaia inside the Kingdom, picked up in volume. It had been doing that more and more lately, and Cindira didn't know whether it thrilled her or scared her to hell.

"No, he's not just on a business trip," Cindira admitted. "But I'm going to look for him. Even if we barely spoke, he's still my dad."

Asla chewed on the statement before her jaw squared. Her head gave a speedy nod. "Then I have no fear for Rex's fate. Even if I had wanted to knock that blockhead's hair implants from his skull for years for the way he treated you, I wouldn't want anything truly bad to happen to him."

Cindira put the old woman's bag on the floor of the cab before crawling in beside her. She'd see her off, assure she'd made the flight. "And Johanna?"

Asla's smile sparkled like that of a mischievous child. "Perhaps best if I don't say. At least until I'm safely outside of the city and halfway across the Atlantic."

TWO

MONDAYS WERE NEVER happy days in the office. That was even more the case when they started with your best friend belting your name like an accusation across the Kitchens.

"Cindira Tieg!"

Cindira felt six sets of eyes turn on her and took comfort only because Kaylie's weren't among them. One of the very few upsides of her older stepsister now being her boss was that bosses had so many meetings. She exchanged a look with her fellow programmers, all of whom had left off sewing bits of code to watch the red-haired social worker stomp across the communal room their division occupied. The human mind leaped at the opportunity for drama here. Beautiful as it might be, code numbed the brain. There were only so many alphanumeric strings of commands a person could write or right before needing a break.

The second Scotia arrived at Cindira's station, her volume went from Hellenistic to microscopic. "Tell me you didn't have anything to do with it."

A quick survey of the room confirmed that the others had burrowed back down into their own work, or at least were acting as though they had. Cindira cleared her throat and attempted confusion.

"Tell me what it is, and then I can tell you."

No wonder why Asla hated actors. It felt evil to embrace lying at this level to the person who had let you use their credentials and crash a royal ball.

"What it is? You don't honestly think that..."

Scotia grabbed her friend's wrist and tugged, pulling her out of the Kitchens, up the hall, and into what turned out to be a janitorial closet. Rectangular devices sat on the edge of charging botic units designed for cleaning. On a shelf, bar-coded white boxes held sanitizing agents and supplies, none of which needed to be closed for the electronics' sake. The air licked her eyes, and Cindira was reminded of the days in the city when pollution required donning ventilating masks.

The door closed like a conviction of guilt, and Scotia picked right up where her prosecution had left off.

"Don't what-is-it me, Cindira Tieg." The finger wag Scotia affected would have pleased a nineteenth-century school marm. "I just heard from one of my contacts that the prince was kidnapped at knife point during that ball you used my invitation to get into."

Cindira played innocent, something at which she'd had much practice. From an early age, the dangers of sharing her ambitions became plain. The Fife twins saw her dreams as targets of ridicule. While Cade had never been one to launch an attack, he did so love following in Kaylie's wake.

"Oh, my goodness. Is he okay?"

"Of course he's okay!" Scotia blurted, as though it was as obvious a statement as water was wet and covered all of New Orleans. "Everyone is saying the security bots were able to save him, but that's not the point. You used my credentials to get in because you didn't want to be there in any official capacity yourself. You specifically told me you needed it so you could talk to him, and this is after showing up at my house in the middle of the night two weeks ago to tell me you blew his avatar up?"

"I didn't say I blew it up. I said we both blew up while I was talking to him."

It was dropping a cup of water on a raging house fire. The intentions were good, but it didn't do much to douse the flames. "I need you to tell me you didn't do anything that's going to have the Authority show up at my house or get me subpoenaed to appear before the Gaian court and rung up on criminal charges."

Cindira laid a hand on her friend's shoulder. "Scotia, you've known me since grad school. Have I ever done anything really dangerous?"

"There was the time you hacked into the school chancellor's systems to expose that chemistry professor cyberraping one of his students during vreal office hours. You know, the one where they were trying to cover it up and make her go away quietly."

"That was an act of justice for someone left with no options." That had to be a good enough excuse, right? "And I'll remind you, seven years later, no one still has any idea it was me who posted the video on the streams. I promise you, I haven't done anything like that since."

"Does that include at the ball?"

Cindira decided to tell a truth of omission. "The person who kidnapped the prince looked nothing like you. Believe me, there's an entire palace of witnesses who would look at your avatar and state definitively that you were not the person who was involved."

"You know that I'm professionally trained to see around the corners of that enormous wall you just threw up, right?" Scotia huffed, pressing the finger pads of her right hand to her temples and shaking her head. "I'm not going to ask why. I'm not going to ask anything. Just please, tell me honestly, is there any way this could ping back on me?"

"None. Your credential was read to get me in, and I created a UX record afterward to show you jacked out a few minutes before anything... dramatic happened."

"Only you didn't actually jack out then, did you?" She tilted her head to the side. "You know that's illegal too, right? Editing UA and UX records?"

The terms meaning a "user entry" and "user exit" respectively. And yes, she did, but she wasn't about to admit that out loud. Finally, when Scotia saw that there would be no response, she tamed her tone.

"I don't know what to say. I used to wish you'd finally live up to your potential, make a difference with your abilities instead of just winning us a few hundred greens at the hackdomes now and then. Not that I don't like the money. But hacking data logs, using a friend's kindness to undertake actions which could negatively affect them, skirting around the truth when confronted?" Scotia shook her head. "This is the kind of thing I expect from my VIA patients, not from you."

"I'm not a chiphead. I just..." Cindira sighed, letting her head hang down. She looked up to see the edges of her friend's face softening. "I was wearing a good disguise."

The ice storm clouded Scotia's expression in a heartbeat, drawing her gaze up.

Darn it. "I didn't steal anyone's avatar. I borrowed one from a deceased user." Never mind that the user in question was her own mother, and that while only technically illegal (because a user's avatar was supposed to be permanently off-lined at their death), no one had ever been formally charged with that crime. "I got to the ball, took one look around at all the rich, famous, and powerful people there, and knew immediately I didn't belong."

"So you didn't see what happened to the prince?"

There was an air of hope in Scotia's tone, one that turned Cindira's mouth sour. Maybe that was what deceit tasted like. At least she'd skip the details and not dig herself in any deeper.

"I overheard Kaylie and Cade talking about it at the senior staff meeting this morning. I know the basics of what everyone is saying." That was completely true, and in the reflection of that fact, Cindira felt a little like her ship had been set straight. "The prince is pissed off but fine. Security is cracking down on all units, of course, trying to see if they can find the jackpod the hacker used to get in."

Which they wouldn't. Cindira hadn't used a jackpod. Instead, the brilliant piece of tech her mother had left behind and which had recently come into her possession had done the trick. The slippers were high-tech moldable silicone embedded with trillions of translucent nanites. They allowed the wearer to dip in and out of the vreal at will from anywhere. The only problem was that, while both the shoes were still in Cindira's possession in the real, she'd lost one of them in the vreal while saving Francisco Batista and escaping the Kingdom. She wasn't sure why that mattered, but Laporte reconfirmed her worst fear: she had to wear the shoes in both environments for the tech to function.

To make the shoes function again, she needed to get the missing slipper back from the prince in the vreal. Just how she was supposed to do that, she had no clue.

"Okay, fine." Scotia crossed her arms, nodded, pinched her chin. "Corporate is already pissed off at me right now over the Tagentry Charity Gala I'm helping to plan, and if they saw my invite was used by someone besides me to get into the Kingdom—"

Cindira reached out, putting a hand on her friend's shoulder. "Trust me, Scotia. There's not a single coder in this company that can do what I did, and the way I did it is completely untraceable."

"By AI, by bots, maybe. It isn't as easy to fool human eyes." Any tension left Scotia's shoulders. She leaned her head against one of the storage racks. "I would have kinda liked it if you had pushed Kaylie off a balcony or something while you were there."

"That... wouldn't have been a good idea. The safety protocols in the Kingdom allow for in-vreal damage to replicate in pain sensors on the outside."

"Holy shit. No way." The redhead's eyes widened. "How has that never gotten back to me? That's savage." Then an odd smile drew up the corners of her mouth. "But that just makes me wish you'd have pushed her even more."

They peaked out in the hallway to make sure the coast was clear before exiting. No reason to raise suspicions that they'd been conspiring.

"So, Tagentry Gala?"

"Oh, yeah. Tagentry." Scotia's brow creased before remembrance ironed it out. "I got a special waiver from Plaxis to go under temporary contract with them. It's not anything technical. No trade secrets being shared or anything. I'm just a guest speaker and coordinator, helping them to organize a fundraiser for St.

Dymphna's. Plaxis signed on as a corporate backer too. Imagine that? Your stepmother and Hugo Ferrente are on the same side of something."

"Odder things have happened." They strolled back towards the Kitchens. "St. Dymphna's? Isn't that the chiphead hospital?"

Just because the Kingdom had been the industry's most exclusive, luxurious, and immersive vreal since it launched over fifteen years ago didn't mean it was the only one, and it certainly wasn't the first. Vreals had been available for four decades at a wide swath of price points, and for a variety of needs. Like anything technological, however, virtual reality was a tool, one that could be misused. Addiction to jacking was its contribution; the dopamine and wish fulfillment made possible the newest form of self-harm. St. Dymphna's had been founded even before Gaia had launched. It was said that it never turned away a patient, no matter the ability to pay for service.

Sometimes a patient was admitted and treated, able to return to some form of an existence based in reality. Sometimes they dug even deeper into the vreal as their bodies slowly ate themselves. Oh, there were ways of keeping someone in the vreal healthy on the outside, but that level of care was beyond even what St. Dymphna's could provide, no matter how generous their donors. Only the uberwealthy could afford the biobotics and configure jackpods that allowed for round-the-clock external care.

"How many times have I told you, we prefer to call them Vreal Immersion Addicts."

"You yourself just said chiphead not two minutes ago." Cindira pointed back towards the janitorial closet, as though to remind Scotia of the scene of the crime.

"That doesn't count. It was an accusation at a friend, not a diagnosis of a patient. But anyway, yes, the VIA Care Facility," she said. "You wouldn't believe how many families use St. Dymphna's as a dumping ground, like they're throwing something out. They show up and check in their dad or sister or husband and then never come back. Don't visit. Don't come to claim the body when—" Scotia cut herself off, pursing her lips. "Anyway, yeah, sad. I know Tagentry is one of our competitors, but they really care about the cause. They raise tons of crypto each year during this event."

"And I'm sure with you as their speaker and organizer, they'll raise even more."

Cindira pressed a finger against the scanner outside the Kitchens. "I'll be happy to donate. Just let me know how."

"Really? Thank you. I know they'll appreciate that. I'll get the donation vector from the coordinator and zip it over to your comque later today."

The door beeped, and a sliding sound let them know the lock had disengaged.

"You know, I hear there's a high-stakes match at the Stadium tomorrow night." Scotia folded her arms over her chest and leaned against the door frame. "Perhaps the Mistress of Cinders could turn that small donation into a not-so-small donation."

"I can't." She reached up to push the door open. "I have some special projects right now I need to—"

"Cindira."

Both women jolted as they stepped into the Kitchens. Johanna Tieg might be a woman long past her youth, but she possessed a stature that would still arrest the beating heart when she was long dead in her grave. Tall, curvy in all the right ways despite her age, she wore her blond hair pulled back in a fierce bun and her lips pulled back in a scowl. She took one look at Scotia, and that was enough to send the social worker buzzing back to her own hive three floors down, leaving Cindira to deal with her stepmother alone.

The coder cleared her throat and remembered what Laporte had said. The tiny AI-powered botic was right: until Cindira was sure she could find out what had happened to her father, recover the lost shoe, and figure out whose attacks were threatening Gaia's stability, she needed to keep the status quo. She'd need all of Plaxis's resources at her disposal, and she wasn't about to get that by finally turning on Johanna after all these years.

"Good morning, Johanna." Cindira conjured up a tiny smile. "How can I help you?"

Johanna's head jerked towards Cindira's desk. A box was there. It hadn't been there when she and Scotia had left the room just a few minutes ago.

"You can help me by collecting your personal effects," Johanna said. "You're fired."

THREE

THEY RODE DOWN THE elevator in awkward silence: Johanna, staring straight forward, Cindira, and Laporte — rescued from her desk when no one was looking and nested in her jacket pocket. She hadn't needed an entire box to gather her things. A lunch sack, a few datapads of schematics, one with a romance novel she'd never admit to anyone she'd read, and a little golden statue designed to look like a spool of thread and a needle slid from side to side as she shifted her weight.

Johanna spared a sideways glance at the box. "Is that a Stitcher?"

The award was given to the best design each year, for coders by coders. It was the only thing connected to her "secret" work for Kaylie that meant something.

"Yes, it is."

That answer was as simple as it was sharp.

"You won it?"

Oh, so that was Johanna's angle, open hostility.

"Does that surprise you?"

Johanna took a moment to give Cindira a diagnosing look before turning her eyes back to the elevator doors. "I'm surprised that you have only one. Jealousy among the Kitchens staff, though I don't know if that's because you're Rex's daughter or because you're so much better than them. They know they could never compete."

There was kindness somewhere in those words. Suspicion immediately scratched at the back of Cindira's brain. Johanna Tieg was not a woman who gave compliments freely. They were only down payments on favors forthcoming.

But before Cindira could say thank you, her stepmother went on.

"I'm sorry for that scene upstairs just now. It wasn't my intention to embarrass you in front of your colleagues."

"You really mean that?"

Johanna's shoulders twitched. "It's not good for employee morale to see someone they respect let go, and so publicly. It's going to affect productivity."

Ah, so it wasn't about any kind of sympathy. For a moment, Cindira had fooled herself into thinking that somewhere under the reptilian shell of her soul, Johanna had culled an iota of compassion. But would she really want her to? Wouldn't that require some level or reciprocity? The last thing Cindira intended to do was find a connection with the woman who'd murdered her mother.

She pulled a long breath, taming her instincts. The time to force Johanna to settle up for her sins would come, but now wasn't the time. Status quo. The term was becoming her mantra. What would the Cindira Tieg version from two months ago say?

"Maybe you could tell me why you did it," Cindira worked to keep her tone even. A shaky voice might give her away. Was there any way Johanna had found out the truth: that the woman who confronted her in the Kingdom disguised as Omala Grover was, in fact, the daughter they shared? "When we discussed working together on locating Dad, you never said anything about firing me."

"It's a ruse, and I didn't have a choice. You'll need time and resources to find Rex. I couldn't give you those unless I told Kaylie why she was no longer allowed to exploit your time." Johanna looked directly at her for the first time since they got into the elevator. "This work needs to be done discreetly. We have no idea who's working against us, and what connections they might have."

"So you're not really firing me." The truth revealed itself as Cindira worked out the scenario. "I see, then. You needed word to get back to whoever has Dad that I'm no longer at Plaxis. True, I've never become a rockstar designer like some others in the

Kitchens, but those who know, know."

"Kaylie knows, and that's why you've never grown the cult following the others have. She wouldn't share you with anyone." Johanna grinned in Cindira's peripheral vision. "So many compliments on your designs, not just of her dresses, but all the things you've done in Alsace and the palace gardens. The First Lady of Azeristan offered a king's ransom if you'd design her daughter's wedding gown. Not you, specifically, mind you, but she told Kaylie as much."

That her skills were so highly prized wasn't what caught Cindira's attention. "They held the wedding in the vreal?"

"On the grounds of our palace last year," Johanna confirmed. "It was a very secretive operation, so of course everyone who's anyone found out about it. I'm surprised you didn't."

Cindira tried to shake the confusion away. "I don't really pay attention to what goes on inside the Kingdom."

And that truth had gotten her into this situation to begin with.

THEY ARRIVED AT THE boarded-up brick building at the edge of town about twenty minutes later, taking a tiktok instead of one of the executive craft kept at the ready for senior staff. Seeing Johanna pile into a commoner's cab was like watching a diamond be set in a tin ring.

"Our movements must be kept as covert as possible."

It was just one more bizarre statement after another, starting with "You're fired." For a moment, Cindira thought she ought to remind her stepmother that tiktoks were inexpensive and plentiful for a reason: the Authority, like peacekeeping organizations in most major cities, had sewn in any number of video and audio devices, making patrolling the streets not only cost-efficient, but underwritten by the very population they infiltrated. Then she remembered Plaxis hadn't gotten where it was today without having certain... understandings between the Authority and its senior staff. Even a fool would put down a hopeful wager that this particular tiktok had gone dark to the Authority this morning.

The cab rolled away on its one large wheel, leaving the two of them alone. Cindira rolled her wrist over the edge of the box, looking down at the comque.

"You'll find that has little use here." Johanna fished around in the leather bag hanging off one shoulder. "The entire building and a two-meter perimeter around it are in a wireless dead zone."

It seemed true enough. Instead of the typical ready data that displayed when the device detected its wearer was looking at it—date, time, temperature, AQI, battery level, the number of waiting messages, et cetera—she found only digital ants. Blue dots scrawled left to right, filling the screen in a single line, and then disappeared. A single line of text hovered over them: LOOKING FOR SIGNAL. As far as Cindira knew, the city-wide wireless network was only blocked in high-security facilities. The city prison, for example, as well as Gaia's administrative center on the north end of town. Though, given that both were also surrounded by twelve-foot walls constantly paraded by highly armed Authority members, what was the difference?

It was funny how the theaters of security rose highest on those who paid for the extra protection and those from whom they were meant to be protected. In the meantime, the audience was left to fend for itself from both street and stage.

"A warehouse?" Cindira looked up at her stepmother. "What's inside?"

"The last remnants of your mother's company."

That didn't make sense. "Plaxis was my mother's company. Until she sold all her shares to you and Dad, that is."

Johanna's gaze was soft to the point of sympathy. "Hardly. Gaia Labs was hers. And your father's too when it started, of course. But when they broke up, they broke up the company too. Your mom kept the humanitarian-project side, and Rex developed the commercial for-profit side. In the end, we consumed Gaia Labs back into Plaxis for its own sake."

"Because it didn't have any cash centers to sustain itself." Cindira had heard this story before. Studied it even in grad school. Learning about your parents' personal lives in an academic framework was the ultimate out-of-body experience. "Dad gave me an abbreviated version of it once when I first joined the company in one of his rare episodes of wanting to spend time with me. But that still doesn't tell me what we're doing here."

Johanna sucked in air through her teeth. "I think there might be a clue to where your father is inside."

Cindira's head lashed in her direction. "What?"

"Every physical thing that was purchased by Gaia and not integrated into a Plaxis facility is in this building," she said. "I'm not sure why we didn't just pitch it. Rex wants to keep it. I think he sees it as some kind of potential museum. Or maybe he's a pack rat. Or maybe there's still something in there that he's not ready to part with."

"Again, not seeing the why."

"You always were so impertinent." Johanna rolled her eyes once before schooling herself into a sober demeanor. "Like I said, for security, this place is a dead zone. Even if the equipment and files in storage here are fifteen years or more old, there's still a lot of sensitive data. There's not supposed to be any relays coming in or out of it, data wise. But about three months ago, around the time your father disappeared, there was a singular massive data burst."

Cindira's eyebrows knitted together. "A hardwire connection?"

"It would have to be. I had some of our analysts look closer, and they found there actually is one active line that runs from the building. A security monitor might explain that, but it doesn't explain a 2.5 petabyte download. All our attempts to tap the data for analysis remotely were blocked by a security bot that makes our Yuchi look like a kindergartner fighting with crayons."

Cindira bit her tongue before saying that she'd actually been the one to make Yuchi look like that.

"I even sent some of our guys in," Johanna continued, "but they couldn't find anything in the building with an electric pulse, other than the machines that creates the wireless connection gap."

"I'm not a hardware or network architecture specialist, but that might have been enough to do it." Even Cindira wondered if whatever data had surged inside might not have been placed in the building for that very reason. "So, what, your theory is that whoever has Dad got info from him that this might be a way to get to the source code?"

"More than that, I think Rex is the one who caused the data surge. I think he has had access to the source code this whole time, and he hid it on some device inside this building."

Cindira felt a thrill go through her, chased the next moment by terror. Rationality caught up with her animal brain, and the implications made themselves plain. "You want me to find the device?"

"More than that. I want you to find the device, tap the download, and figure out not only what in the hell that much data was, but what the source was," she said. "If you can upstream the data connection, you'll know where Rex is. Or at least, where he was three months ago."

Was she actually hearing what she thought she was hearing? "This is what you fired me for?"

"You're still an employee, just off the books, paid in cash, and kept out of sight." A clinking metal-on-metal sound tinkled before the woman beside her lifted her hand to reveal a set of keys. "The investigators who were here three months ago set up a new hardwire connection to do their work. It's still on and quarantined from the one they couldn't find, so if there's any viral content in all those petabytes, the infection shouldn't spread. There's a Sink prototype that's been reactivated too. A little smaller and buggier than what we have in the Kitchens, but functional."

Johanna approached what turned out to be a door covered by one of the pressed silicate boards that matched the ones over the windows. The key slid in without trouble. Rather low-tech security, Cindira thought. Johanna seemed to read her thought as she dropped her keys back into her purse.

"Sometimes, the old-fashioned ways are better."

A feminine gloved hand reached out to wrap around the heavily painted wooden board that served as a door, its uneven bottom scraping pavement as Johanna pulled. Behind it, another door, but one of far more substantial build. Instead of a typical handle, something that looked like a wheel from one of the replica antique boats parked in the aquatic museum nearby was mounted in the middle.

"What you're seeing now"—Johanna vaguely motioned to the brick walls— "is a small remnant of a building that used to dominate this area of the city. Currency was physical then, and this is one of the places the US made and stored it. No amount of interface coding will get you in. Rex and Omala picked this place up at an auction before you were even born. Your mother did have a taste for hopeless things."

Cindira closed her eyes against fury, her teeth grinding the way they always did when Johanna casually impugned her mother's memory. If Laporte could leap out of her pocket at this very moment without fear of discovery, he'd lecture her on the importance of patience. Luckily, Johanna was too busy fidgeting with something on the door to pay attention to Cindira's machinations. There was a keypad, one that some convenience lockers she'd seen in her travels still used, a basic three-by-four grid of buttons, each with a character printed in faded script. Johanna's lithe fingers danced over the set, a string some twenty digits long. Always a fan of puzzles, Cindira's mind quickly mapped the numerical grid, assigned the alphabet to combinations that were often used in certain coding shorthand and worked out the puzzle.

"I love you, *mera pyaar*?"

"Is that what those numbers represent?" Johanna's hand passed to an embedded dial hatched with white marks. Her hand froze. "Funny, I never knew. I thought Rex would have changed it after..."

After you killed my mother? The thought leaped into Cindira's head before she could stop it, her head daring her tongue to tell the woman before her she knew the truth. That she would pay. That even if it just turned out the Rex had left her, she deserved it, along with two ungrateful and selfish children.

She did none of that.

Back when the focus of her life had been not standing out, Cindira found filing down her emotions a great benefit. Now she realized how ingenious that strategy had been. Ever since the day Francisco Batista had shown up at Plaxis, setting off a chain of complications, Cindira had no choice but to feel. It was a survival tactic. Still, no one would have been able to convince her that compassion could be so painful. This was the woman who had stolen away her father, killed her mother, and made her feel smaller than a grain of rice washed down the sink for most of her life. She didn't want to feel sad for Johanna. She should delight in the fact that this remnant of her mother's love for her father remained still and pained her. Mera pyaar was a term of endearment Omala used, but only for Cindira herself.

Suddenly, Johanna shook her head. "It doesn't matter. Your mother set the code, and I didn't get where I am today by refusing to acknowledge facts. She must have assumed you'd come here someday, and of course, she loved you. But I thought—" Her voice died away, as did her awareness, until Johanna shook her head. "It doesn't matter."

A few buildings remained in Andorra where Cindira had spent much of her schooling from the "Before World." That's what everyone called it, anyway. Not just before GAIA had taken warfare online and given the planet a chance to breathe after years of conflict, but before so many nations and superpowers had dissolved into bickering microregions, all of them skirmishing over borders, resources, sovereignty... A few treasures survived from antiquity, structures too magnificent for even postmodern man to destroy. The pyramids of Giza, for example. But even though Cindira had toured eighteenth-century fortresses and nineteenth-century piazzas, few examples of twentieth-century architecture remained. It simply had not been built to endure the way older structures had.

And yet, undoubtedly, Cindira was certain that was what she was looking at once they'd passed the doors.

The hall stretched on forever, walls of dark red brick and gray mortar suggesting this one building occupied the entire city block in San Francisco's depopulated industrial zone. On both left and right, doorways built under stone arches were covered in metallic doors, each with the spinning captain's wheel like the one Johanna had opened to let them into the building. A battalion of saucer lights hung from the smooth, white-washed ceiling that undulated in a rippled wave pattern as far as the light permitted her to see, illuminating pockmarked cement floors cut into an artificial attempt at tile work.

"Welcome to what we now call 'the black box.'"

Cindira took a few steps forward as Johanna closed the door behind them. Unlike when they entered, the locks sealed themselves. "I can't believe this is where my mom started it all."

"And your father." The eyebrow had been shaped by professionals to act as their own back slashes with the slightest movement on Johanna's part. "So many people overlook Rex's part in Plaxis's origins. As great as your mother was, she wasn't a monolith. Many hands were lent to her over the years from all corners of the globe. Still, I suppose it is hard to praise a candle when the torch burns beside it."

To the left, one door varied in design, more modern and plain than the others. The material was definitely a polymer, not a metallic slab. Instead of a spinning combination wheel, there was only a single rectangular biometric grid.

Johanna jerked her chin. "I asked that your thumbprint be registered into its security latch. See if it's functional."

Years of mistrust made her hesitate. Could this be a trap, a way to take Cindira off the field? Johanna had gone out of her way to make it look like she was being fired in disgrace. No doubt that across town, in the breakrooms and corridors of Plaxis HQ, the gossip transport was making the rounds. Whatever theory had floated to the top of why she'd been let go, Cindira knew from experience that Plaxis had a one-way door where employees were concerned. Also, since moving out of her family's compound a week ago, none of the neighbors would question that they no longer saw her coming through the back gate like clockwork each night. Maybe Scotia would raise some concern, but preparing the fundraiser was going to distract her. Her friend might not believe it if Johanna came up with some excuse about why Cindira was missing. By the time Scotia's curiosity was piqued enough to encourage her to act, she could be in a watery grave at the bottom of the bay.

Finally, after a few moments of inaction, Johanna's hand reached out and grabbed Cindira, forcefully pushing her thumb against the sensor. "You and I are going to have to work on our trust issues if we're going to have any hope of finding your father."

Big words for the woman who admitted to killing my mother.

The door swung open of its own accord this time, and Johanna didn't bother to close it, even preceding Cindira inside.

"Any device or node inside this building goes through the secure ad hoc connection I mentioned. The interface nodes will be in the middle of the main hall, with enough cable to stretch to wherever you need to work," she said, crossing to a group of ceiling-high server towers and pushing a half dozen buttons. "All your work is going to need to take place inside the brick perimeter of the building. I had the old employee gym and lounge converted into something approximating a studio apartment."

She came to a stop where she stood, next to a pile of five boxes equaling her in height. "You expect me to live here too?"

Johanna blinked in confusion. "You can't be running about in the city to-and-fro. Do you really think whoever has taken your father would hesitate to come after you? We can't work together to find him if you get kidnapped too. Stay here and keep working. Now..." Her stepmother pointed to another door on the opposite wall. "My advance team told me that they've outfitted the living quarters with a bed, personal supplies, and enough tab food to keep you fed for two weeks. If you need to construct any tech, you'll find chips and assembly equipment in the anterior closet. Not to mention all the junk and scrap that's stuffed into every corner of this place. Start your search for the hard line on the south side of the building. There are more boxes of... well, Rex would hate to hear me say it, but trash there. And you—"

"Johanna, wait." Cindira dropped into an old metal chair nearby. "You've made all these arrangements without even asking me how likely it is I can pull off whatever you're thinking, let alone if I was willing to."

The statuesque blonde clicked her fingernails against her palm. "Sorry, but you do remember the discussion we had in my office after the prince was kidnapped, don't you? You said you love your father and that you'd work with me. Well"—she motioned to the room at large—"this is what working for me looks like."

"Of course, I love my dad and I want to find him. That's not the point." She chose her words with extreme deliberateness. "It's just, when we talked about working together out of sight of the public to avoid any suspicion, I didn't think you meant locking me away from the world! I know my life looks simple to you, but I'm still free."

Johanna took time drawing in a breath, all while narrowing her eyes, as though working through her options until finally she reached a decision. "Is that all the thanks I get for putting you here to protect you? You're right, your life is simple. That's why you don't understand what's really going on here. After what happened with the prince at the ball last week, everyone with known hacking skills is being watched. That especially includes you. No, you're not a famous code designer, but others in the Kitchens are, and each of them has seen what you're capable of. If you got detained for questioning by the prince's people or Authority, they'd read you like a cheap gossip stream. You've never had a very good poker face. You're too... what's a good word? Genuine."

"And you seriously don't think Kaylie or Cade would give me up if they thought it would get rid of me?"

Johanna dropped her hand and shook her head. "Please, Cindira. I know the three of you have never been close, but they wouldn't betray you like that. Especially since you're not guilty of anything. At least nothing to do with what happened to the prince. They all know your only access to the vreal for years has been through the Sink in the Kitchens. You don't even have an avatar to jack into."

Her deceased mother's admonishment carried to her over waves of memory. Johanna was a mother, and she loved her children. Cindira had to respect that, even if her opinion on the character of her stepsiblings varied dramatically.

She took another survey of the room or, as she might think of it, her prison cell. "So, what happens if this works? I find out where Dad is. What then?"

"Then we rescue him."

"With what army?" The question seemed obvious to her, as well as its answer. "The major nations of the world disbanded their land forces when Gaia was successfully implemented. Unless you'd like to hire mercenaries, in which case they'll kill Dad."

"If you think finally hacking the source code the better option, by all means, have at it."

"And we're back to that, are we? You realize we hand over the source code to whoever did this, the best thing they're going to do is copy it for their own use, and the worst is... Well, I think you know what the worst is."

Johanna nodded. "And while it would hurt me to have our company go under because of the loss of a trade secret that important, I don't know how it would matter if Rex isn't there to run it with me."

Our. The moment the word had passed Johanna's lips, Cindira had been filled with a warm and squishy feeling, like she might be part of the family at last. Then came the stark reminder: Johanna's only concern was Rex. And as much as Cindira joined in the desire to save her father, she couldn't let go of what the destruction of Plaxis would mean.

The Kingdom annoyed her and mocked her mother's legacy, but it employed thousands of people the world over.

And Gaia... Gaia had saved the world.

Johanna resumed, dragging Cindira from her thoughts.

"But I'm positive it won't come to that. Not now that you've finally decided to work with me."

Johanna said it like Cindira had been given the choice all along. Less than a week had passed since the coder had shown up at her stepmother's office. The intention had been simple: confronting Johanna about the confession made while Cindira was in disguise. Instead, Cindira had been let in on the secret that her father was not only missing but being held for ransom.

For the moment, Cindira just nodded, however. "I'll do my best."

"Good." Johanna turned, her heels beating as she started back towards the door. "I'll check in with you daily for updates. You still have a message box on the internal employee communication system, yes?"

"Assuming it wasn't terminated when I was." Cindira wanted to point out that the archaic text-based systems were among the easiest to hack, and there wasn't much point in stashing her in a highly secured secret building if anything she relayed out of it could be decoded by a first-year programmer.

Not that she would send any messages of importance. There was no way in hell Johanna was getting her hands on the source code, and little chance this wild idea of hers about analyzing a data dump was going to yield any fruit.

"It wasn't," Johanna confirmed. "We keep all employee inboxes open for thirty days after termination to allow for debriefing and project hand-off. Just one last warning: you probably haven't had to do too many projects using hardwire connections. You'll find the relay times are a little slower than what you're used to with the city wireless grid. But I wouldn't jack into the vreal or go outside of this building if I were you. And no matter what you think, you're not a prisoner here. You remember what the entry code to the building was, don't you?"

"I love you, mera—"

"Yes would have been fine, Cindira," Johanna said, cutting her off. "I suggest you don't leave, but if someone does come after you here, I also suggest you don't stay."

FOUR

FRANCISCO POURED HIMSELF a cup of coffee from the silver-plated service set on the dining room table, confirming that he was, in fact, in the real.

Jackpods tapped into the human brain, both reading and writing waves that corresponded to tastes, textures, smells, sounds... The hyperreality could fool you. The vreal's weakness, ironically, was its perfection. You never splashed a few drops of tea on the heel of your hand while pouring there, not unless you were intentionally trying to. The vreal aimed to optimize. Nature had no such qualms about pleasing the expectations of men. Each fiery liquid drop burned truth. He was in San Francisco. This was the real.

The table in the royal residence had been harvested from Denmark before the ocean claimed back that which its citizens had burrowed. Made of dark-stained walnut, with a scroll hewn on its edges in a simplistic repeating pattern and rather long, the impressive piece was believed to be of German design, with room enough to seat forty. Forty-four, if his guests didn't fear intimacy. Six months into his reign, and Francisco couldn't remember there ever being more than three for dinner. Having a real-world palace in tandem with the one inside the vreal where the government seat lay was nice, but probably unnecessary. Twin settings of linen placemats, assorted silverware (yes, genuine silver), and one marble-carved salt and pepper shaker had been set in place by the palace staff before his arrival.

Normally, when Francisco entered, it was to find his attaché busily engaged in any numbers of conversations simultaneously, both through the comque wrapped around his wrist, and up to three data pads spread over the table in an arrangement to please the most particular of card dealers. But as Francisco poked around the tomatoes and eggs on his plate, it was under Carlos's dedicated gaze.

The prince made certain to chew and swallow before speaking. "I think you have something to tell me."

The old man's cheek flushed. "I suppose I shouldn't be surprised that you can read me so well after all these years."

The attaché in the real was a man with a medium build, deep olive skin, and thinning salt and pepper hair. Of course, in the vreal, with the design of his avatar under his control, Carlos appeared to be a contemporary of the prince himself. That was nothing new; men of power and influence for centuries ran from time. Cosmetics, shapewear, hair dyes... Your hair must remain black into the grave, an ancient dictator was rumored to have said to his protégé. Don't do anything to remind the masses that you, like mortal men, grow old, or that so much time has passed since first you seized control. How could it, if you're still young?

Francisco shook his head as he measured out a spoonful of sugar. Today's coffee was extra dark. "Not so much. I can see what's on your cover, but I can't predict what I'll find in your pages."

"In another life, you might have been a poet."

"And in another, a king. Another, a beggar. And maybe I will be in a life still to come. For now, I'm just a prince, even if I'm one with no actual land to claim as mine."

Carlos left off the lyrical to return to the mundane. "I've just finished an analysis on the third bombing, the one that happened in the museum district."

The prince grimaced. On so pleasant a morning, it was easy to forget that someone had blown him up two weeks ago. Virtually, at least. After hackers had bombed public areas of Gaia's capital city twice in as many weeks, the royal office had been quick to remind everyone that violence in the realm didn't affect real world damage. If someone died in Gaia, as often happened in the wardomes, they'd wake up in a jackpod back in the real, psych shocked but otherwise unharmed. The latest attack, however, outside a museum housing the oldest digital artifacts from the early twenty-first century, was a bold move. Even if the two-dimensional abstract NFTs showed the simplicity of the age, it was still part of the vreal's heritage. Two Kaplans and a Yin-Zhu had been destroyed. (Francisco did doubt they'd be missed.) But the true damage was worse. Galleries and gift shops could be reprogrammed; the source code damaged in the explosion, sadly, could not. A prominent artist-in-residence, present when the bomb went off, also had leaked the story to the real media. Her avatar had been destroyed, as had, in her opinion, the NDA she'd signed. Oh, his lawyers were filing a breach-of-contract suit, but as the old American saying went, the cat was out of the bag.

Francisco let the hot liquid run down the back of his throat, closing his eyes, swallowing, rejoicing in the bittersweet echo and the aroma that tickled the tip of his nose. "And?"

"And..."

Carlos buffered silence between them. So much so that Francisco was forced to open his eyes and glare just to end it.

The attaché drew little circles with the tip of his finger on the table. "My conclusion remains the same. Plaxis's corporate interest will always come before our political and humanitarian pursuits. Gaia exists solely at its leisure, with its cooperation, and under its oversight. Security protocols written into the heart of the source code that form the backbone of our parallel platforms are breaking down. Without access, we cannot fortify them. When we're attacked next time—and we will be—we'll only be able to defend ourselves to the degree that they allow us. That's why you must find a way to get access."

"I would remind you that when I showed up there in person and demanded as much, as you recommended, Johanna Tieg basically told me to go screw myself."

"I doubt she said it like that."

"You're right. She was more diplomatic. She shoved her daughter in front of me and implied that I might be interested in screwing her instead." Francisco stuck his knife into the jampot. "Tieg claims Plaxis can't access the source code either. Given what happened at that ball, how easily that hacker got in and got away with what she did, Tieg may have been telling the truth."

"Or was the kidnapper a plant?" Carlos leaned forward, hovering over the table. "How do we know the bandit wasn't working for Plaxis? Their shareholders are whispering, Francisco. There are rumors that Rex Tieg has gone missing because the platform is starting to crumble under its own weight. They might want an 'other' to point at and blame."

"If they wanted a distraction and a scapegoat, they would have killed me. Dead monarchs make better martyrs than live ones who get away."

Not to mention there was no way someone working for Tieg would have shown up wearing an avatar shaped like Omala Grover.

Someone working against her, however...

Francisco wasn't sure if he believed the adage "the enemy of my enemy is my friend" always held true. The Fake Omala Grover may very well turn out to be the bigger threat than the real Johanna Tieg. Although if the bandit had been there to kill him, she'd blown her chance when she handed over the very knife that she'd held to his throat without even being asked so much as to put the weapon down.

She had claimed she was saving him.

Saving him from what? Saving him from whom?

Carlos guffawed. "There's no way they could have built the Kingdom on top of a foundation of which they did not even know the composition."

Francisco set down his coffee with a great deal of deliberation. Every generation assumes idiocy in the one before it as to whatever is new, his grandfather had once told him. But it is ignorance only. A wise man would take time to explain, not to chastise. Carlos didn't lack intelligence; he lacked understanding. He was a member of the last generation that had to send its young men and women off to real battlefields to die true deaths.

"Speaking of poetry, do you think you could write some?"

The abrupt turn of subject made Carlos blink in surprise. "Its quality might be questioned. I may not reflect pathos, or even woo a woman into bed."

That brought a smile to Francisco's face, if only in passing. "And yet, you have no firm foundation in writing poetry, only a vague concept of what came before. There are centuries of dead bards whose work would serve as soil for yours to grow." He grabbed the hunk of bread from the side of his plate, took a bite, inhaling the sweet smell of pork. "The vreal is like that," he said, chewing his food and his words at the same time. "We need to know that the ground we build on is firm, but we don't need to know about the tectonic plates beneath it. Omala Grover invented the Purusha language to build her vision of the vreal, but she didn't invent coding. And we know enough of the bones of her work to make new bones that look just like it."

"Tectonic plates have a way of slipping every so often." Carlos grimaced before pivoting their conversation back to its intended path. "Recent events force me as your advisor to recommend something we discussed only in passing once before: Gaia uncoupling from Plaxis. We must be free to secure our own interests and, dare I say, hack into the source code on our own. Every explosion destroys more, and soon the platform will grow unstable."

The gilded coffee cup became the sole recipient of Francisco's gaze. He leaned back, pushed by an idea with the force of wind to his soul. "You're talking about La Isla del Después."

"Ay, ya!" Carlos swatted the air with both hands, as much to clear it of childlike notions as their native tongue. "The Island of After: a fantasy wrought by a woman consumed by fantasy."

"A concept of a new world by a woman who actually birthed one." The cup became boring. Francisco lifted his head to meet the other man's gaze. "You and I have both read the sealed files with Grover's notes from when she and Rex Tieg were creating

Gaia. She knew that giving war a virtual landscape was only a first step, that Gaia would have to evolve and become an arbiter of action in the real world as much as it was in the vreal to have any enduring effect. But she herself dismissed those early visions as naïve. A single entity which can control all has the power to exploit all."

Carlos clicked his tongue. "I'm not talking about world domination, Francisco. All I'm talking about is how Gaia survives in the vreal. As head of an independent vreal nation, the first of its kind, you'll emerge as a true leader. You'd have tangible power. But keep the status quo, and Plaxis could pull the plug anytime they want. Or worse, have the pug pulled on them. But if we declare independence..."

"A nation that stands alone falls alone."

Francisco knew that much from experience. For his native Andalusia, the first to sign the initial Vreal War Accords, consigning its conflict resolutions to Gaia's wardomes, the backlash eventually led to his father, the last Batista King, being slashed across the throat and left to bleed on the steps of his own palace. Eventually, most of the world did ally and join Gaia, but not before Francisco's family had lost its crown, its honor, and most of its fortune making the platform possible.

"We'd be sitting ducks," he continued. "Without the security that has Plaxis at our back provides, hackers would pull us to pieces in days."

"Your Majesty, they're pulling us to pieces now."

Nothing silenced a contrary tongue like truth.

Francisco pushed his chair back from the table but didn't rise. Nor could he force himself to lift his gaze. If he did, Carlos would see the point he'd just scored in the shattered confidence of his features. Logic and veracity could counter any argument, but Francisco didn't know how to put into cogent words that he wouldn't move to make Gaia an independent nation for no other reason than, in his gut, he knew it was wrong.

Luckily, Carlos didn't feel the need to volley another blow.

Instead, he picked up his napkin, ran the stiff linen across his face, and surrendered it to the crumb-strewn plate on the table before him.

"Before I served you, I served your father. As ruler of Gaia, you have as much of my loyalty as did the King. If Gaia falls, war moves back into the real. The entire planet will quickly be right back where it was twenty-five years ago, and all the sacrifices made by your family will have been in vain."

"I won't let that happen."

Carlos reached out to lay a hand on Francisco's knee and squeezed. "I'm not laying this at your feet, mi niño. You're a prince, not a god. But I also hope you don't invite the problems that made Gaia such a blessing into its politics."

"Meaning?"

"Even the Pope has the Swiss Guard." Carlos pulled back his hand and fanned his fingers through the air. "Being a man of peace doesn't mean you march into the world of men armed with faith alone."

It was a good point, even if Francisco wasn't keen on the example his mentor used. "I suppose we could benefit from a limited defensive force loyal only to Gaia, not Plaxis. If their activities are confined to our platform and don't affect the Kingdom, Tieg couldn't take issue. But where would we find anyone willing to work for the meager wages we could pay? The VR corporations recruit the best of the best, and under such brutal contracts that they'd never be able to pick up and leave for another competitor."

"You leave that to me." Carlos stood and pushed in his chair. "You'd be surprised how invoking Omala Grover's legacy can lead the blind to see and the crippled to walk."

Francisco busied himself with buttering a piece of toast, more to divert his eyes than to have something to eat. "Any update finding out who the kidnapper was or if there was really a threat on my life?"

"A real threat? She held a knife to your throat."

Francisco tried to hide a chuckle. "If she had wanted to kill me, she'd have done so when she whisked me away in the coach."

"Perhaps she had second thoughts."

"She?" He lifted his eyes the tiniest bit. "Are we sure of that?" Or did you just answer my first question?

"I admit, we aren't." Carlos grinned, bowing his head. "No, Your Highness, our joint investigation with Plaxis hasn't resulted in any clues... yet. The only thing we can say for sure is that it wasn't the namesake of the avatar she was wearing. She wasn't Omala Grover."

"Ghosts make poor hackers, and even worse dance partners."

Carlos nodded, paused, then lifted a finger. "Have any other details from that night resurfaced? Perhaps she inadvertently mentioned something that might connect her with one of the known hactivist groups or if she had some greater agenda. Did she give some clue about what she hoped to achieve by taking you from the ball?"

The truth tiptoed on Francisco's tongue and threatened to leap, but he bit it back just in time. Having one's mind jacked into a virtual reality platform allowed impossible things to be experienced in the artificial environment. An undamaged nineteenth century European city that he ruled... Soldiers who were killed in the line of duty one moment, only to wake up safe and sound in their jackpods half a world away in the next...

A shoe that appeared to be made of glass that had slipped off a young woman's foot, which now existed in his hand whenever he summoned it into being, but which none other could touch.

The first time Francisco had jacked in after the ball, he'd been surprised to find the item resting in his right hand. He'd been even more surprised when he attempted to give it to one of his aids with a request to investigate its coding, only to have it disappear the moment he let the young man take it.

The second and third cycle of it appearing in his hand, then vanishing in the aid's, was no less disconcerting.

And with the second and third aid?

They'd all been sworn to secrecy, and Francisco, still unsure he wanted his would-be kidnapper found until he had a better understanding of her intentions, had come up with a plan: to find her, he just needed to find the person who could hold the shoe. Outside of attempting to hand the shoe to every person he met, however, he still wasn't sure how to put his plan into action.

Francisco rose, taking his coffee with him. "Form an ad hoc committee."

"Sire?"

"To discuss your proposal," Francisco said, like it was obvious. "Can Gaia declare independence, and if so, should it? Keep it a tight group, though. I don't want to touch off rumors. Find me someone you think would support it, someone you think would oppose it, and get me someone who can tell me what that would look like from a technological perspective."

Carlos's eyes shone. "So you believe we should declare our—"

"No, I don't." Francisco cut off whatever wild weed of a fantasy had sprung up between them at that moment. "But having a contingency plan that I can present to Plaxis will give Tieg something to think about. It might finally get her to open up."

"Still think she's holding back on you?"

Francisco turned a rueful smile away, setting his gaze on the windows overlooking the gardens. "She's holding back something. I'm sure of that. Rex Tieg's extended absence from San Francisco has let her dig her claws deeper into the daily running of the company. We should see where he is if we can, make sure he's aware of what's been happening in Gaia. Rex might be an ambitious, elitist bastard, but he believes in Gaia's purpose. Johanna sees us as nothing more than a tick feeding off her corporate profits. You say we should uncouple from Gaia? That may be. But if Johanna's thinking the same thing, I want it to happen on our terms, not hers."

FIVE

IT HAD TAKEN YEARS, but finally Johanna had managed it.

She'd made Cindira scared.

Night owned its own chorus, complete with the bass sounds of the bay: tenor boat horns coming and going across the waters, and a smattering of high-pitched tweets and chirps she hoped were bugs and not spy botics. Just enough fog to pick up the lights of the streetlamps above, each of them flickering on when they detected her movements, as though saying to anyone in the shadows, there she goes! Of course, nobody lived in the Warehouse District. Rumored to be haunted, she'd heard. Probably contaminated. Years ago, when San Francisco had been part of a larger nation and not the Pacific States, tactical weapons were made and stored here. The closest neighbors Cindira found at the end of the block outside were a few scrawny cats and the rats they chased.

The former eyed Laporte on her shoulder as she passed.

"Do you really think the people who have your father will look for you?" the botic asked.

Cindira shook her head. "But out here, who knows who else might be?" She pulled the folds of her jacket closed. "I'd be an easy mark, Laporte. Get me in the virtual, and I can defend myself with a butter knife. Here in the real? Not so much."

The mouse must have feared an invisible threat as well. It buried itself in her dark brown locks. "Can I suggest you make haste contacting Miss MacAvoy so we can go back inside?"

Tilting the comque into view confirmed they were now far enough away from the warehouse. The signal indicator flashed green in the projection's corner. "I agree."

If she had thought Scotia was nerve-racked this morning in the janitorial closet, now she was positively having a breakdown.

"Where are you?" her friend yelled and whispered at the same time. She must have been in a bathroom stall or tucked into some corner out of someone's sight.

"I can't tell you exactly where for security reasons." Hers or Johanna's remained to be seen. "I'm safe, and I'm still in the city."

"Good." Scotia nodded at her own statement before her face fell. "Right? I mean, everyone's saying Johanna fired you, and coders don't just get fired. They usually leave lying on a cart or in Authority custody."

"Not fired, just reassigned. I'm working on a top-secret project, but don't tell anyone. If they ask you anything, tell them you think I was let go because of the hackdome tournaments. Don't sound sure about it when you say it, though, or they might think you know something more."

"Okay — but Cindira, it must be, like, really top secret." She brought her face close to the camera node on her comque, making the projection of her face on Cindira's side take on an unnatural angle. "Kaylie showed up at my desk about an hour ago and demanded to know what I know."

Her forehead crinkled as her face screwed up. "She came to you? Why didn't she just go to Johanna?"

"Probably because Johanna never came back to the office after she left with you this morning," Scotia said. "I was half hoping you were calling to tell me you hacked a tiktok and sent it off the pier with her still inside."

Cindira bit back the memory. There'd be a certain poetic justice if Johanna left this world the same way she'd murdered Omala, but that wasn't the kind of person Cindira was. Something she sometimes regretted.

"I would never—OH MY GOD."

A pile of garbage nearby shifted. Cindira spun, putting up her arms in the way she'd done as a battle avatar so many times before. Luckily, the old tom who jumped atop the trash bin knew better than to take her seriously.

"Cindira!" Scotia's voice was louder now, demanding. "What happened?"

"It's okay. It was only a cat." She pivoted the camera node up before her well-meaning friend could alert any local raccoons as to her whereabouts. "Anyway, I'm fine, but I have to go. I just wanted to tell you not to worry. I'm going to do everything I can to get this done quickly so I can come back."

"Oh, god, please don't do that."

Cindira grimaced again for the second time in as many minutes. "You don't want me to"—she minded her words before giving anything away—"accomplish my task?"

"Oh, no. No, that. I know you'll do anything you set out to do. I mean don't come back," Scotia said. "Or give it a good think before you do. I'm not sure what you're doing. I'm not asking. But you're doing it away from here. Don't be so quick to put yourself back under their boots, Cindira. Learn to walk on your own."

Johanna's workers had done a good job. Cindira was pleased to find the coder bay operational. The data stream over the hardwire connection indeed was a little slower than what she was used to, but she compensated in short order by decreasing the optical upload density. It wasn't as if she'd be designing dresses here and putting them in Kaylie's closet. The speed at which the Sink prototype manifested images and tracked movement was much more important.

Laporte, unusually catlike, lay on its belly with its chin resting on the control pad. "I wish there was more I could do to help, miss, but I'm afraid the building's blackout zone means I'm unable to connect to the wireless grid as well."

"You could help me by telling me who this supposed fairy godmother is." Cindira kept her eyes on the command pad as she aligned the security clearance codes to access the Kingdom and pull it up into view.

The mouse lifted its head. "As I said, I am sorry, but I'm unable to do that. She asked me not to say anything unless told I could do so."

Her mouth ticked up into a half-smile. "Must be one hell of a hacker, is all I can say. I didn't think there was anyone else around better than me at manipulating the vreals. And if she needs to protect her identity for now, fine, I get it. You just let her know I'm thankful that she saved my ass, but I'd like to meet her if she ever thinks it safe."

"I know she feels the same."

Finally, images inside the glass tube took on definition. Looking like a giant cylinder turned upside down on the floor, the Sink allowed the coder to stream live views of anywhere inside the vreals. Unlike the larger, more powerful, and more state-of-the-art Sink in the Kitchens, however, she was disappointed to discover that this render was read-only. Cindira only hoped that whatever she found in her continued investigation of her father's whereabouts would require no manipulation to explore.

"Is that the gate to the palace?" Laporte sparked to life, scrambling to the top of her work console and getting a better view.

Cindira nodded, her finger turning clockwise circles on her control pad, zooming the view forward. Soon the gates were past, and the scene shifted to the ballroom, empty now of anyone except NPCs and VAPORs. The pre-programmed servants and mutable objects had no purpose without active avatars to serve and service, but it was easier to let them run continuously than constantly switching their functions on and off.

"I want to start by checking to see if my father's avatar is still where it was during the ball."

Meaning lying in a bed in the upstairs wing of the palace reserved only at the Tiegs' or Fifes' request. While the "first family" of the Kingdom had a vreal residence a short carriage ride from the palace, the royal suites were often used to host corporate meetings or hold gatherings for Plaxis's VIP customers. Past a corridor of antechambers, behind a door unguarded and, thankfully, in a room unoccupied, she found him.

Should she be happy or disappointed that he looked much the

same?

Cindira sat back, pulling her knees into her chest and resting her heels on the lip of the chair. "Laporte, it occurs to me now that I have seen an avatar in the vreal like this. My mom's, when I jacked in for the first time in ages a few weeks ago. Does it mean that my father's also d—That he might be deceee—"

The words caught in her throat.

The mouse shook its head. "It means nothing. If you'll recall, your childhood avatar was also on hiatus next to your mother's. All it means is that your avatars were alpha series."

Relief was quickly pushed aside by curiosity. She fetched her cup of tea and pulled it to her lips. "What's an alpha-series avatar?"

"As the convention suggests, they were the first functional profiles launched into the vreal. Well, into your parent's platforms, at least," it said. "They're always on, and don't go into offline storage when their owner jacks out. It allows for a quicker jack-in time. It's also part of what makes the silicone slippers able to function so well, letting you slip in and out of the platform with ease. Your mother was an enthusiast for efficiency. And speaking of the slippers..." The botic turned around in place. "Can you also access Gaia from this unit? Maybe we can look around where you and Yuchi had your confrontation. The slipper may still be in the vicinity."

It wouldn't solve the problem of how she was supposed to retrieve it. Without a jackpod, and especially without both slippers in her possession in the vreal, how was she supposed to jack in and get it back? Still, it was a first step.

She leaned forward, typing a few commands into the console. "Yeah, just a second."

A gentle breeze blew, making the spring of grasses reaching out from a pile of rocks sway. No signs of a struggle were plain from where she watched. Without a bewildered prince and a samurai trying to kill someone, the meadow where the public exit lay almost looked pleasant. Luckily, they'd stumbled onto it at a time of day when no users were present.

Which piqued her curiosity. "I don't see it, but maybe someone picked it up, not knowing what it was?"

How did such a small botic click its tongue? Cindira really wished she understood more about hardware and botic design.

"Impossible, miss," Laporte informed her. "Not just anyone can handle the shoes. Your mother's design of the virtual representation came with very specific user requirements."

She manipulated the viewer controls, performing a thorough survey of the area. "Do you know who else is on that list, because I'm not seeing them."

"I don't. I was your mother's assistant, and to the extent it is possible for someone such as me, her friend. But she did not tell me everything, only that which she thought I needed to know."

"Yeah, that makes two of us."

The mouse sniffed. It nearly sounded like a chuckle. "Having said as much, the shoe may have had a homing function I'm not aware of, a command to place itself somewhere your mother thought it would be safe if she ever lost it. Besides efficiency, Omala also practiced the art of contingency planning."

"Now, that sounds like Mom."

Obviously, a manual optical scan wasn't about to turn up anything. The Kingdom was a vast platform, the geogrid it manifested covering thousands of hectares. It would take weeks of roving the grounds to turn up the shoe. Cindira doubted that would be her mother's way of finding a lost slipper as well.

"WWOD?"

Laporte's head tilted. "Sorry, miss?"

"WWOD," Cindira repeated.

She stood up and crossed to where she'd put down the cardboard box that she'd carried out of Plaxis the day before. The good thing about the slippers being made of soft silicone was that they rolled up compactly. No one would have bothered to look inside the small sewing kit from her desk (sometimes she liked to stitch together fabric in the real to better study its nature). The slippers rolled out in her hand the moment she sprang them free, and she wasted no time sitting back in her chair and crossing one leg over the other.

"What would Omala do?" Cindira said as she swapped footwear. "It's a little thing we coders are taught in training. Mom designed things in unique ways. Our professors were reminding us to think beyond our understanding and to see design in a bigger framework. Not that it worked for most people. She wasn't exactly public with most of her coding theories, right?"

"That's true, but I still don't understand what you're getting at."

The silicone slippers activated the moment she thought to turn them on. How, she wasn't sure. They had no indicator lights, no projection nodes to render data. All Cindira could say for sure was that she felt their presence. There had to be a transmitter in them, and if she could tap the signal, then it should only take a few command lines of Purusha Plus to...

The view tube went gray, flickered, and then clarified into a completely different scene.

"There."

Gone was the castle in the distance, the quaint medieval village festooned with floral arrangements and kitschy shops selling customers on any number of VAPORs and upgrades. Present was a much more recent tribute to a European city: the Hague.

"I can't use the shoes to jack in, but I think there's a way I can use the real world shoe's signature to home in on the missing slipper's location in the vreal." The viewer zoomed from clouds to the rooftops, down into the streets and into a building Cindira recognized, passing through the walls like they were air. "Ah, Congressional Hall. Mom used to have an office there. She must have programmed the shoe to relocate in the event it became separated from the other."

As much as a mouse could experience a jaw drop, Laporte did. "Amazing ingenuity."

"Yeah, Mom was good at that kind of thing."

"Not her," Laporte said. "You, miss. It never would have occurred to me to try something like that."

Her cheeks flushed, though why she should feel embarrassed didn't make sense. Maybe this was what pride felt like?

"Thank you, Laporte."

Suddenly, the scrolling view stilled. Cindira knew the shoe must have been somewhere in the scene that filled the Sink, even if in a drawer or perhaps even setting on a floor. What she saw, however, swept any relief she'd felt when her plan worked away, and replaced it with an overwhelming sense of dread.

The shoe was in plain sight.

Being held by the prince.

SIX

IT WAS THE MOST PERPLEXING thing he'd ever seen, and for a man who'd spent his late teenage years hacking into vreals and corrupting their code, that was saying something.

To the eye, it was just a woman's shoe. Made of glass and with the smallest heel, it wouldn't have been comfortable in the real world. This kind of thing could only be made for vreal wear. But was it the thing an avatar could don and run about in to-and-fro, fighting high-security bots?

And why could no one but him handle it?

"Sire?"

A knock sounded at the door, forcing Francisco to snap to attention. He shot to his feet, looking for some place to store his treasure.

"Just a moment." Francisco wasn't sure why he wouldn't just show it to Carlos. He'd told his attaché all about the bandit who kidnapped him and what had happened, but he hadn't told anyone about the shoe belonging to her. Was it because he wanted to crack this mystery himself, or because he wanted to protect the bandit?

With the glass shoe secured in the top drawer of his desk, Francisco sat back down and tried to make himself look absorbed in the documents set out across the workspace. "Come in."

The moment Carlos opened the door, Francisco knew he wasn't as slick as he thought. His mentor slipped in, looking around the edges of the room as though he expected to find someone there.

"I thought I heard someone in here with you."

That set Francisco's face sideways. "Why?"

"I thought I heard... whispers."

Could he have been saying his thoughts aloud and not realizing it? It didn't matter. Giving into further speculation would only draw attention that Francisco had already decided he didn't want.

The prince cleared his throat. "Did you have something you needed to tell me?"

Carlos snapped to attention, pivoting to the desk and helping himself to the guest chair. "Yes, Your Highness. The meeting you requested me to arrange? I've set it up for the day after tomorrow at noon."

Francisco grabbed his fountain pen (an archaic writing instrument, to be certain, but one he rather enjoyed using in the vreal) and made a note on the paper before him. "And who did you find to be our pro and con?"

"Congressperson Yo-Yo Hsu of Macau and the Prime Minister of Ethiopia, Eshe Aster."

"Hsu? Good choice. She's one of the most senior members of the Gaia congress. She's a purist, has hated the idea of Plaxis, a corporation owned and ran by multicryptoaires, hosting our platform for as long as she's served. There's a stack of letters in the monarch's secured files filled with her strong-worded opinions. She'd jump at the opportunity to uncouple us." Francisco shuffled to the next page in his stack. "I'm not as familiar with Aster."

"She's only been in office for a few years, but she's given several speeches crediting Plaxis's humanitarian efforts and dedication to Gaia. Her country has been plagued by several border and resource issues for decades, and Plaxis paid for their Gaia membership for the first twenty years to help them stabilize the North African-Western Arabia region."

"She definitely would have a fig in the basket to keep things as they are." Another page, another signature. Francisco signed off on the document with a flourish and sat back in his chair. "And for tech support?"

"I'm still working on that. I have a few lines out, but no one's bitten yet." Carlos ran his hands over the ornately carved arms of the chair. "In fact, I have a meeting with one now but back in the real, if you wouldn't be needing anything here from me for a while?"

"No, by all means." The prince waved a hand through the air. "I'll see you at the residence after I jack out."

For the first time that he could remember, Francisco wished office drawers in the vreal had locks. Carlos hadn't been gone two minutes when the urge to take the shoe back out overcame him. His correspondence would have to wait.

With one hand on the shoe, he used the other to tap a button on his desk. The AI assistant wasn't a person; it was a complex set of algorithms and databases, but Pele's voice still sounded female.

"How may I assist, Your Highness?"

He lifted the shoe to eye level. "Identify the VAPOR in my hand."

A momentary pause. "The prince is not holding a VAPOR."

He felt his eyebrow quirk. "What am I holding then?"

"The object in your hand cannot be identified," Pele said in a flat tone. "It does not match the description and build of any items registered in my database."

Curiouser and curiouser. "Best guess?"

A series of muted tones was played to let the user know Pele was, in fact, working. Finally, after a few seconds, the tones stopped. "It appears to be a jackpod."

"Damn it."

Francisco let his hand and the shoe fall to the desk. "Sorry?"

Pele repeated her statement. "I said, it appears to be a jackpod."

"No, I heard that," Francisco said. "I mean after that. Did you cuss? I didn't think you were programmed for—"

"Oh, no, he can—"

Francisco shot to his feet. "Who's there?"

No, Pele hadn't cussed, but someone else had. A woman. And her voice sounded vaguely familiar.

With only silence for answer, Francisco lifted his hand and shook a finger. "Whoever you are, remove your tap from this room. This is the personal office of the Prince of Gaia. You're breaking international law and facing a possible jail sentence if you're caught."

"He really can... What? No, I can't do that ... Because it's stupid, that's why... He's not going to know."

Suddenly, Francisco felt like he was listening to one side of a comque chat. The woman was having a conversation, the other party as invisible to his eyes as she was.

"Who are you?"

"Someone who's smart enough not to tell you the answer to that after you just threatened me with jail time," she said.

Well, his mysterious interloper had him there.

"I promise," she continued, "I didn't mean to spy on you. I wasn't trying to find you at all. I was looking for..."

As the woman's voice drifted off, Francisco tried to think of the most obvious answer. "You were looking for the glass shoe." As it turned out, obvious things were obvious. "You're the bandit who saved me."

"Yes, and it's a silicone slipper, actually."

"Not according to Pele. She says it's a jackpod."

"And that's why the artificial part of artificial intelligence is so important to remember."

Francisco laughed despite himself. Truth be told, he should be reaching for the button on his desk, the one that sent a signal back to Gaia's real-world facility in San Francisco. It would tell his security team that he needed a system lockdown and immediate assistance. But he didn't think that was true.

"Will you at least tell me your first name?"

There was a long pause until a gentle "No."

"Okay." Francisco shrugged. He had to ask. But the fact that she wouldn't say told him one thing: her name must not be common. What fear would there be in saying Sarah or Padma or Lin? Such women were a byte a billion. "That night of the ball, you said that the people after me were the ones who lost the most when war went online. My security teams have been ferreting out all our available intelligence networks and haven't been able to uncover anything like that. Can you at least tell me where you got your information from?"

"I was making a guess. I might be completely wrong. I had a feeling that night that you were in danger. Can we leave it at that?"

"People at my level don't usually take dramatic actions based on feelings."

"People at my level don't take dramatic actions without them. Why else would you do anything, unless you felt it was right?"

He could hear the smile in her voice, and it brought one to his own. "Touché."

"Your Highness, that slipper isn't yours."

Francisco pivoted to his desk, running a finger over the back heel of the shoe. "I know, it's yours."

"And I need it back."

"Gladly." He lifted the object and held it up in offering. "Come get it. Or don't you trust me not to arrest you on sight?"

"I have no reason to trust you."

"I think it goes the other way on that, miss. You are the one who held me at knifepoint."

"And then I gave you the knife the second we were away from the palace on our way to fight a samurai."

"In retrospect, maybe you should have kept the knife."

When she laughed, his heart lifted, as did his smile. It had been a while since he'd charmed a woman like that. Francisco had forgotten how much he enjoyed it.

WHICH WAS A SILLY THOUGHT TO HAVE. Was he actually flirting with the woman who might have killed him if she'd wanted to? Should she really get that much credit for not killing him? Attempted murder started so few romances. At least he knew for certain now that the woman he was talking to was, in fact, the bandit. He hadn't told anyone else that his kidnapper had disarmed herself once they were alone.

Francisco pushed his hands into the pockets of his slacks and sat on the edge of his desk. "Do you spy on me often, Bandit?"

"I told you, I didn't mean to do this. I was looking for the slipper, and, no, I've never spied on you before."

"Are you disappointed you found me instead?"

"I..." Even with the odd audio quality of her voice wrapped around the room, he could hear her swallow down a reaction. "Your Highness, are you... Are you flirting with me?"

"Maybe." Francisco stepped forward, the same way he might if he were near a young woman with which he wanted to talk more intimately. He had a feeling she could see him, though he wasn't sure how. "Or maybe I'm just attempting to woo you in hopes that you'll reconsider and come collect your shoe from me in person. I am the prince. I could issue you a pardon, if I felt it was warranted."

"Do that, and you'll undermine your own authority and risk weakening Gaia. Besides, I can't be interested in you."

"You can't be interested in me?" That was the strangest rejection he'd ever heard. "Gaia is a democracy. You can choose to do anything you like."

"If Gaia were the real, I might take you up on that. Unfortunately, out here in the real world, where there would be... complications."

He blinked. "You're married."

"I'm not, but it has nothing to do with that. I have people I need to protect, and there's no way you could issue a formal pardon without filing my identity in the Congressional records. I need the slipper back, without you finding out who I am. I'm sorry, Your Highness, I really am. You... You seem like a great guy."

The sadness in her voice struck him in a way that he wasn't prepared for. Suddenly, Francisco found his sympathies getting the better of him. "Is there anything I can do to help?"

"Give me back the slipper. Leave it somewhere no one would see it. I can locate it no matter where in Gaia or the Kingdom it is. I'll collect it as soon as I'm able to get there."

Ah, so they were back there again.

Francisco turned to his desk and placed the object in question on the corner. "I suppose that means we're at an impasse."

"I suppose it does."

That was it then, unless he could think of some other piece he had to play on the board. Obviously, the hacker who'd pulled off what she had and showed up in his office without being seen or heard could evade anything his security could do to trace her.

"So where does that leave us, miss?"

Francisco waited for her answer for a minute. Two minutes.

"Miss?"

But no more answers came.

SEVEN

"MISS, IF YOU PLEASE!"

Startled, Cindira bolted up and hit her head on a lamp hanging over the bench.

"Sorry—ow!"

She rubbed the spot, hoping it wouldn't leave a mark. Only then did she round on the mouse sorting diodes atop the workbench.

"What was that for?"

Laporte didn't deviate from its work. "You've been humming that song for hours. It's setting my teeth on edge."

"Setting your teeth on edge?" Cindira blinked her confusion. "I'm not that bad of a singer."

"Your notes are near enough to pitch, with less than 5.8% deviation on average, but that's not what I mean."

If for a moment she wondered at the botic expressing emotion, any doubt was cleared by that comment.

Shortly, Laporte continued. "I've been tracking your efficiency for the last three days, and I have observed a steady drop in your productivity whenever you take to song."

Cindira rubbed the back of her neck. It wasn't that the mouse was wrong; it was that he was attributing an effect to the wrong cause. It wasn't the singing, but the reason she felt like singing that was slowing her down.

It didn't make sense. It wasn't like Cindira had never had a boyfriend. True, not a serious one, and most of them turned out to think dating a famous person's daughter somehow upped their own social ambitions. They all learned in short order that social ambition wasn't something the daughter of Saint Omala had a particular interest in. If she did, her attraction to Prince Francisco Batista de la Reina would at least have some justification. As it was, she found her mind too often turning back to the way his voice sounded toward the end of their brief talk through the prototype Sink—a phenomena which still defied explanation.

"Can I remind you that your father is still missing?" the mouse chided when her thoughts had taken her away again. "Not only that, but we've as yet turned up no trace of anything in this facility which sates your stepmother's inquiry. Between you and me, I feel much better if we could get that out of the way, and hope there's a way for you to integrate back into Plaxis HQ."

"I would have thought you'd be happy to have me out from under the thumb of my mother's murderer. I'm at least thrilled not to be constantly a whim away from Kaylie. I think this the longest I've ever gone without having to do some project or another for her."

Cindira pulled down another crate of technological bric-a-brac. Random parts or tools, even some useful surplus, were bountiful in the warehouse, but in two and a half days of search, they'd turned up little else.

"I don't know why we're searching through these boxes. Obviously, whatever downloaded 2.5 petabytes is going to have an actual cable coming from it. It's also going to be hot as hell."

Even if storage devices were now the smallest they'd ever been, you couldn't push that much data and maintain it without creating heat. Nowhere that she'd been inside the facility seemed particularly warm, let alone had the type of venting that would be required.

"We're going through these boxes to see if we can find enough spare parts to assemble a jackpod."

Cindira's hand froze in midair, a cooling fan in her clutch. "What?"

Laporte swam about the dish, emerging with three blue diodes in his snout. He scurried out of the bowl and spit them out into a special pile on the counter. "We know where the silicone slipper is, now all we have to do is get it. I know you can hack into the Kingdom with my help, but we still need a functioning jackpod to do it. Since you can't leave the building—"

"I can leave the building."

"Since you shouldn't leave the building," Laporte amended. "Our only hope is to build one from scratch."

"Laporte, I know that I'm the best coder of my generation. But you must be thinking of my father, the renowned hardware architect. That, or you have me confused for a techanic." She dropped the fan into the crate and heaved it across the room, where they'd designated a different workbench for holding the things they'd already examined. "I can't build a piece of hardware that complex. I certainly wouldn't subject myself to its use if I did. Not to mention it would take weeks to do it."

With a grunt, Cindira made her best attempt to pull down the next crate, one at the very back of the workbench and covered in grease.

"Why won't this thing move?"

Laporte scrambled over to the table and scurried around the backside. "It's attached to the workbench."

"Attached?" She stopped pulling and tried to see what the mouse saw. An overhang of the shelf above blocked her view, though. "Why would anyone bolt a storage box on a workbench?"

"Not bolted, miss. It's connected via a wire array."

A thrill went through her, but the mouse quickly nipped it in the bud.

"Not a data cable," it said. "It's some kind of corded metal thing. I would posit that it's use is mechanical. I can't see where it runs to; somewhere under the desk, it looks like. Maybe if you try to pull it out instead of up, you might have some leeway."

Mechanical? That only brought more questions. And if there was one thing with which Cindira had a problem, it was leaving questions unanswered when there might be a way to solve them.

Steeling herself in case the contents turned out to be heavier than expected, she grabbed two dusting cloths from the sorted pile and wrapped them on the corners of the desk. She was going to look like she'd wrestled a tiktok's innards when she was done, but at least she'd know what this mechanism they discovered did.

"Ready then?" The grip was better now. "Go!"

"Ladylike" was not a word one would have used to describe the sounds she made. The crate wasn't heavy, but whatever lay on the other end of the cord wasn't going to give without a fight.

"Pull!" Laporte had appointed itself crew captain, sitting on top of the workbench and barking out orders. "Put your back into it!"

"Not. Helping." She tried to sink down so that the crate in her arms was parallel with the ground, reducing the energy required to move it out by not also having to move it up. Unfortunately, it also reduced the range of her muscles.

"You're thinking of the box as a weight. Think of it instead as a pulley!"

If her face hadn't already been contorted from exertion, Laporte's words would have made it so. What was it saying, think about it as a pulley? Pulleys distributed weight over a greater surface area so less effort was required on the working end to pull. If the box was the pulley, then...

"Oh!" Cindira planted her feet, hoping that she wasn't about to break her back. The polished concrete floor didn't look like it would exactly cushion her fall. "Okay, here it goes."

It all happened at once then. Cindira shot up straight, pulling the box tight to her chest, before falling back like a board. If her head hit hard, she'd be done for. The day, the week, or forever, she wasn't sure—nevertheless, done for. Instead, she was pleased when the tension on the cord equalized with her mass, and she was left leaning back, her body at a forty-five-degree angle.

It was then that she heard the click, and a door that had not been there a moment ago appeared on the wall to her left.

EIGHT

SHE STARED AT THE BODY and asked herself the same questions that she had been asking for the last hour: How was he still alive? Who was he? Why had someone hidden him in the old Gaia Labs warehouse and supplied him with enough renewable biobotics and supplies to last half a century?

The monitors plugged into the first-generation jackpod in which the body lay refreshed, displaying the report Cindira had asked its interface to compile. She scrolled through the data and reached two preliminary hypotheses. Either there was corruption, or the frail man with thinning gray hair and a sickly pallor inside the machine was the new world-record holder for the longest jack ever.

"According to the logs, this man has been in a session for over twelve years."

The mouse sniffed the air. "That is quite a long time."

"Oh, this makes no sense."

A closer look at the jackpod also added to the mystery. Most of the hardware required to make jacking possible was housed inside the shell of the machine. You couldn't have critical connections exposed hither and yon and risk one of them accidentally being disconnected. Pull the wrong cord at the right moment, and you could fry someone's mind. But as her eyes adjusted to the light, Cindira realized something else. Some tubes contained liquids of several viscosities and colors which seemed to move, though if it was into the machine or away from it, she couldn't tell. Possibly both.

A memory tripped. A photo opportunity for the Tiegs to look charitable and compassionate: Johanna holding the hand of a frail, brown-skinned woman sewn into stasis, Kaylie and Cade standing behind her, looking somber. On the other side of the bed, her father had squeezed her shoulders as she'd stood in front of him. "New Omala Grover Memorial Wing of St. Dymphna's dedicated; family members attend dedication and comfort the afflicted." That's how it'd appeared in the news feeds. Cindira also remembered how Johanna and her children had broken the pose the moment after the picture was captured.

Her father had lingered, and after a moment, she swore she heard him say, "Amen."

Scotia probably knew who had coined the term "chiphead" to describe the addiction. Cindira didn't, but everyone knew the toll it took on society. It was so much easier for a young mother to escape to a tropical beach than listen to her children complain. The working poor could escape to a low-grade vreality where they were the boss, where everyone deferred to them. There were stories of children found half-starved and neglected while their parents spent hours wasting away inside jack dens. Even the rich weren't immune. In some ways, their addictions were worse. Children of privilege bankrupted generational wealth to afford the latest, the most exclusive, the "in-vreal" fashion or tech of the day. Morality-challenged coders built worlds where widows and widowers of war escaped into customized platforms where their dead one's avatar could be programed to replicate the relationship they'd shared.

Part of the solution had been outlawing avatar retention. When someone died in the real, it was now an edict that any avatar they'd had in the vreal be deleted or permanently archived within ten business days. In the meantime, techanics adapted hospice jackpods for chiphead use. At St. Dymphna's, they could live out their final days or weeks in a self-contained world filled with VAPORS (back then, still called NPCs), where they wouldn't have access to their bank accounts or be able to hack into those of family and friends and keep paying what amounted to exuberant fees for the poor to keep up the illusion of a gilded world.

The machines at that hospital that day had looked like this one. Jackpods with additional inputs and outputs that fostered the body and allowed access for the biobotics: tubes to carry food, those to carry away waste, and electrical stimulation nodes to force muscles to move, staving off the worst effects of the corporeal atrophy. The body inside had been "sewn" in and all vital physical functions and requirements met while he continued to exist in the vreal.

But could that keep someone going for over twelve years? The patients at St. Dymphna's rarely survived more than a few months, a few for a year. Had that been by design, or could the jacked human body survive indefinitely?

Could the mind?

Cindira finished her survey of the space by opening the machinery of the jackpod housed beneath it. She wasn't a techanic; she didn't know what half of the parts beeping and flashing in front of her did, but she knew what the large cable plugged into the network port was for. Now that she'd acclimated to the room, she also heard the unmistakable no-pitch hum of the ventilation system, felt the baby hairs on her neck flutter as the air flowed around them. The heat was being pulled from this room, yes, but likely there was another room beneath or next to it which housed a superserver and the cooling units necessary to keep it from overheating. She'd bet a fine amount of greens that on the roof of the building, directly above them, two exhaust vents were well hidden, by design or with money, from environmental regulators. The silvery covering on both walls and ceiling suggested some sort of wave dampening material. Johanna had said that her people couldn't find any sort of electric pulse in the building matching the expected parameters, didn't she? That would explain why.

"Laporte, I believe we've found our data device."

The mouse botic sniffed the air. "This is a first-generation jackpod. Someone's hacked it up and specialized it, true, but I don't believe it's capable of retaining that amount of data."

"I wasn't talking about the jackpod." Cindira turned to it. "I know you don't currently have a connection to the wires to research, but do you know how much data the human brain can hold?"

"I wouldn't need a connection to the wireless grid to speculate that it's in the neighborhood of 2.5 petabytes."

"Bingo." She shifted her gaze back to the man in the jackpod. His chest rose and fell with a constant rhythm. Beneath his eyelids, movement approximated those of a person experiencing REM sleep, the level of consciousness at which dreaming could occur, and which a jackpod closely reproduced. "Should we... Should we wake him up?"

Cindira wasn't sure if she was asking Laporte or herself.

"I'd suggest it against it for the moment, Miss," the mouse said. "There may be a good reason he's been hidden away here for so long."

"Such as?"

The mouse scuttled over the clear glass of the jackpod cover, taking in a different vantage of the poor soul within. "I'm only speculating, but in the early days of your parents' work, there was a suggestion to use their new platform not only as a world congress and for war, but also as an alternative to prison. It was thought, especially for those with a long or life-term sentence, that being trapped in the vreal may be more humane, and perhaps even have greater prospects for rehabilitation, than to be housed, caged, and isolated."

The disgust raced up her spine and tugged on her. Cindira took a step back. "He's a criminal?"

"Again, miss, I can't say. I'm only analyzing my databases and trying to find the most likely reasons someone would be permajacked in such a conspicuous way." Its eyes shifted, a myriad of colors flashing across them. "I'm still unable to connect with the wireless grid, but I do have in my memory a mention of a prison volunteer for the beta test, and a confirmation that the individual was inserted into a pumpkin vined off Gaia."

Confusion cocked her head. "A gap in the database, or just something you didn't have a reason to access?"

"Hard to say. Your mother designed me to have access to almost all Plaxis's resources, but sometimes even I... What is the human idiom, hit a brick wall?"

In a building comprised of brick walls, that term had never seemed more apt.

"There are elements of this that point toward an answer," the botic continued, "but every time I try to dig down and analyze, something in my internal algorithms forces me out of the subroutine."

She nodded, but it was only an acknowledgment that she'd heard, not that she understood. She looked around the room, trying to see if there were any clues, but found little more than random pieces of jackpod parts and general-purpose tools.

"Miss, I think I've found something."

Cindira turned to see that the mouse had moved to the side of the machine pushed against the wall. Its little head peeked up like that of a creature looking over a fence.

"There's a servicing tag posted here," it continued. "A listing for a techanic on the other side of town, and an indicator light suggesting the unit is being monitored remotely."

How, Cindira wondered. The shielding on the building shouldn't allow for it. Not unless the monitor was also tied into the hardwire connection, which would mean it too had been hidden in this concealed room for over a decade.

"According to the San Francisco public records I have downloaded in my memory, there is still a techanic at the same address as the business listed on the service tag. The name is different, though. It could be they rebranded, or it could also be someone else entirely."

Cindira looked back over her shoulder, as though she could see the overly fortified exit to the rest of the world through the many brick walls between. Technically, she would only have to step outside and be away from the building to ping them. Walk a block as she had the other night, and her comque could pick up a signal, letting her make an inquiry conveniently. But as one of her professors at school had been fond of saying, convenience comes at a premium, and that premium is often privacy. The techanic was a public business. This storage facility was part of Plaxis, even if abandoned. There could be many reasons someone would try to hide something away from the world here, ranging from the benign to the horrifying. Even though her comque was secure from Plaxis's security protocols, that didn't mean the techanic's was. Anyone could be listening. She couldn't risk it.

"I'll go in the morning."

Laporte leaped back atop the jackpod. "Miss?"

"To the techanic," she clarified. "I can't risk calling. Plus, if it turns out they don't know what I'm talking about, they'd probably just hang up on me anyway."

Tiny feet with tinier nails scuttled along the glass. "Do you think it is wise? I'm no fan of Johanna Tieg, but she was right when she said you being about could be dangerous. Whoever has your father may look for you, especially now that you're no longer with the company. Searching eyes grow wide before they narrow."

Cindira shook her head, not believing herself what she was about to say. "This guy didn't end up here by accident. Someone deliberately sewed him in, set up enough biobotics to keep him going for a while, then hid him. Maybe he volunteered for... whatever this is." She motioned vaguely to the machine. "But maybe not. I'm not ready to say I know anything about how this is even possible, let alone what that much data downloading to a human brain implies. I want to be extra cautious about this, especially before I tell Johanna that I've found what she asked me to find."

The mouse's tiny head bobbed. "I'll come with you."

"No." Cindira slashed the air with an open-palmed hand. "That part of town is too dangerous to take you to. If someone realizes that you're such advanced tech and not an actual mouse, you'll be off to the black market faster than the fall of rain."

"I'm aware of the crime statistics for Inner Sunset, which is even more reason that you shouldn't go alone."

Something about that statement gave her pause. "Why would

you know that?"

"I... I think I spent some time there, once upon a time. I... have records directing me to find... someone in that area of town."

Coincidence, or yet another dead end? "Do you know who or why?"

The botic sniffed the air. "My files have either been blocked or deleted. It could have been a confusion, a malfunction. There were times early in my existence when my command and subroutines still required fine tuning."

Two sides of the same coin, and no way to know which one was the lucky side. But that wasn't as important as the bigger question: who was flipping the coin?

"Laporte, how long has it been since you were initialized?"

"I came online in 2129, miss."

"And your creator?"

"Your mother, of course." It answered the inquiry so matter-of-factly.

She nodded. "And who have you served since your inception?"

"I serve your mother." The tone remained the same, the answer in the botic's concept as obvious as the first time it said so.

Cindira crossed her arms over her chest. "My mother is dead."

"Yes, miss. She died in 2133."

"And if the data I'm pulling up here is accurate, VRip van Winkle here went under in around 2136." The mouse didn't dispute that. "So, who could have edited your files?"

Focus. Cindira breathed in, breathed out. As many wonderful things as she could do in the vreal using the code, it didn't change the facts. A program was a complex set of binary questions, and the answer to each one sped a command down a channel of negative and positive responses.

"Laporte, is there anyone else besides my mother who has access to block or delete your memory files?"

"Besides yourself, and then only to the degree that she delegated, no."

Anyone else hearing what the botic had just said would take the response for an answer. Cindira wasn't anyone else. It wasn't an answer; it was a qualification and obfuscation.

She swallowed, sighed. "Is there anything besides my mother with access to block or delete your memory files?"

Its eyes flashed green, then yellow, then red. "Subroutine 'Eat this message.'"

"Eat this message?" She ran a hand through her hair, pulling on the ends. "What in the hell does that mean?"

"It's the only solution I can find to your query, miss. Even though your mother designed me to be a sort of portal that could peek into the real from the vreal or vice versa, I have a complex series of algorithmic self-defense mechanisms. That subroutine allows me to delete or permanently black-box any information of which my possession creates a direct threat to a user."

"Did that subroutine trigger around our friend here?" She vaguely motioned to the jackpod.

"I have no record of it, but I wouldn't, would I? All I can say for certain is that I can't tell you I haven't not triggered that subroutine."

"Even for someone like me, that's confusing." Cindira clapped her hands together. "It's been a long day. We'll look more into this tomorrow. For tonight"—she turned towards the door—"pleasant dreams, VRip."

NINE

FRANCISCO HAD NEVER followed celebrity culture. He was only aware of Kaylie Fife's renown as a fashion icon because the people who prepared his daily briefings thought he might want to know. He didn't. But considering she was the young woman who'd recently become Plaxis's official liaison to his royal offices, he expected her to arrive in some outlandish, bright pink costume meant to inspire fear and/or lust. Instead, he discovered Kaylie in a smart business suit that would have made her fit into any row of the Gaia Congress.

Something strange was afoot.

"Your Majesty." She tilted her head, her eyes challenging him. "Remind me of the etiquette in the real. Am I supposed to bow?"

A backhanded insult. Not that someone would blame Kaylie for her hostility. The last time they'd met in the flesh, Francisco had been presented as Detective Frank Batista, working on behalf of the Gaia security forces to investigate Plaxis's business practices. His sources inside the company had reported that Miss Fife had "blown a motherboard" when she'd learned who Francisco truly was. He wasn't sure if it was because of the deception, or because he'd tugged at her romantic gestures (no doubt equally engineered) just long enough to learn what he'd wanted to know, then quickly forgotten she existed. Any worries that he might have insulted her were dismissed even quicker. Kaylie had been told to flirt with him (by her own mother, no less) to distract him from his work, no doubt.

No, Francisco hadn't changed his mind. He still thought there were secrets about Plaxis being kept hidden from him and the World Congress, but he'd decided that Kaylie wasn't the one hiding them.

Francisco looked up from his tablet only long enough to motion to a chair across from his desk. "I'm only royal in the vreal. To the best of my knowledge, that position, while respected, hasn't been recognized by any real-world nation. Here, I'm just Frank." He pointed to the guest chair on the other side of his desk. "Come to try and seduce me again, Miss Fife?"

"I don't think there will be a need for that today." Kaylie sat down, opened the briefcase she'd brought with her, and got down to business. "Since the unfortunate incident that occurred at the royal ball, we've been reviewing security protocol with both Plaxis staff and your own Gaian team. We've finished the preliminary report. I'm here to review our findings and present suggestions on some changes we can make. Assuming that now is a good time?"

Her manner, professional. Her inquiry, sincere. Maybe there was more to Kaylie than his brief experience and intelligence reports suggested. Perhaps she wasn't a petulant, spoiled trust-fund baby who'd had her whole life handed to her on a platter. *Once upon a time, you were that kid, Francisco.* A little voice inside his thoughts had been growing in volume as of late. Having his entire world turned upside down when he was fifteen had borne in him a sense of compassion that previously lay outside his experience. His recent years of dealing with people from his own background had taught him that compassion shouldn't be reserved just for the poor.

"Security protocols?" Francisco sat back, swiveling in a slow arc in his chair and putting his data pad down. "Why go over them with me? Aren't those built into the system?"

She looked away sheepishly. "Some are. But I also understand from Carlos's strongly worded letter that a certain security option we currently have in place in the Kingdom didn't meet your approval."

"You mean the whole 'physical injury can be replicated outside of the platform thing'? Yeah, not my favorite." Francisco raised a hand, feeling along the base of his throat. "Though I'm sure being held at knifepoint wasn't exactly your doing, I still didn't enjoy it."

Kaylie cocked her head to the side. "You seriously can't believe that we would let the Prince of Gaia be stolen away by a hacker and put in actual danger, right? Come on, Frank, you're smarter than that."

"I am smarter than that, and I'd really prefer if you called me Mr. Batista."

Her face screwed up. "But you just said..."

He presented a hand to stall her words. "But then I heard you say it, and I didn't like it."

She huffed, the little blue pupils in her eyes wobbly. Kaylie Fife was not a woman often denied, and that was inclusive of all areas of life. At least in her professional space, she stayed on task. She continued as though he hadn't just handed her an insult to go with her injury.

"At the end of the day, the Kingdom is a place people come to be entertained, but it's also a place fraught with real-world consequences. Imagine if the rulers of two countries whose forces are currently engaged in the war arenas inside Gaia were to cross paths in the Kingdom. Words are exchanged. A heated battle takes place. Soon they're at each other's throats and one of them kills the other... even if just virtually. Early studies into that kind of situation suggested the players would be likely to carry their conflict out in the real world as well, and then what is the point of Gaia if that happens on the regular?"

Francisco blinked his surprise. Kaylie was many things: young, ambitious, spoiled rotten, and sexy as hell. Just because he didn't like her didn't mean he'd deny the truth. But informed and rational weren't tags he often filed for her in his mind.

She sat back, stretching her hands over her head. Yes, his eyes followed the rise of her chest. It was hard not to. She was just so damned...

Francisco fidgeted in his seat. "I suppose I see your point."

Her hands dropped to the side, even as a little smile picked up the corner of her eyes. His attention, and her effect on him, hadn't gone unnoticed, it seemed. "Rex decided early on the best way to prevent vreal conflict from the Kingdom spilling over into the real was to give such encounters real-world consequences. Which, of course, we could be liable for."

"All of this is true, but none of it explains what you're planning to do instead. I'm going to need you to get to that quickly or get out even quicker."

The corners of her mouth pulled back into a straight line. "I'm here to prevent any further attempts at regicide."

His eyebrow lifted suggestively. "I thought you said my kidnapping was only entertainment?"

"That's our official statement." Rather than pull out the strings of their previous discussions, Kaylie pressed on. "If you're going to be in the Kingdom regularly, we can't overlook the likelihood of copycat criminals. If they can't get to you here in the real and few would dare try in Gaia, that's their next best option."

"Plaxis vets and tracks every client while they're logged in. I know one of your clients can show up in fantasyland disguised as anyone and using any name they choose, but you know who they really are, don't you?" Francisco shrugged. "Do you really think they'd be so bold as to take me out, knowing they couldn't get away with it?"

Only after asking did Francisco realize how self-evident the answer was. A woman had kidnapped him in open sight and surrounded by witnesses, and neither Plaxis nor Gaia security still had any clue who she was.

"You don't think there are people who would be proud to call themselves your assassin openly?" Kaylie grinned. "I'm sitting here in the real, considering undertaking the act myself and wondering what shoes would work best for the occasion."

The air froze between them, as did Francisco where he sat.

She stared at him.

He stared at her.

And then they both laughed, Kaylie throwing back her head and letting out a very unladylike cackle.

The prince was not a man without a sense of humor, though perhaps its edges had been smoothed over time and with a great deal of vigilance. But it was a laugh. A genuine, unprocessed, ugly-but-true laugh. Such a slight gesture, one that reminded him that the woman opposite him was real. Vain and aggressive at times, perhaps, but still... real.

And you don't know who the masked woman really was. You're becoming obsessed with your projections of who you want her to be, not who she was.

The recollection sobered him, as did the dwindling mirth. When they both sat there in silence again, Kaylie held up the black cylinder in her hands.

"This is a retinal mapper."

"Eye scans?" Francisco wiped away the last remnants of his smile. "I haven't heard of those being used for a security feature since every third-world hospital could reproduce anyone's with a basic bio printer."

"And in the real, that's true. But in the vreal..." Her voice tapered off as she pushed a few buttons nested into the smooth lines of the device's contours. Around the circular end facing his direction, a soft glow emanated. "Retinal maps aren't part of a typical avatar build. If you ever looked deeply into someone's eyes in the vreal, you'd see they lack the typical definition present in the real. You might also fall in love."

"Have to admit, I don't do that much."

"Which one?" Her eyes peeked up, even as her head stayed angled to work the device. It made her look... what was the English word, comely?

Flirtation: Kaylie's second language, and she had near-native fluency. But unlike the blatant attempt before, when her efforts had been not only transparent but overdone, Francisco found that this time he was actually enjoying her suggestive stare.

"Neither." He grinned, leaning forward ever so slightly, taking a good survey of his guest. Her eyes weren't blue. They were a distinct shade, somewhere between a storm cloud and the cerulean sea, with tiny flecks of brown near the center. "But maybe that's been to my deficit."

"Yes, well, just keep in mind that we can't hide the complexity once it's embedded." She buried her smile inside a professional demeanor. "Anyone looking into your eyes and with a bit of knowledge of security will know. That's why I'm going to suggest you not look anyone directly in the eyes in the vreal unless you have complete and utter trust in them. A hacker could lift the map, and any security measure locked by your retinal scan is useless then."

"It doesn't sound like it's that reliable of a security measure, then."

"And that's why we're also going to create another redundant bio-attribute." Her eyes flitted away. Kaylie bit on her bottom lip and flipped the scanner over, pointing to a rough, toothed section on the end that would slip over his eye. "A DNA sample."

Had she just said what he thought she'd said? "You want to take my blood?"

"We only need a single drop. I promise you won't feel it."

The pain wasn't what concerned him. "As you probably know, Miss Fife, I've refused several requests to add my DNA to my profile already." There were secrets in his blood, secrets that even Carlos didn't know.

Kaylie fidgeted. "I am aware of that, yes. But, Mr. Batista, consider the fact that someone has already tried to kill you once."

"In the vreal." Francisco took to his feet and paced to the window. "The DNA profile only helps secure the jackpods. I've had no worries about the security of my physical person while I'm jacked in. Not before I was a prince, and certainly not afterward, when my jacks are always from the security of the Palace of Fine Arts. A DNA attribute doesn't do anything to protect me in the real."

"I know, but I've been advised to give you every security tool we have at our disposal." She put the scanner back into her bag. "If you want to refuse it, however..."

"No, wait."

The finer features of her face remained in professional stoicism, and the distinct conflict between the presentation he'd been given today and the one he'd first had while visiting Plaxis for the first time made Francisco question his own conclusions. Perhaps Kaylie wasn't the licentious minx who threw herself at anyone with power and influence. Perhaps that was just her persona, who she was forced to be when others were looking and she had to perform a part.

Her brand, but not her spirit.

Who are you truly, Miss Fife? Can I trust you?

"I'm not sure why you're staring at me like that, but it's starting to make me nervous."

"I'm sorry." Francisco shook himself from his thoughts. Was he blushing? Princes weren't supposed to blush. Kings certainly did not; that was one of the few lessons his father had managed to convey, as useless as it had seemed at the time. "I was just thinking... You're different than the last few times I saw you."

It was as though he'd announced that he'd caught her stealing credits out of her mother's bank account. Kaylie's eyes went to the wall. She pulled in on herself, scooting to the edge of her chair. "I told Cade I should apologize."

"Cade?" Francisco scoured his memory for the people who'd been at the party that night. "Is that your boyfriend?"

"What? No, ew." She grinned. "Cade is my brother. You met him at Plaxis, but you probably forgot him. My mother always says I'm the light and he's the shadow. You never notice him if I'm around."

Now that she mentioned it, he remembered the existence of the other Fife sibling. "Oh, right. I..." He cleared his throat and straightened. "There's... a problem with my DNA."

Kaylie's head quirked to the side; she pursed her lips.

"Not a problem, I mean, more like a quality," Francisco amended. "It's unique, and I'm worried if anyone finds out about it, they might think certain things about me."

"All medical information is held in the closest security. It would violate the law for us to share anything, and there's only four people... excuse me, three people who would have access to them."

Francisco's left eyebrow arched. "You sound unsure about that."

"It's only because we recently lost one of our high-security clearance workers." Kaylie held up the cylinder in front of her, turning a dial, and its gentle white glow shifted to blue. "I promise, you can trust us. In fact, I'll personally handle the data myself and make sure no one else has access to it."

"Your mother?"

Kaylie shook her head. "She's distracted at the moment. She doesn't even know I'm here."

He felt his shoulders ease as he relented. Francisco melted back into his chair. Kaylie wasted no time in making her way around the desk, bringing with her a fragrance of roses and jasmine.

"Tilt your head back and try to keep your eyes open, but blink when you need to, okay?"

Keep his eyes open? He'd do that, but he found himself slowing his breathing, drinking in her scent.

A corner of her mouth twitched. "It's called Gardens of Versailles."

"Sorry?"

"The perfume. Supposedly it's what the Gardens at Versailles smelled like."

Suddenly, a flash. White light blazed. Red veins. His heart took off. An image burned bright in his sight. The shoe, like it was floating there in the air. Francisco jerked back, his chair hitting the wall, banging.

Kaylie was there in a moment. "Mr. Batista!"

Francisco gasped. Something had just hit him in the chest, knocking all the air from his lungs. He tried to swallow his overreaction, but now his pulse was spiking for an entirely different reason. A touch. A woman's touch. How long has it been? Kaylie's soft fingers wrapped around his wrist, her eyes charting his face, looking for injury.

He held up his hand to cover his eye and was surprised when he pulled it away to find a crimson smudge. "You said it would be just a drop?"

"It would have been, but you panicked, sending your blood pressure shooting up." Kaylie's eyes went to the ceiling. "Do you want me to send for someone?"

Francisco cut her off. "No, it's okay. I'm not hurt." He blinked, the image of the shoe fading from what must have been his mind's eye. Where did it come from, and why?

Her face screwed up. "Maybe I should come back another time to scan the other eye. It won't collect blood this time. The one drop is enough"

He waved away her offer. "No, please, just get it over with."

Kaylie leaned forward, bringing the floral aroma back into proximity, the feel of her leg brushing his outer thigh driving all thoughts from his head. Through obstructed sight, he could just make out her smile. She moved the device to the other side, and Francisco reached up, laying his hand over hers, nudging the device into better alignment. This time, when the flash came, there was no other result than his body giving an irrepressible bounce.

Kaylie lowered the device and raised a full smile. "Thank you for your patience. I'm finished."

Francisco found his mouth suddenly dry. "Already?"

"I could just stand here and look into your eyes longer, if you want me to." Kaylie raised a finger, tracing the ghost of a path along the corner of his right eye and down his cheek. "But I'm not sure I could continue to do it in a professional capacity. They are very pretty eyes."

The gravity. Francisco had forgotten about the gravity. It had been so long since he'd had time for something as inconsequential as romance. There was a kingdom to rule, conspirators to find, a father to avenge... What weight can one give the heart when the world pushes its weight down on you? Even though he'd mimicked the expression with the same woman a month ago, that hadn't been seduction. It had been a strategy. There'd been no engagement of desire in the act. But now...

Now, he very much wondered what it would be like to kiss Kaylie Fife. And from the look in her eyes, she wondered the same thing back. But that would have to wait.

The door opened at the other end of the room, and the pull between them dissipated. Kaylie pulled back both in body and in spirit, arms tucked in, eyes turned to the floor, as Francisco swiveled in his chair, locking eyes with whoever had just walked in. Had they been discovered?

In an act of utter mercy, Carlos only said, "Shall I leave, Your Highness?"

Francisco turned back to his desk to see that Kaylie had already tucked away the scanner into her briefcase and was closing it.

"Carlos. Perfect timing," she said. Perhaps a little too fast? "There are a few new security procedures we're implementing that I'd like to review with you."

Carlos looked over Kaylie's shoulder, the woman now between them, a knowing expression in his gaze. Men with power making things possible for their intended conquest had no short history, even if it was a history to which Francisco had never contributed.

"Retina scanning," the prince said, though his corrective tone might have been interpreted as: Please don't embarrass me. There's nothing going on.

But any hope for continued détente exited as Carlos said, "Is that what you kids are calling it these days?"

Francisco rolled his eyes. And then Kaylie turned and gave him a wink.

And he rolled his eyes the other way.

Carlos motioned with a sweeping hand towards the door. "Miss Fife, my office is just up the hall, two doors on the right. If you'd like to wait there for me, I'll be along in a few minutes, right after I see the prince to the jackpods."

"Yes, of course." Kaylie turned one blushed cheek over her shoulder as she attempted a mild curtsy. "Your Majesty."

Before Francisco could remind her he wasn't, in fact, royalty, she and her briefcase were halfway to the door.

"Kaylie?"

Her eyes were wide as she spun. Had it been the first time he'd called her by her first name? Certainly aloud, he realized.

He paced forward, his eyes lowered. "I... It was good to see you."

She turned, the sun coming out from behind clouds. "You too, Frank."

A moment later, alone, Carlos turned back with an amused expression. "Now, that's something I wouldn't have predicted."

Francisco reached for his datapad, half hoping his dignity was somewhere underneath it. "Don't, Carlos. She's Plaxis's official liaison to my office, and she was only here on their behalf."

"The near kiss was for professional reasons, then?"

"It wasn't like that." But Francisco couldn't overlook how his pulse perked up at the notion. "Besides, I'm far too busy to—"

Carlos cut him off. "To what? Have a little fun? Or worse, an actual relationship? You know, Francisco, your father wasn't much older than you when you were born, and he balanced both a crown and a child."

"One moment of attraction, and you already have us married and expecting."

"Ah, so you do find her attractive!"

Fine, he'd give an inch. "I said I don't have time, not that I lack eyes."

"It wouldn't be without its official merits, you know."

Francisco looked at his old mentor with a creased brow. "What?"

"You and Kaylie, a couple."

Before the prince could field any further protest, Carlos continued. "Consider the optics. You are the Prince of Gaia, and one of the world's most desired and eligible bachelors. She's the symbolic princess and heir apparent of the Kingdom. There are some, I'd dare to place a hopeful wager, who would have their tongues loosened by a chance to gossip, and who knows where that could lead?"

"If my spies are to be believed, I know exactly where it leads. I'd be kicked to the curb via her bedroom."

"But while you were on your way, you might engage in pillow talk unfettered."

Francisco stopped in his tracks just as they reached the elevators. "You're not saying what I think you're saying, are you?"

Carlos grinned. "Is it so shocking a proposal? Bed sport has been a tool of rulers since Cleopatra and Caesar."

"And look how that ended."

"You'd want to be cautious, of course. But beyond any strategic gain, it might also do you some... mental good."

"No, and we're ending this discussion now." The elevator opened, and Francisco stepped in. "Besides, if I took Kaylie to my political bed, I'm not sure Johanna Tieg wouldn't come along for the ride."

"Well, they say politics makes strange bedfellows."

TEN

HE ARRIVED TO HIS JACKPOD at 11 p.m. San Francisco time, when most of the city's residents were just settling down from their day, tucking into bed, or perhaps checking on the morning forecasts to learn if the pollution levels would warrant breathers. In Gaia, however, it was the start of the workday.

Not all the Kingdom's administrators and diplomats were based in San Francisco, of course. In fact, very few were. What would be the point of a virtual reality crossroads where both war and diplomacy were waged, if it required one to travel to access it? Officially, the room in the basement of Gaia's real-world HQ was referred to as the launch pad, but unofficially.... Jackpods were often called coffins on the street because of their uncanny resemblance to the old-fashioned way to bury the dead (still practiced in some of the more rural areas of the world, Francisco had heard). Instead of being ashed, the deceased was placed inside a "coffin", a wooden box built just for the purpose, then placed in grounds with others who'd received the same treatment. What better name, therefore, for an underground facility which housed so many jackpods than that of those grounds?

The Graveyard.

It took ninety seconds for the security detail to run the standard protocols.

Outside doors secured? Check.

Transmission clarity and bitrate sufficient? Check.

Power flow consistent and backup generators available via emergency launch? Check.

Wardome ingresses and egresses locked until jack of the royal office complete and confirmed? Check.

No Gaian monarch had ever suffered a casualty because of a

blackout or network surge, but techanics insisted these tended to be the weakest links in any virtual system: dependency on systems designed by men had the same faults as the men who built them.

Francisco belted himself in and lowered the floating array of wireless sensors that the machine would use to tap into his brainwaves, both writing and reading the electrical currents in a constant loop.

The operator swiveled in his chair towards the command board. "Destination, Your Highness?"

"My office, as usual, Pete."

Maybe she'll come again tonight.

Since he'd taken office seven months before, Francisco had made a habit of walking the city before reporting to work. That was, until the bandit had visited. Only audibly, sadly. He still had no idea what she actually looked like. She certainly was not Omala Grover as she'd appeared to him at the ball. Francisco had begun to wonder if he was suffering from a case of Stockholm Syndrome but dismissed it. The prince hadn't decided to like his kidnapper, but he certainly was intrigued by her prowess and gentle demeanor. As a student of the vreal, a former hacker himself, and as the victim of the crime, could he be blamed for his curiosity?

Pete hit a few buttons and the outer lid over the coffin lowered. "See you when you pull, Your Highness."

The buzz started, an electronic hum of the jackpod firing up, scrambling and surveying Francisco's thoughts. One set of diodes read his synaptic patterns, the system and his brain agreeing on terms, and then a reorganization of his thoughts occurred as the jackpod broadcast into its occupant's thoughts, sketching out a VR overlay. All this took place in the time it took Francisco to exhale one deep breath. He closed his eyes on the real and opened them the next instant inside the virtual world.

The tension in his fists eased, the first sign he had been clenching them. He opened his eyes, watching as the wire frames of his office filled in, blossoming with both depth and scale. The vreal didn't exist anywhere but on servers secured by Plaxis in a secure location, far from San Francisco. And yet, it was the only place in the world where Francisco had felt truly at home since he'd lost his own as a teenager.

But as the prince acclimated and prepared to make his way to his desk, he realized his desk wasn't there. Nor the lamp he'd designed himself. Nor the picture of his father in a gilded frame. In fact, he wasn't in his office at all.

Had Pete messed up? A system glitch perhaps? Where was he? Should he abort?

Thoughts fragmented as Francisco searched memory and the view before him for any hope of something familiar. There was nothing to be had. The room: plain, mundane. A sofa and two matching side chairs in a shade of green that hadn't been in fashion for decades formed first. Side tables made of questionable substances flanked the furniture. Marble, maybe? Acrylic? Four white-washed walls boxed the room, and under his feet, a tile with a checkerboard pattern, a monotone grid stretching in all directions.

Sitting on the couch, a woman.

The room might be unfamiliar.

The woman was not.

He couldn't help the smile that played across his face, nor the way his heart raced with anticipation. "Taken me hostage again, have you?"

The bandit, her hands crossed in front of her, her brown sari hinting at a pair of legs crossed underneath.

"Your Majesty." Her eyes closed, her head bowed, and then those large, amber orbs peeked up again. "We need to talk."

Francisco cocked a hip. He'd suspected the kidnapper had to be one hell of a hacker, but pulling his avatar and consciousness into a pumpkin while jacking through the most secure server in the world? She was unreal. Not to mention, far too bold for her own good. Didn't she realize that even now, his security team back in San Francisco would be counterhacking her, that she'd be found out and exposed in a matter of minutes? As much as he'd longed to see her again, the way it had come about frankly pissed him off.

Surely, she could have approached when people weren't waiting on him, when no one would be running around asking what happened to the prince and why he hadn't shown up?

Somewhere and sometime when they could be alone...

"What, no knife this time?"

A line formed between her eyebrows. "Knife?"

"Yes, knife." His hand reached for the door handle and tried to turn it, only to find that it didn't have one. "Don't you remember? You, me, a coach ride, and a samurai trying to kill us both?"

"Samurai?" She searched the air with her eyes, only for them to brighten, followed by the rest of her features. "Ah, you must mean Yuchi. She was Rex's idea, of course. He had a thing for martial arts flickers that I'm afraid he never quite outgrew. In any event, I'm afraid you're confused. I'm not who you think I am. I'm not the woman from the ball. She's not available right now."

"The woman from the ball?" She said it matter-of-factly, and somehow Francisco knew she was telling the truth. "Do you know who she is?"

The woman across from him nodded. "Oh, yes."

Pressure was building behind his eyes. "Who?"

"I won't say."

"I am the prince of this realm. I demand that you tell me."

Hearing his words, his tone, his relapse into being the entitled son of the King of Andalusia, a little voice in Francisco's head chastised: Apologize this instant and stop being an ass. But if the person before him really knew the truth of who his mystery abductor/savior was, something his own security personnel hadn't been able to deduce, he was going to find out.

But before he could present either threat or theory, the Omala skin before him rose, crossed to him, and pinched his cheek.

"You know what I've always loved about you, Paco?" she said, pulling her hand away after she'd left the right side of his face red. "Your passion."

Brow furrowed, thoughts swirling, Francisco felt the ire drain away, replaced by confusion. "Sorry?"

She grinned. "I was afraid you lost it, but I see now it's still there, buried. You've been hiding it for years, haven't you? Scared that whoever came after your family will come back and get you too if you make too much noise. You're not the only one doing that, sadly."

Francisco tracked "Omala" as she crossed into an extension of the room that he'd swear hadn't been there a moment before. A dinette set sat under a single burning bulb hanging from the ceiling by a thin, ratty wire. The plastique coverings had been worn by age, the metal frame blossoming with corrosion at their joints. She sat, a cup of tea appearing in her hand from nowhere.

"You called me Paco."

Omala sipped the tea. "I did."

"No one's called me Paco for years."

"I'm sorry to hear that. I thought it was endearing."

He reached up to the table, as if by instinct, and found a cup of tea in his own hand too. He looked down, refusing to believe it was there. Even in the vreal, objects didn't just magically appear out of thin air. Everything had to be coded or called up, and to keep the mind from shock, mundane ways were usually employed to introduce new items to a scene. Fickle human thoughts and their ability to deal with lapses only to a certain degree and such... Still, it required action, purpose, intent.

Had he intended to drink tea? Could he have unconsciously called up a command board and coded himself a cup? "Sleeping coding," as he'd once heard it called.

"If you prefer coffee or even something alcoholic, I'd be happy to accommodate." Omala drew her own cup to her lips, blowing across the surface. "Of course, here in the vreal, the alcohol doesn't have the same effect. Not unless you have a good imagination and great follow through."

"It's not that... I was just wondering... No, thank you." He gave up trying to reason and pulled the cup up. But when he tipped it back, nothing came. "It's empty."

"Is it?" Omala dared feign innocence.

"Why are you acting like that? You know it is." He let it fall on the table. "Did you really bring me here to tease me with riddles and give me empty teacups?"

"No, I'm not trying to riddle anything." She leaned forward on her elbows. "I brought you here because you need to save the kingdom."

"I have nothing to do with the Kingdom." It was an automated response made routine by the many inquiries and invites he'd received since assuming the royal office the previous year. His predecessors, it seemed, while well-intentioned men and women, still partook of the luxuries afforded by Gaia's ugly stepsister platform. Attending the ball at Johanna Tieg's showcase palace had marked the first time Francisco had ever set foot inside it.

Officially and legally, that was. His brief hacks as a teenager, during which he'd lacked proper skills to evade security for long, didn't count.

At least, that's what the judge who'd heard his case and sealed his juvenile files had said.

"I should have been more precise." Omala's mouth widened, more a sympathetic smirk than a smile. "You need to save your kingdom, Gaia, which will require, much to my dismay, saving the Kingdom as well. I'm here to tell you how."

Pretense eked away as Francisco's tone turned bitter. "And just how are you going to do that? And from whom am I saving anything? The Kingdom is fine, while my so-called kingdom seems to be on some master hacktivist's hitlist." Well, this was no longer interesting or helpful. Maybe he'd been better off when he was only talking to her as a faceless voice. "Look, I don't know who you are, how you brought me here, or why you look like Omala Grover, though it's a popular choice lately for people who show up claiming to be there for my own good." That part was more to himself than her. "I have meetings with some of the best coders in the world to get to. They're trying to figure all this out, so if you'd kindly just"—he made a shooing motion with his hands—"send me back to the launch or forward me into Gaia, I'll get to it."

She leaned forward, balancing her chin on the tip of a finger, elbow pressed into the table. "Why couldn't you drink the tea?"

The sudden change in subject reduced Francisco to a blinking squirrel. "Sorry?"

"I said..." She stood, circling the table with methodical steps, a tiger sizing prey. "Why couldn't you drink the tea?"

"Because the cup you gave me was empty."

"And why was that?"

She stopped right in front of him, her amber eyes glistening. "Because you didn't fill it."

For the first time in his memory, Francisco was getting a headache while in the vreal. "How am I supposed to fill it?"

"It's your teacup."

"But there isn't any freaking teapot. I don't even know how you had any tea in yours, or where the cups came from, or how... ¡Joder!"

Cussing was always done in his native tongue, otherwise it didn't feel like cussing.

The path towards violence wasn't one he trod frequently, but he knew the way. Luckily, Francisco also knew when to step back, close his eyes, and retreat to peace. Self-admonishment took the form of a deep breath and silencing thoughts. Funny how his mind knew the sensation of fresh air filling his lungs was all an illusion, a series of correspondence between the platform and his mind, recreating the electromagnetic activity in his own head so that his subconscious felt the effects of what his vreal body experienced. When he opened his eyes and spoke again, it was deliberate speech.

"I don't understand anything that's going on right now."

When she snapped right in front of his eyes, the prince felt his chair join his body in jumping back. He crashed to the ground, and by the time he looked up again, the room he'd been in was gone. All that remained was him, her, a damp earthen floor, and the single light bulb burning above, its cord stretching up into an abyss.

"That is the first bit of intelligence you've expressed since you showed up here."

"Thank you?" Honestly, did she mean it as a compliment or an insult? Francisco pulled himself into a seated position, his legs crossed.

Omala's hand eased down her side, tucking the flowing sash and skirt of a brown sari. "I'm afraid I can't hold you here much longer. Your mind will only let me stretch a moment so far without damage. Just remember this: all you must do when the moment comes is to fill the cup."

He tipped his head to the side. "Tea is going to save Gaia?"

"The tea is a metaphor, dear boy." Omala leaned forward, laying her hands on both cheeks. "I gave you the cup, but you're going to have to search for the teapot on your own. I brought you both together once, but no matter what the people say about me, I'm not a saint. I can't make miracles happen. The pieces are on the board. Right now, that board belongs to you." She leaned forward, planting a kiss on his forehead. "Remember that. I think those you keep closest to you are trying to make you forget."

Francisco's mind was awash in grays and blues, but he focused on the dash of red streaking through the middle. "Not a saint?" he asked, his eyes wide as she pulled away. "Oma—Ms. Grover, is that really you? You're... You're alive?"

"You've always been one of my favorites, Paco. For that reason, when you were young, I gave you gifts that in hindsight you weren't ready for, nor that you'd yet earned. I turned them off for a while when I saw what you did with them. Ah-ya, breaking into the Kingdom and trying to corrupt its code! Why would you do something so reckless? Luckily, the real showed you some mercy and treated you legally like the child you were back then. And while you're not a child anymore, I'm still not sure if you're ready. I hope so, because we're running out of time."

Francisco wondered what in the hell she was talking about, but he was still concerned with his first question to ask another. "How are you alive? I watched your funeral. I've visited your grave."

But before she could answer, the world and all the universes spun. The light above coughed out. Everything was black.

And then, it wasn't.

Francisco rolled once. Blinked twice. Made three curses in succession. He was in his office now, the contents of his vreal workspace just as he'd left them the day before. But outside... Outside, something truly unique was happening.

It was raining.

It never rained in the vreal. The coding allowed for day and night, even a variation in cloud cover, but the coders had said precipitation in such a large platform was a task unto itself, an impossible mess and unnecessary bother.

But the rain, he knew, always washed away the grime. In the real, anyway.

He looked out the window, and then down.

On the windowsill sat the single glass shoe.

Fill the cup.

Finally, Francisco understood.

"The bandit," he said to himself. "She's the teapot."

And the source code was the tea.

ELEVEN

LIFE HAD ACCUSTOMED her to waking up in lonely places, but never with the knowledge that a living mummy was sitting in storage on the other side of the building.

Cindira was relieved to discover that hot water was one luxury her current accommodations provided. Of course, living in the guest house of her father's estate, that had never been an issue. One of the richest men in the country could easily afford the exuberant costs associated with such an indulgence. Many of life's crueler facts had become known only after her mother had passed and when, shortly after, Rex and Johanna had shipped her off to boarding school on the other side of the world. There was a chance that her screams still echoed through the halls of L'Espoir from the first time she'd taken a shower there. So much energy had been tied up in running the wireless grids and all the tech grafted to them that using any to heat water beyond a bare minimum proved politically unpopular.

She pulled on her clothes and tied back her long ebony locks. As she'd done since the day of the ball, Cindira also made sure to put the silicone slippers on under her socks before slipping on her shoes. If an opportunity arose for her to reclaim the missing glass slipper in the Kingdom, no matter how slight the chance of that happening, she didn't want to be caught unprepared.

Laporte emerged from its charging pad, the botic equivalent of crawling out of bed. "Good morning, Miss Tieg. Do you require breakfast first, or would you like to depart immediately?"

Cindira slipped off the cot and pulled on her shirt. Johanna might have given her food and basic facilities, but she hadn't thought far enough ahead to give Cindira any change of clothes. "Nice try, Laporte, but you're still not coming. In that part of town, somebody would rip you apart for scraps or sell you on the black market if they found you. You're not the only botic around, but one as small and grabbable as you would be an easy score."

"I'm much more than a botic, miss."

"Exactly my point."

A sophisticated concordance of programming and superior exterior design sometimes made Cindira forget that Laporte, for all its utility, had its limits in understanding human reality.

"Stay here. I won't be gone long. I just need to ask these techanics if they know anything about what we found yesterday. That's assuming that whoever is running that place now has any connection with who owned it back then."

The little creature bobbed its head. "As you wish, but would you grant me leave to place myself outside of the dead zone around this building at least? That way, if you require my help, I'll at least be at the other end of your comque."

"I'm only turning it on long enough to call a tiktok. I don't want to take any chances that somebody will track me."

"Then you shouldn't take a tiktok. The reason they're so inexpensive and accessible is because their primary function is to patrol those areas of town where crime most occurs. The audio, video, and user data feeds straight into Authority's database."

Cindira's face screwed up. "I'd forgotten about that."

She'd never found herself in a place where it mattered if she was tracked by Authority. Actually, with a moment of hindsight, it explained why the Ferries on a de facto island just offshore, was such a den of inequity. Accessible only by boat, it was one of the few places in town the tiktoks couldn't access. Sometimes she forgot that being reliant on technology meant that it could be reliant on you.

"I saw an old-fashioned bicycle in one of the storage closets yesterday as we were cataloging contents. You know, the ones without any motor, that you actually have to pedal? The air's not too bad today. I could take that."

Laporte didn't thrill at the suggestion. His argument that the tires would surely be rotten by now were dismissed when she showed that they were a high-quality eternal type, not subject to air pressure or much maintenance. Only then did Laporte reluctantly agree that, all things considered, it may be the best option she had. Cindira wrote directions on the back of an unused lab manual, donned a hat and sunglasses to help protect her identity and her skin, and made for the double set of doors that led out of the building.

It rolled open just in time for Kaylie Fife to look as surprised as Cindira felt.

The coder stumbled back. "Kaylie?" She rolled the bicycle between herself and her stepsister. "What... What are you doing here?"

Instead of an explanation, the blonde squared her shoulders and planted hands on her hips, looking the younger woman and the bicycle up and down like she was giving her a physical.

"And just where in the hell are you off to, riding that antique? My mother said she told you to stay here until you were told you could leave."

"It was a suggestion, not a command. And as it so happens, I am on my way somewhere, and I don't have much time, so..."

"Wait! I need a... something from you."

Cindira stopped, halfway toward sliding past, and pulled back. "Something?"

Kaylie pushed pinched fingers together. "A... A favor." The way the blonde stretched the word made it sound like one of a foreign tongue and she wasn't sure of the pronunciation.

Kaylie had been in Cindira's life since she was a child. In a happier home, they might have grown up as true sisters, or at least friends. The five-year age gap and forced distance, both emotional and physical, that Rex and Johanna had introduced by sending Cindira away to boarding school hindered any chance of it, sadly. Perhaps that was the reason Kaylie had taken so readily to being her stepsister's pile driver boss, and why Cindira had let Kaylie get away with so much. Obeying Kaylie's wishes paid the bills and kept Asla employed by extension. Even though Cindira would have preferred more autonomy and recognition, she was proud of her work. But in two decades, never had there been a hint of supplication, certainly not any favors, which might suggest reciprocity.

Rapid blinking failed to clear up the confusion, leading Cindira to ask, "A favor? There's nothing I could give you that you couldn't buy six times over."

"That's true. There's nothing you could give me. But there's something you could do for me." Kaylie stepped back, her hands bracing the metal rod that served as a banister on the exterior stairs. "Nobody else codes my clothing in the vreal as well as you, and I need something fit for a royal engagement."

Simultaneous streams of ice and fire shut down Cindira's back. She came all the way here... for that? "One, you have at least a hundred dresses in your files that I've made for you already. Take those to anyone in the Kitchen and have them make a few modifications. Switch out a few attributes, and no one will recognize it as something recycled. And two, what royal engagement? Are you seeing that Sheikh again? You know that's only going to end in heartbreak like it did the last time."

Kaylie's nose crinkled. "For your information, I have a meeting with Prince Francisco de la Reina tomorrow morning. I don't need a ball gown. I need something... appropriate as business attire, and you've made nothing like that for me. It's my first trip to the Royal Court, and I thought it would be best if I looked"— she mocked finger quotes—"presentable."

A thousand images passed through Cindira's mind's eye. Not that she was seriously considering the task. But before she could make any random suggestions, Cindira clicked her tongue. "Wait, tomorrow morning?"

Kaylie started. "Yes, at 10 a.m. Why?"

"Because if you have a 10 a.m. meeting with him local time, you're not meeting in the vreal. You're meeting here in the city, at the Palace of Fine Arts. You know, Gaia HQ."

Its old name suited the ground better. It was one of the few remnants of the old city, and even the Kingdom had a hard time competing with its beauty. So beloved was the site that, when sea levels rose a century before, great expense allowed civic engineers to excavate beneath its foundation and build a platform that allowed it to float. In essence, the grounds were now an island, the counterpart to the Ferries on the east side of the city. A domed cupola outside the palace proper served as one of San Francisco's primary wireless grid transmitters.

"If you're going there, you need an actual business suit, not one made of pixels and photons," Cindira continued. "And that is where my talents fall flat. But I'm sure your mother could suggest a tailor. She's always finely dressed."

It was true, even if the woman had murdered Cindira's mother.

Rather than express any sentiment of gratitude, Kaylie's face curdled. "Thanks for nothing and for making me haul myself all the way out to this dump. Oh, and thanks too for getting fired. Half the Kitchen already hates me, but now that they assume I had something to do with you getting canned, the rest of them came online in that campaign too."

Cindira cocked a hip and attempted to shelve her lack of sympathy. "That's easy to fix. Just tell them the truth. Tell them that your mom fired me."

"If I was going to tell them the truth, that wouldn't be it, would it?" The sharp edges of Kaylie's expression smoothed and softened. She threaded her arms over her stomach, looking to the ground. "I know it was just a stunt for anyone watching, so they don't know what you're really up to over here. So they don't know that you're looking for Dad."

The coder took a step forward, out of the portal. "For Dad?"

"Yeah, you know, our father, Rex?" Condescension thickened her sarcastic tone. "Does that surprise you, that I call him that? I know you still only think of him as your dad, as your mother's ex-husband. Haven't you ever put yourself into my shoes and seen it from my perspective? He's been my mother's husband longer than he was Omala Grover's, and he's been a much better Dad to us than that horrible man my mother used to be married to."

Rare had been the occasions when any of her acquired family—Johanna, Cade, or Kaylie—had mentioned Christopher Fife. It had never been done with any ounce of kindness or tenderness. Cindira took the hint that his existence was something none of them were too eager to resurrect, even in memory. But perhaps his ghost lived on in other ways. Cindira had always been so focused on the ways the twins and her stepmother had treated her that she'd never stopped to consider how others had treated them. Maybe Kaylie wasn't broadcasting vitriol and spite; perhaps she was only projecting and redirecting it.

Before she was fully cognizant of what she was doing, Cindira found one hand clutching the handlebars and the other on Kaylie's shoulder. "I'm going to find him."

Kaylie's eyebrows knitted, a curved "v" forming in the center as she looked with wet eyes back up. "You... You better. 'Cause you, you know..."

They stayed like that for a moment, a rock in the river of their tumultuous relationship. Finally, Kaylie turned on heel and made for the stairs leading down to the street. "Fine, I'll find a real business suit. Anyway, Yumi Nigani says a woman should change her fashions like she changes panties."

"So you'll be going naked then?"

The blonde stopped at the bottom of the stairs and spun back to glare at her stepsister, mouth askew. "If that wasn't so clever, and if you hadn't been let go, I'd fire you for that."

"If I still worked for you, I'd still be working for you."

In so few words, Cindira laid out a tapestry of meaning. She waited, wondering if Kaylie would pick up any of the loose threads and pull at them. There might have been some emotion in those big blue eyes, but the next moment, Kaylie pulled on her sunglasses and waved toward the north end of the street. In the distance, several blocks down, a black luxury transport that had been motionless lurched, its lights flickering like an automotive equivalent of giving a thumbs up. The car pulled to the curb, and no sooner had it come to a rest than a man leaped out, throwing open the cab door and offering a hand for Kaylie's use. He wasn't a driver; cars hadn't needed those for almost a century. Goodness forbid that someone want for a foot massage or a whiskey sour in the short commute between one part of town and another. The valet was probably also a bodyguard of sorts, Cindira realized, as he closed the door behind Kaylie and took time surveilling both the street and Cindira herself before crossing in front of the car to get to his own door.

"Well, that was awkward." Cindira looked down at her feet to see Laporte joining her observation. "Did she really think you'd snap to attention and do her bidding?"

Cindira leaned back against the door, lacing her arms over her chest as, down the street, the transport turned a corner and disappeared from sight.

"I think, Laporte, that you don't quite understand what just happened." She pushed off, turning to close the portal but leaving it open enough for the mouse to crawl back inside. "That wasn't a heartless boss feeling entitled. That was a woman admitting she was scared and coming to me for armor."

"You're right, miss. I'm afraid I don't understand."

A deep breath cleared the scaffolds from her brain. Cindira tried to rebuild facades using the same materials. "Kaylie has suddenly found herself in a position of authority she didn't deserve, and that didn't intimidate her because she thought she'd have me behind her—or under her, at least. Now comes the first challenge she's facing without me in the background, having to assist the prince using her brain and not her sex appeal, and she's terrified." She nodded, as though agreeing with her own thoughts. "That was Kaylie being vulnerable. That was her begging for help."

The mouse's tiny head bobbed. "It's too bad you're not able to help her, then. Assuming that's something you'd want to do."

Cindira bit her lip. Would she help Kaylie out of the goodness of her own heart? She wasn't sure. Just now, however, she'd felt she might.

Regardless, her sister's need for fashion wasn't her problem, and every moment she lingered here was another she wasn't working on those she had already decided to take on.

Cindira lifted rolled the bicycle beside her, making it bob and jerk with each step of the stair it hit in its descent. "Get inside and stay hidden if anyone shows up. I promise, I won't be long."

TWELVE

FRANCISCO STEPPED OUT of his office and made his way down the hall. He had to see for himself if it was true. More importantly, he had to see if it felt true.

The main lobby of Congressional Hall stood empty, except for a single service clerk, a young man whose eyes widened when he saw the prince approaching.

"Your Majesty." He bowed his head, then looked up, and seeming to think better of the notion, buried his chin in his chest once more. "Can I be of assistance?"

Francisco pointed vaguely toward the exits, three circular doors flanked on either side by two of the more typical double-hinged variety. "Do you see that too?"

The young man's jaw became slack as he followed the indicated direction with his eyes. "The doors, Your Majesty?"

"No, not the doors. What's going on outside."

The young man made a longer, but no less confused, survey. "Do you mean the rain?"

He jolted when Francisco clapped him on the shoulders. "Yes, the rain. Exactly, the rain." Then, pulling his hands back, Francisco used one of them to slick back his black hair. "I needed to know I wasn't delusional."

"No, Your Highness. It started about ten minutes ago. There was a rush of congresspersons who ran in then, but none since." He hitched a white-gloved hand over the brocaded purple uniform shoulder. "They were all asking me if I had umbrellas in case it was still raining when they left later. I looked in the lobby aide's manual for instruments and VAPORS I could request from my terminal, but there wasn't a listing for umbrellas. All that to say,

I hope that's not what you're here to ask me for."

Francisco dropped his hand and shook his head, his eyes still fixed outside. "No, that's not why I'm here. I'm here because..."

Because he wanted to step outside and feel the rain. Because rain meant renewal, meant hope. Rain washed away the ash and left the world refreshed. But that was in the real. What did it mean here, in the vreal? A part of his soul longed to move forward, but his wariness overrode his want.

"There's nothing in the source code that creates rain. In the real, water is so integral that we never think about how dramatically it alters everything. It's not just the state of something being wet; it affects different materials in different ways, even more so as a function of time. It would require so much code to encompass the power of something so elementary." He finally brought his eyes to the young clerk, not surprised to see the young man holding back his judgement but confused none the less. "It was very dry where I grew up, and so damned hot at times. I always wished for the rain. It brought comfort, especially when I felt unsafe."

The boy leaned in slightly, as though he were inspecting the prince's chin. "I see. That explains it then." He stood back at attention. "The umbrellas, not your feeling unsafe, Your Highness."

The prince grinned suddenly. "But I feel safe now."

"I'm glad to hear it." He rolled up on his toes. "Will there be anything else, Your Majesty?"

Francisco shook his head, extending one arm out to the side, holding an open palm at hip level. "Oh, yes, my boy. We're going to need umbrellas."

By this point, Francisco was certain this poor lobby boy was positive that the sovereign had gone mad. Maybe he had. How else could Francisco explain the fact that he felt like he had been the one to conjure rain?

"I understand, but as I've already mentioned—"

"Shhh." Francisco pressed his eyes closed, ignoring the concern rolling off the clerk and recalling his previous train of thought.

"She was shoving me out of wherever it was she had stolen me, and I was scared. I didn't want to feel scared. I wanted to feel safe. And then I showed up here, and it was raining. So how would I make an umbrella?"

"Maybe if you were wet?"

Both Francisco's eyes rounded on the boy. "Brilliant!"

"What? Sir, wait, you shouldn't go out there. Wait!"

But he couldn't wait. Francisco leaned back as fat raindrops sloshed his forehead. He ignored them, ignored the sense of being drenched. Bits of code aligned in his thoughts, a combination of geometric renderings, data attributions, and relational interplays. It had taken him months in the labs beneath his grandfather's palace to even synthesize a virtual piece of paper, and that was barely three-dimensional, but he'd done it. Then a glass. And water. And eventually, fire.

But an umbrella? It was so much more complex than anything so elemental. Still, if he could get the coding just right...

Joining the sovereign on the dais before Congressional Hall, the boy brightened when an object took shape in Francisco's hand, then solidified. Shaft, aperture to push open the canopy, the frame, the material wrapped around the frame... Achievements were no less significant just because they were small. Even the prince had to smile when he pulled up his arm and found the umbrella fully formed in his grip.

All formality fled. The boy rushed to reach for Francisco's side and tugged at the prince's arm. "Whoa, how did you do that?"

The prince allowed the boy to take the object into his hands, turning it over, running his fingers over the exterior frame, digesting the manifestation of what was otherwise a bunch of alphanumeric characters. "I don't know. Purusha, I guess. Years of study. You study, right?"

Most of the clerks that handled mundane, frankly unnecessary tasks around the city were upper school or college interns, either with an interest in political science, virtual world design, or objective coding.

The boy nodded. "At Delft, sir. I'm in my first quarter."

"Wonderful school." Not that Francisco had any basis to know. He'd left the university after the first semester, having learned that there was little their VR studies departments could teach. "We need talented architects. If you ever need anything, you let my office know, and we'll see what we can do."

Francisco couldn't have gotten a better reaction if he'd just transferred the kid a million greens. "I will, sir. Thank you. Oh!" Suddenly cognizant of his job, he dropped the new umbrella into Francisco's hands and moved to open the door. "Have a good day, Your Highness."

"Thank you, son. I will."

THIRTEEN

THE SHOP DIDN'T LOOK like much from the outside, but it had two distinguishing characteristics that separated it from the surrounding buildings: a complete lack of windows and filtration pipes sticking up at regular intervals from its roof.

Memories lingered of her childhood days growing up in the city, when dangerously high AQI readings meant wearing a personal air filtration mask as the norm, not the exception. Only in the last four or five years since Cindira had come back from school could you leave home without giving it much thought. The buildings completed during the "gloom years," as they had come to be called, still bore the evidence of such considerations. Glass had been insanely expensive. Using it in a commercial building on a street dotted with adult bookstores, seedy hackdomes, and drug dens, all crumbling remnants of a city falling in on itself, meant something shady had gone down. Techanics made a good living, but not enough to build something like this place to pre-2140 code.

The room Cindira found herself in could be called a lobby. Against a whitewashed cinderblock wall stood two rickety guest chairs with faded red backing. A counter, waist-high, was covered with small baskets of random parts, each with an attached plaque suggesting price in greens and yens. A legit business then, and one heavily regulated. The Pacific State's official crypto still held value, but nowhere near as much as the gov-free ones. On a wall behind the counter, sales posters. Were they actual paper? It didn't seem possible—this wasn't a museum—but why else would they be in anti-UV frames?

Looked like the owner had a penchant for antiques. Somehow, that seemed in line for a profession which specialized in keeping old technologies running for those too poor to replace them.

"Hello?" Cindira leaned over the counter. The door that must have led into the workspace rested partially open. From her position she could tell there was a light on in the room beyond, though if there was anyone in it remained a mystery. No answer came, but now that her eyes and ears were adjusting to the environment, she heard something... musical. Not distinct enough to make out specifically, but the tinny noise had both rhythm and percussion underlying it.

A moment more and she leaned a little further, her midriff brushing the edge of the products on the countertop. "Hello? Is anyone here?"

She almost fell off the counter when an old man's face tilted into the door frame.

"Oh, a pretty girl!"

He wore a smile framed by a long, thin white beard that brushed the top of his clavicles, the outline of which was visible through the thin material of his purple shirt. The balance of his bald head glistened in the light, except for the halo of hair that started just above his ears and ringed around towards the back. Dark brown eyes shone, and even though he was turned her direction, Cindira felt as if he were looking past her at something behind her.

The bottom half of his body joined the top, and the old man shuffled towards her at a pace that was both hurried and slow. "Picking up or dropping off?"

"Neither. I'm looking for... a quote, I guess?" she started, choosing her words with great deliberation. She knew her comque was off, but she found herself wrapping her opposite hand around it all the same. "I have an... um, unusual situation."

"One you don't want anyone hearing about?" The old man's smirk doubled in depth as his eyes traced down to where she'd masked the microphone on her device. "We don't accept contraband here. I know those thugs over on Third Street say we do, but we don't. They try to implicate us in something so Authority will crack in and shut us down. Not true. No contraband."

Her hands went up to her shoulders, open palms out. "Oh, no! It's not contraband. It's just something... old. Valuable, you see, and I..."

A long, skeletal index finger flashed up in the air, the old man telling her to wait. Cindira nodded, even as she kept her pose, and watched as he bent over. With his own hand on the edge of the counter for support, the old man flicked something underneath and out of view. Not a second had passed when her comque gave out five succinct beeps. She pivoted it in front of her, double checking its display to see if it could be true.

"You forced a hard restart of my comque?" Cindira held her arm out at length to be certain she wasn't seeing things. Her thoughts became a chicken coop, each one scratching and bulking. "What about no contraband? Last I knew, base-code wipers? Pretty illegal."

"Controlled, not illegal. Techanics have a special license. Necessary in our line of work sometimes." He tapped his own wrist. "We have about three minutes before our devices completely reset and sync with the grid. So, what do you have then? Some valuable antique or animech? Maybe a wheellie-do?"

"A wheellie-do?" She repeated the phrase like the words of a foreign language. "Weren't those popular, like, a century ago? I've only seen those in antique museums."

His gracious manner soured. He swung his hands dismissively through the air. "Ah, bah! You think it's so old? That I'm so old?"

"Well, no, of course not. I'm just saying, I didn't expect..." She examined more closely what he had said. "Wait, how old are you?"

That was the wrong thing to say. He turned, mumbling curses below his breath as he hobbled his way to the backroom.

"No, wait, sir. I didn't mean to insult you. I just... Oh, please don't go."

Cindira didn't know what had possessed her. She wasn't the kind to cut lines or go somewhere without permission. But that's exactly what she did. Through the doorway, a room filled with a few busted jackpods, domestic botics, and every imaginable piece of tech affordable in the lower classes, dotted at intervals with industrial waste.

The old man was halfway through the workspace, his back to her.

"Sir, please, I—"

A lunge, and her best intentions came to a complete and utter stop when she ran into a chair.

A chair? No, she'd have tripped on a chair. It must have been something taller.

Or.... Someone.

She looked down with as much confusion as a second man looked up with a tight jaw and flaring nostrils. Well, no, not a man, really. More of a boy on the edge of becoming a man — and he wasn't happy.

"Who told you that you could come back here?"

He had the voice of a twelve-year-old but the presence of a disgruntled Authority officer with years of service under his belt. Hands balled into fists and anchored on his hips, he looked like a pissed-off mom. A 3D print of a name tag on his chest said "Warren."

"You deaf, lady?" Warren took a step forward, and Cindira reflexively fell a step back. "I said, what do you think you're doing?"

"I was trying to apologize to the old man. I mean, older man. I didn't mean to call him old. And I..." Cindira realized that her slippery words were losing her ground. She cleared her throat and stood up straight. "I have a first generation Dreamzone NNIP jackpod that needs..." A social worker? A coroner? "...attention. It had a service plaque with your information on it."

His stare remained fixed, but the eyes shifted, one eyebrow arching. "The only G1 we service is at the Stadium, and if it needed anything, Talia would have called us."

The same hackdome where she and Scotia used to swindle people in the tourneys? She'd competed there many times and would have known if one of the bays had a first-generation unit. Would have known because she would have refused to compete using one. The term "coffin" originally came from that generation of devices, and it wasn't only because of their shape.

Cindira pushed the thought out of her mind. She had to stay focused.

"Well, it didn't technically list you." She took a chance, softening her expression and sliding forward on one foot. "It was a different techanic shop that was at this address before you. I was hoping maybe you just rebranded or something, and you could just help me... um, diagnose an issue with the machine."

Diagnose sounding so much more approachable than "help me figure out why there's some guy who's been broadcasting from it for years and why he was shoved in a hidden closet of an old Plaxis warehouse."

"The shop that was here before us?" Warren shot a confused glare over his right shoulder, back into a line of metal shelves where the old man must have disappeared, before turning back. He shook his head once. "Sorry, that wasn't us. Can't help you."

Desperation picked up her feet and the tone of her voice. "Please, I don't know where else to go, and the guy I found who's been jacked into it for so long and—"

The hand slapped over her mouth too late. Like most teenagers taking in something from an unfamiliar adult, the one before Cindira had worn a doubtful squint since the moment she'd started talking. Now Warren's suspicions seemed confirmed, like he'd finally determined what she was really after.

"Some guy jacked in?" He buried a laugh in his shoulder. "Correct me if I'm wrong, lady, but you can't jack in from a broken machine."

Cindira admitted defeat on that part. One reason she rarely lied was because she was so bad at it. "No, I don't suppose you can."

"Good, so you do have a basic idea of how technology works," Warren said. "Sounds to me like you don't have an issue for a techanic, you have one for St. Dymphna's. I don't know why your kind always runs here. You think we're some kind of chiphead hospice?"

"I know that's what this looks like, but believe me, it's not. He's—"

"Your boyfriend, your father, your pimp..." The kid enumerated what must be the usual suspects on a finger with each additional member of the list. "We specialize in hardware, not psychology. Wouldn't matter if it was Saint Omala herself. We don't do extrications."

Cindira didn't have much time to react to an invocation of her mother's name as the old man stepped out of the shadows, leaning on a plastic cane. How he'd circled around from the back of the service bay without her noticing was anyone's guess. He took two more sliding steps forward.

"We'll do it. We will help you."

Warren, the man-boy, didn't waste a second. "Come on, Gramps, you know she's full of sh—Ow!"

The old man's cane made a brilliant weapon, Cindira thought. Just enough to pain, not enough to injure. She covered her mouth with her hand again, but this time with a giggle. Warren was too busy rubbing the spot on his backside where the old man had struck to care about her reaction.

The old man ignored his grandson. Using the same cane for its intended purpose, he took a few steps forward.

"This new generation," he said, waving away the whimpering boy. "They lack tact."

Cindira looked at Warren. He wasn't that much younger than she was, truth be told. Was the comment meant for her as well? She'd have to step carefully, just in case.

"The guy in the machine isn't my anything," she said, staying focused. "I have no idea who he is or how he got there."

Or what kind of mass of data someone may have dumped into him to store, because who would go looking for a human body when trying to find a data dump?

"Understanding how he got there and, more importantly, how he survived for so long like that, could help me to help someone else."

"And so, my grandson was partially right." He stopped, the tip of his walking stick beating a percussive period on the statement. "At least by proxy. You're not asking this for yourself."

Slowly at first, then with more ease, she nodded. "I think if we can get the man I found out of his situation, it might help me help my father."

"If your father is permajacked, it might be more efficient to help him instead."

It was the logical suggestion. Except, of course, for the obvious. "I don't know for certain that's what happened. You see... I know where my father is in the vreal. I don't know where he is in the real."

"Talk to him and ask him then, dipshit. Ow!"

This time, when the old man whacked Warren's backside, Cindira flinched too. It wasn't necessarily that she thought it hurt that much. The old man was weak, and the teen was just shy of fully grown. It was more that she seemed to be the one causing the discord.

"Obviously, she would have done that if she could have," he said, chastising Warren. "When's the last time you heard of a chiphead exiting the vreal because someone said please?"

"My father's not a chiphead."

A saccharine smile spread across the old man's face, shadowed by condescension. "Of course not, sweetheart. And we don't really care if he is." He leaned in. "Let's start with the basics. Where did you discover this Chadwick Chiphead jacked in to the first gen?"

Cindira gave a vague description of the area of town and how she'd come across her discovery, leaving out anything that would reveal her identity or Plaxis's involvement. When she was done, the old man shook his head.

"You're not lying, but you're not telling us the whole truth."

Warren huffed. "Come on, Gong Gong, people don't just find jackpods in storage closets filled with biobotics. It's obviously hot, and the only thing worse than being caught dealing contraband is being caught with hot goods. She probably needs this guy's retinal scan to get into an account or open a door or something."

"If all I needed was his retinal scan, and I was desperate enough to steal his body and the jackpod he was in to get it, why wouldn't I just pop his eye out and carry it around with me?"

Even imagining the act turned her stomach, but she wasn't about to let that on now. Instead, Cindira watched a welcome sight: Warren's head lowering, his chin sweeping to the right. Contemplation. That idea had hooked him.

The grandfather poked his stick in Cindira's general direction. "Look at her, you fool. Obviously, she's not a thief. She's scared. She wants to make sure she hasn't come across something that's going to get her killed. That's why she's here." The old man waved a hand through the air before shuffling towards Cindira, extending that same hand in greeting. "I'm Chen Wu, and this is my grandson, Warren. And as much as I think he's being a little prick, these are hard times. Our fees for this kind of service are fixed. Our silence is negotiable."

Cindira's stomach dropped into her shoe. She reached down to her comque and tapped its interface. The device was on, but it hadn't yet reconnected to the wireless grid. She did so now, turning it on just long enough to check her wallet. Sadly, she found it just as light as she remembered. She'd used all her untraceable crypto to move Asla out of the country and keep her off grid. There was a little more legal, aka traceable, currency in her accounts—her last official paycheck from Plaxis, she suspected—but the last thing she needed was for someone to notice she'd spent it here.

"I could code something for you." Cindira searched their faces for a sign that it might be of interest. "I know that doesn't sound like much, but trust me, I'm not the average coder. If you don't ask me how I'm able to make something work, I can stitch together whatever you want."

Chen sighed, then turned. "We deal in hardware, lady, not programs."

Cindira pivoted, putting herself in his path. "I know, but as the ancients used to say, you can build the biggest sail known to man, but if the wind doesn't blow, who cares?"

"We already have all the diagnostic software we need."

"It doesn't have to be diagnostic. I could build you a simple vreal with a few days of work." A few days she really didn't have time for. Even now, who knew if it was already too late for her father.

"A new vreal in a few days?" The old man threw back his head and crowed. "Ha! That kind of thing takes months, and that's with a whole team working on it."

Not if you can think in Purusha Prime. Not that she'd admit that to them. Desperate as she was for help, there was no way to float that without them knowing just what she was capable of.

But maybe... "I can hack, and I mean anything, any platform."

Chen stopped in place. "Hack?" When he turned this time, there was an intensity in his eyes that hadn't been there before, like she was a work of art in which he'd just noticed a new detail. "That's illegal."

"Only if we get caught." Sweat beaded in her palms. "Come on, there must be something drifting out in the vreal you'd like access to. I can cloak your avatar and make it look like it's just attributes of my own. That way, it will be me they come after if anything does go south. We trade silence, and no one need know we ever met."

His jaw worked. "There's a pumpkin that housed on the Plaxis servers, but it's quarantined. Could you get me into that?"

She straightened her back, felt a ripple of ice plunge into her chest. Quarantines didn't happen often. Something had to go really horribly wrong with a critical or indispensable pumpkin for it to be iced and not deleted. There was always a risk of pulling back the infection if they were opened willy-nilly. "That's risky."

"That didn't sound like a no." He mused another moment before nodding in agreement with his own thoughts. "If you can get me into a certain pumpkin for about fifteen minutes, then I can help you figure out who your Jack Doe is."

Warren cackled. "Yeah, right, Gong Gong. Why not ask her to get you an audience with the Prince of Gaia?" He swung an arm up, pointing digits. "No one can hack Plaxis platforms. It's impossible."

Cindira stepped up to Chen, and extended a hand. "Agreed."

She smiled when he closed his grasp and shook. But if she had expected an attempt at hubris to convince Warren, she was sorely mistaken. He narrowed his eyes when she looked at him, his jaw tight.

"You got a lot of balls for a chick."

She wasn't sure if it was meant as a compliment or an insult. "I was hacking into some of the most secure systems in the world when I was in elementary school. I can get you in, even if it's in quarantine." Reality, though, still existed. "But you'll have to give me a little more context. A pumpkin's place shifts around on the servers every time the security and archival units re-stack the platform. Without a fixed position and no official way to check Plaxis's directory, I can use a piece of metadata to locate it."

"Metadata?" Chen said. "I've never heard of that stuff being of much use for anything anymore, not since neoblock-c became standard encryption."

Cindira gave him a nod. "And since no one takes metadata seriously, its security features don't get updated these days. That also means it's the easiest thing to exploit. And just to show you my word is good, I'll pay in full beforehand, and you can back out of the deal if you feel I don't deliver."

Good Gaia, was she really saying this? Even if she had a few perks for being the daughter of the CEO of Plaxis, it didn't cover exposing industrial secrets or security weaknesses inherit to the system, both illegal under the national penal code. Cindira still wasn't sure what the connection between the data downloaded to the man in the hidden closet and her father's disappearance was, but instinct told her this path would get her somewhere. Even if it didn't, she felt like she owed it to the man in the machine. Maybe he was jacked in on purpose, but she'd heard rumors of it being one way to deal with a problem. They couldn't get you for murder if he didn't kill the person and keeping someone on ice might prove useful later if they had some particular knowledge of something.

For the moment, Cindira's proposal had seemed to stifle Warren's objections. She swallowed her moral qualms and continued.

"Last I knew, there were over six hundred pumpkins in Plaxis's patch," she said. "Not sure how many of those are quarantined. Maybe a dozen or two? But if you can give me a data point, I should be able to narrow it down to the one you're looking for."

Chen for the first time looked unsure. He gave his grandson the side eye as all his features screwed up. "What kind of data point?"

What kind indeed? At Plaxis, she'd occasionally needed to go inside a pumpkin to update dirty code, but she'd always had its precise location given to her. She'd discovered the metadata flaw by accident when someone had misreported a color file that had lost several spectra of red.

"Do you know its creation date or when it was last accessed? Maybe the designer's registration number? I can find a needle in a VR haystack, but first I need some way to find the haystack."

"Date of last access, you say?" Chen drew down the points of his barely-there beard. "That would be the day Bas died."

"Oh...kay." She bit her lip. There wasn't necessarily a reason a death date should automatically be a reason for concern, right? It wasn't like these two had killed whoever Bas was. Just to be careful, however, she decided not to ask anything she didn't absolutely need the answer to. The most dangerous thing someone could take was somebody else's secrets.

"We'll also need to jack you and me in," she said. "Preferably two coffins side by side. It will be easier for me to keep our presence off the books if I only have one network node to camouflage."

Chen looked at his grandson. "Speaking of the Stadium, maybe we should stop by and perform our maintenance a little early this month?"

FOURTEEN

THEORETICALLY, THERE shouldn't be a point at which a virtual structure ended, but there also shouldn't have been a reason for Francisco to render himself dry and presentable merely by thinking it. Unlike in the real world, the vreal came without physical limitation. A building might appear as a shed on the outside but render as the Taj Mahal once entered. Like measures of time, however, early tests suggested most human minds hesitated when confronted with a mismatch of dual visual perceptions. A thing either was or it wasn't, and eyes, even virtual ones, needed to be trustworthy for the mind to follow. Hence, a sort of virtual building code had been adapted: "internal" space could not exceed fifteen percent of what "external dimensions" implied.

As Francisco rounded the last of a series of turns, he was certain that whoever had designed the Congressional Hall had played fast and loose with those standards. It went on forever.

Dual sets of dark brown eyes swung his direction when at last he entered the room. One, Francisco recognized as an Asian representative, a thorny senior member who was as shrewd as she was opinionated. She had sandstone skin and long, brown-black hair twisted atop her head like wind-worn mountains. It was the kind of look that suggested she could be from anywhere and nowhere.

"Your Majesty." Carlos had had his back to the door, but now stood, head bowed. Once protocols had been sated, he reached out an arm to indicate their guests. "You already know Congressperson Yo-Yo Hsu of Macau, and may I present the Prime Minister of Ethiopia, the Honorable Eshe Aster? Both have agreed to serve as members of the committee."

"Honorable Miss Hsu, Prime Minister." Francisco turned to each of the women in turn, bowing his head in recognition of their roles. "I'm so delighted that you agreed to assist in this highly sensitive endeavor."

The two women exchanged narrowed eyes and wrinkled foreheads, informing the prince immediately of the truth.

He leaned into a chair, his hands flexing over the ornate carvings of its frame. "You don't know what that endeavor is, do you?"

It was Prime Minister Aster who answered, her words like tiny pebbles tossed over cracked and dried earth. "Your attaché mentioned something about exploring a reorganization of Gaia's infrastructure and the sovereign's role within it."

A crude explanation, if not entirely incorrect. Francisco lifted an index finger when Madame Hsu cut in.

"About time for it, too." She tapped the edge of the table with bony fingers before continuing. "When the congress was first organized as a democratic monarchy, I thought we'd accomplish so much more. So far, those who've held your office have shown little appetite for flexing the muscles a supreme seat provides. I've had many discussions with your predecessors on the topic."

The problem with a VR avatar, as well as one of its benefits, was that one could present themselves as any iteration of their own body. There were regulations against it—guidelines suggested that an avatar should have its coding updated every three years to reflect natural real aging—but rarely were such policies enforced. Francisco often forgot the youthful faces he saw daily might belong to elders many years his senior. If he recalled correctly with Madame Hsu, his administration was the fourth during her own tenure.

"Yes, Madame Hsu, I consider myself a student of my office, and I've read several registered opinion statements you've authored on the matter."

It was a genuine statement, one that neither endorsed what the congress person had said, nor contested it, even if he found its implication unbearable.

Madame Hsu blinked, her brown eyes drilling into him. "Then you agree."

"Of course he doesn't agree," the Prime Minister answered on Francisco's behalf. "Gaia was founded as the world's conflict-resolution platform, but members take part of their own free will. If you disenfranchise that choice, then the rulings here become edict. While the throne may hold power of this city, its power does not extend outside these servers. Isn't that right, Your Highness?"

"There are certain situations in which my authority can be extended to other Plaxis platforms, but no, you're right otherwise."

Francisco cast one dubious look at Carlos, who sat across the table, humor in his eyes but face flat. There would be no hope of rescue from those quarters.

"I think..." The prince cleared his throat and dared to sink into the seat before him. "That, as Thomas Jefferson said, a little revolution now and then is a good thing." He waited a moment to see if he could garner any reaction from the statement. When none came, he continued. "Jefferson, he was an eighteenth-century American philosopher, statesman, and slaveholder."

The Prime Minister rolled that over her tongue. "Slaveholder? Is that from whom you take historical lessons on precedent?"

Francisco didn't try to argue the counter. In his studies of millennium history, a discipline in which he'd only recently developed an interest, he'd found that monumental historical figures usually held positions in conflict with current standards. America's own founding father was a prime example. A phenomenal mind which understood the natural rights of freedom, who at the same time held the bonds of others.

"If the lesson is sound beyond the person who said it, and even more so if it was contrary to aspects of their own character and yet, they still found their way to what I see as a righteous stance? Then yes," he said. "William Shakespeare also said through one of his characters, 'The evil that men do lives after them; the good is oft interred with their bones.' I think in these times we're able to go back and dig up those bones a little better, is all."

The statement left both women confused as to how to counter. He didn't give them a further invitation to do so. Instead, he passed to Carlos, excusing himself from their company.

"Will we be joined by the other representative soon?"

Carlos kept his voice low. Needlessly, it turned out. The two women had decided to debate each other when the prince's attention shifted. "He should be along soon. I thought best for him to arrive separately. This all may go nowhere, and rumors might spread if someone saw the two of you walking towards the same meeting. Fewer lips speak fewer words."

Polishing his chin with his palm, Francisco nodded. "But someone is coming to represent the technical challenges, right?"

Though maybe that wasn't necessary after all. With his new abilities in the vreal, maybe Francisco no longer needed to rely on others. He'd made it rain and then pulled an umbrella into being just by thinking it. Cleaving a vreal nation away from its host of nearly three decades and defending its borders couldn't be that much more advanced, could it? For the moment, though, it might be best to play along and not let anyone know what he could do. Until he could explain it, and, frankly, until he knew it wasn't a fluke, Francisco needed to keep "vreal magic" under pocket.

Carlos pulled up his watch—a vreal representation of his comque on the outside—into view, interfacing with data. "Yes. In fact, he sent me a message just a few moments ago saying he was walking up the hall and that he hoped—"

Before the sentence could land, the door opened. Francisco wheeled around, ready to welcome their guest, when his world turned red.

Hugo Ferrente de Miguel was more than a man in Francisco's world. He was an apocalypse. Once upon a time, the two had been thick as thieves and twice as dangerous. Their academy instructors had called the prince "Hugo's thin shadow." That was, until Hugo's family underwrote the coup that left Francisco's father dead, the Batista family holdings liquidated, and his royal title stolen. If betrayal did not destroy a man, it melted away any parts of him that might be soft and hardened the rest.

Francisco didn't remember jumping up. "What are you doing here?"

A defensive instinct, perhaps. Or maybe it was just because, since being surprised at their encounter in the Kingdom two weeks before, Francisco had told himself that if he and Hugo ever crossed paths again, one of them might not walk away.

Hugo busied himself adjusting a pair of white gloves, picking and lifting them to fit the contours of his hands with perfection. Gloves that were unnecessary in a virtual world, that would have to have been coded and fitted specifically to his avatar. In Andalusia, only royalty wore white gloves. In an agricultural region, only a man who'd not known a day in the vineyards or the farmlands could maintain their condition.

"Him?" Francisco swung on Carlos. "I'd sooner burn down Gaia myself than to involve Tagentry. You know who this man is and what his family did to me and mine."

While Hugo's uncle was now king, Hugo himself had founded Plaxis's biggest rival in vreal world hosting. Turned out, the bigger the world got, the smaller it really was.

"Why is this man here?" Suddenly, the Prime Minister was at the prince's back. "Do you know what he has done to my country?"

"Prime Minister, peace." The muscular Spaniard (though frankly, his avatar must have been enhanced in that respect, because Francisco's memory was not that bad) held his arms out to the sides, his shoulders bobbing. "It was my uncle's forces that beat yours in the wardomes. It was a fair fight carried out as was agreed: your best soldiers and coders against ours, for the right to mine the gold reserves near Asosa for six months. Andalusia honored that treaty, returning rights on time, as agreed."

"Returned gold mines stripped bare, which was not agreed," Esther shot back. "You far exceeded your pull rights."

"All involved parties were fairly compensated at market rates, and Prince de la Reina's predecessor, Prince Gallo, signed off on the amendment." Hugo's smile was a poisonous thing. Smug, with a hint of sadistic delight. It curled at the edges, the way a dog did when eyeing a treat held out before it, knowing it was destined for its maw. "I invite you to let my minister of finance know if you've found any discrepancies in our accounting or shortcomings in payments made."

Before another international incident could break out—and judging by the prime minister's whispered curses, that was a growing possibility—the prince crossed to Carlos, yanking him by the arm into the corner of the room. "Tell me you had nothing to do with this."

"I'm afraid I can't." There was a sort of mewling undercurrent, a kind of plea mixed with pity, as if to ask Francisco whether he was too simple to understand the nuances of his office. "You don't need to lecture me about the man Ferrente is. I was there when he stood with the forces that overthrew your family. But this is realpolitik. Gaia has no hopes of achieving any sort of independence from Plaxis without massive technological support."

"You'd replace one master with another." Anger roared within, and Francisco was finding it very hard to stay regal. "At least Plaxis has Omala Grover's legacy at the core of its ethics. No matter in what direction we're pushed or pulled, that always keeps us centered. Tangentry has only him, and the only direction it will take us is down."

Carlos buried his chin in his chest. "Sometimes to get through hell, it's best to let the devil show you the way."

"Meaning?"

"We can't outgun Plaxis if we stand alone. If we really want to debate seriously the chance of declaring our independence, we need backing."

The words pushed Francisco back. "Outgun?"

The attaché's head shook. "I only mean that metaphorically. Tieg won't let us go without a fight. What's that Sun Tzu quote you throw at me sometimes? It's more important to out-think your enemy than to fight them?" Carlos laid hands on both of Francisco's shoulders. "Gaia was founded so we could let go the sins of the old world and save the new one we find ourselves in. Ferrente isn't here as a friend who betrayed you; he's here as a man willing to help a fledging nation rise to its rightful place and offer its prince what aid he can. At least let him sit in for the meeting."

Francisco straightened his tie, cleared his throat. "I don't think so."

The boldest armies in history had never marched with more determination than Francisco Batista de la Reina did in that moment, striding across the conference room to meet his ancient enemy face to face.

"You"—he whipped out an accusatory finger, stopping only inches from Hugo's chest—"are not welcome here."

Hugo's hands flew up to his sides, as though it were not Francisco's finger but a weapon pointed at him. "I was invited."

"As the ruler of Gaia, I hereby rescind that invitation. You have ten minutes to exit the program on your own terms, or a security bot will escort you out. Painfully."

Even in the vreal, Hugo towered over him, a fact made clear when the men stood chest to chest. "Think about this, now, Your Majesty. It isn't just about you and me. This is about Gaia. Plaxis has some of the best coders and lawyers in the world. In fact, they have the only ones Tangentry couldn't woo away. We're your best shot if you decide to go through with this."

"Are you really that determined to take another crown from me?" Francisco stepped into Hugo's chest. "You'd have to kill me first."

Both women, silent till now, gasped. Truth be told, Francisco found himself in awe of his own bravery. A man who'd been born to privilege, condemned to poverty, and risen again through his own merit didn't easily let his place go, however. He waited, chest heaving, thoughts storming. A scatter of cracking knuckles raised the hairs on the back of Francisco's head. Logically, he knew that no physical harm could come to him here inside Gaia. Unlike the Kingdom, Hugo could pull a knife and ram it into his heart, and Francisco would wake up back in his secure jackpod in the city. But the emotional and political consequences would be real.

Hugo's jaw tightened, then relaxed. His head lowered to his chest as he took a step back. "Paco, please," he said, using the familiar name of their youth. "Take our history out of this. Focus on Gaia and its potential to make our planet viable again. To save mankind from itself. Don't damn your new kingdom by some ill-conceived attempt to avenge your old one. My uncle killed your father, but we were barely more than children. Neither of us should take on the burden of that tragic day. We were friends once. Let me do this and prove that we can be again."

Francisco's right hand lashed through the air, drawing patterns he as only the prince knew. He saw the surprise wash over Hugo's face as first his legs, then his hands, and then even his jaw froze into position.

"Edict 43.1 of the Gaia Charter enables the ruling sovereign to banish any user other than executive administrators from the platform without trial or committee if he or she believes that user poses an immediate threat to other users, himself, or the vreal world as a whole."

In his periphery, Congressperson Hsu sat back, hands folded in her lap, expectant. She'd always wanted to see the Gaia sovereign exercise the full power of their position, to show that they were more than just a figurehead. Perhaps she'd get her wish.

"I enact my powers as prince and banish you, Hugo Ferrente de Miguel, from this platform henceforth and until such time as I or one of my successors deems otherwise." The sound of his snapping fingers echoed. "Execute!"

In the blink of an eye, the place in which Hugo had stood was nothing but space.

Hsu was on her feet in a matter of moments, crossing the room to where Francisco stood, his hand still in the air. She reached up, rubbing his shoulder.

"Finally." She turned then to the prime minister. "He has my support. What about yours?"

Ashe mused, her thoughts impossible to read on her face, until she crossed her arms and leaned back in her chair. "Any enemy of Ferrente is a friend of mine."

FIFTEEN

TALIA GREEN HAD SEEN many people come and go while running San Francisco's best hackdome. Oh, it wasn't its fanciest, its most lux, or even the one with the best cocktails. It was approachable, comfortable, and, because of its prime location on Post Street, highly walkable. Go on about your great vreals and cheap taxis, but they still couldn't compete with the convenience of caveman instinct to graze and hunt on foot.

And frankly, the fewer tiktoks that sped by outside, the better. Talia wasn't certain if the rumors about the low-occupancy self-driving vehicles were true. In an age where you were being watched everywhere, however, it made sense for the Authority to take advantage of the poor's primary form of public transport. Cameras and mics were so tiny and the wireless grid so accessible, the victims of the spying basically footed the bill for their upkeep.

Chen and Warren showed up a week earlier than scheduled, a slender, unassuming woman with black hair, big brown eyes, and the weight of worries on her shoulder in tow.

"My, my, my..." Talia grabbed a towel from the bar, wiping the speckle of suds from her fingertips after pulling down a draft for one of her daylight customers. "I hope you don't expect me to pay extra for being early, or for the extra set of hands."

Chen pulled up his arm, rolling his wrist so his comque was on display. "Need to rent out two of your units for a little while, no questions asked."

"No questions asked?" One eyebrow pitched a slide over her left eye. "Normally that would make me think you've brought a prostitute for a little fun in the vreal where you're still young and virile, Chen, but you've never brought the kid along for one of those."

Talia watched in amusement as Warren's mouth dropped, then flopped a few times, trying to find words. It was funny how young people thought sex was something that had never existed before they'd discovered it, or considered it something the elderly had outgrown. She could tell some stories.

If she was hoping to get a rise out of Chen, though, Talia was disappointed. Not that there was any truth to it. Chen was an ageless flirt, but he knew she didn't let that kind of "jackings" go on in her establishment.

She threw a towel over her shoulder. "So, no questions. Is that just for you, or am I allowed to ask the Mistress of Cinders how she got mixed up with your two sorry asses?"

The dark-haired woman's eyes went buggy, and she schlepped her way across the bar and towards its owner. "Please, I don't want anyone to know who I am, or that I was here."

"I wonder if that has anything to do with you not showing up for the tournament I hosted the other night. The kitty was quite... fluffy." Talia looked back over her shoulder, confirming that her count of a barkeep and her self-involved customers remained true. "Don't worry. The two drinking down there are some of my regulars, but one's deaf and the other is a recovering chiphead. Not sure there's much going on up in the dome except a flashing light next to a door with no exit."

Talia motioned to a nearby table, inviting the trio to sit. Chen took the seat gladly, if shakily, while Warren still studied him suspiciously. Mistress took her seat last, all the while acting like a mouse scared that she was suddenly going to be noticed by the cat.

"Mistress of Cinders?" Chen asked, throwing a look at both women in turn. "What is that?"

Mistress shrugged, her chin buried in her chest. "It's my... handle."

To a casual observer, it would look like a coping strategy, but Talia wasn't a casual observer. She noticed the way the corner of the woman's mouth ticked up into a barely perceivable smile.

She was proud of who she was, and she had every right to be. For more than a decade, Talia had seen every kind of hacker come through the Stadium, from nubile coders barely able to make their battle avatar move to maestros of programming. The Mistress of Cinders bested them all. It was like Purusha Plus was her native tongue. But if that fact was something the woman needed to keep on the down-low for the moment, Talia wasn't about to flip truth that wasn't hers.

It did make her curious, though. "I'm guessing she"—she motioned vaguely at the Mistress—"is the reason for your visit."

Chen tapped the table with two fingertips. "I said no questions."

"And I haven't asked one." Talia leaned back, snapped in the bartender's direction, and held up three fingers. "And something fruity for the kid."

Across the table, Warren scowled. "I ain't no kid, Talia."

"You might be the best techanic this side of the bay, but you're legally underage. You want booze, drink your grandfather's."

Warren crossed his arms over his chest, muttering something, but all Talia picked up was "only buys cheap stuff."

They all stayed quiet as the barkeep set down three half-full glasses of house brew and a red drink in a tall glass capped with a little umbrella. When he was gone, Chen spoke up.

"We need to take a little trip."

Talia pushed her glass to her lips, waiting for something more.

Chen looked left and right, then hushed himself. "We need to take a little trip to the tower."

It was a good thing she had swallowed. Otherwise all three of her guests would have gotten their beer secondhand and sprayed across their faces. She knew being part of Chen's schemes back in the day would come back to bite her in the ass.

"Be that as it may, Chen, you know he isn't here. I have no idea where he is. You made sure of it, and, frankly, I'd like to keep it that way."

"Ignorance is bliss?"

Their host turned to the Mistress in response to the question. "Actually, it's damned frustrating. But it's also not legally damaging. I shouldn't have to remind you that what I do here skirts the fine feathers of the law."

"Hackdomes aren't illegal," Chen said plainly, innocently, like the ingenious child he truly was.

"No, they're not," Mistress added, running a finger over the edge of the table. "But the betting pool and contraband crypto flying around in here each tournament sure are. And if I'm not mistaken, the house takes ten percent for most tourneys."

Want to really know what was going on? The best way wasn't to ask questions. It was to make a vague statement and let the others color in the details.

Chen's attention shifted. He examined his additional hand with new scrutiny and a twisty eye. "And how would you know that?"

When the woman wouldn't answer, however, the old man turned back to her.

"Talia?"

"I keep customers by respecting their privacy, Chen. And I keep customers coming back by having some of the best competitors in the world."

Talia sat back in her chair, pushing a hand into her pants pocket. The pieces were coming together now. She'd never sat down and painted nails with the Mistress of Cinders, but the fact that she'd always had the red-haired chick with her, orchestrating the entry and collecting the winnings, had told her the coder wasn't the throat-cutting type. That, and-or Mistress needed a buffer. She couldn't be directly implicated to have competed in a tourney. Which must mean someone owned her talent. And who else in this godforsaken city could snag talent like that under contract?

"You're a Plaxis codejockey."

The brown eyes widened for a moment, but Mistress said nothing. Which, evidently, was as good as yes.

"You got some chutzpah, Miss Cinders. If your supervisor ever found out I'd let you compete here, they'd sue my bones into dust."

"Don't worry about it. They'll never find out." Mistress said it with such conviction, anyone hearing would know she was telling the truth or self-delusional. "Besides," she added, "I was fired a few days ago. For reasons that have nothing to do with you," she rushed to add when Talia's face went white. "If you let me help Mr. Chen here, it won't violate my contract."

"That doesn't make it any less illegal, I'm betting."

Talia let the silence buffer, hoping one of them would offer a barter. Even with the best of intentions, they couldn't be that innocent or that stupid to think this was a pro-bono transaction. Mistress had the right idea but the wrong numbers. With tourneys, the house kept a fifteen percent cut of the cake. On some nights, that was a significant slice of cake. But if these three were about to attempt what she thought they might be, and they were caught, it would take a whole bakery to clean up the trouble. Then again, having someone like the Mistress of Cinders owing you a favor? Now, that was worth something.

"Well, Mistress." A verbal lilt in Talia's voice served as a metaphorical wink. "Don't take this the wrong way, but I don't know you. Not really. And I certainly have no reason to trust you. Since I suspect you're into some serious underworld pirating shit, given the things you can do in the arena, I'm not sure I should—"

"I can think in Purusha Prime."

Talia's tongue pulled a hard stop. "You mean Purusha Plus."

Mistress shook her head. "No, I mean Purusha Prime. Most complex vreals use Plus; they license it from Plaxis, but it's a derivative, limited version of Prime. And I'm able to interface directly with the system. I don't have to string together code like a toddler putting together blocks the way the rest of the hacks you have competing here do. I have a near-instant stream of consciousness in it. That's how I'm able to win every time."

The rest of the alcohol went down in a single gulp, which was more than what Talia could say about what she'd just heard. If the claim was true, it would fit perfectly into that gap of Talia's understanding about what she'd witnessed every time the Mistress of Cinders was part of the lineup. It didn't change the fact, however, that it didn't seem possible.

"No one but Omala Grover had a composite knowledge of Purusha Prime. I remember back when she and that husband of hers, the what's-his-name that owns Plaxis, were divorcing. The gossip feeds couldn't get enough of it. Someone interviewed Grover when she sold her shares of the company to him, asking if she was worried that he was going to shut down Gaia. She said, and I quote, 'I'm the only living woman who knows how to destroy it, so no, I'm not.' Which means... either you're lying, or she was."

The facts didn't frighten. Every muscle in the young woman's face was perfectly placid. "I've never heard that story, but if that's what my mother said, then, at the time, it was true."

Holy. Shit.

"Your mother?" Talia didn't know why she was breathing so hard.

The Mistress's back straightened. She looked to Talia on her right, Warren on her left, and then at Chen, with a gaze that invited defiance and knew she wouldn't get any. "My name is Cindira. The what's-his-name that owns Plaxis is Rex Tieg, my father. Omala Grover was my mother."

Talia pushed herself away from the table but remained seated. Why, she couldn't say. Was the truth any less astounding at a distance? But sometimes a revelation was like that; it pushed you in the real as much as it did in the head.

Chen, in the meantime, threw his head back and cackled before hitting the table enough to make the remaining liquid in the other glasses wobble. "Well, I'll be a cod-smacked motherfucker."

The old man only gazed with an admiration that clearly made the young woman uncomfortable. She pulled back her chin, tilting her head. "Sorry, a what?"

"Has it really been that long?" Talia ignored the men, instead performing mental mathematics. It didn't take long before it all lined up. "I guess you would have to be in your late twenties now. Jesus, kid, when your mom died, the media was obsessed with you. You were everywhere, on every stream, every page front. And then you just kinda... disappeared."

Cindira shifted in her seat. "Being shipped off to boarding school does that to a person. I lived in Andorra until I finished with grad school. Not that I needed it. I knew more than all the VR studies professors combined when I was in middle school. I just didn't want to come home, and the only way I could have stayed on there was to join the faculty. Obviously, that wouldn't work. I've only been back in the city a few years."

"And... you were... fired by Plaxis?" Warren asked in halting, segmented phrases. "The company your parents founded. The company your father still owns." He sat back in his chair, arms crossed over his chest and a chip firmly in place on his shoulder.

Bless youth, sweet god, because they were never scared to ask the things adults had learned better than to question.

"Yes." Cindira's big brown eyes slid to the side. "And... no. It's complicated, and it would be dangerous for me to tell you why. But I promise you, Miss..."

Here she was, telling Talia she was going to help the old man hack into one of the most secure servers in the world, and she was worried about the kind of formality?

"Green," Talia said. "Talia Green. And for what it's worth, I believe you, both that you're the daughter of Omala Grover and what you say about your knowledge of Purusha. Hell, I've practically seen you show it in my hackdome downstairs. But please understand that this place which I have spent years building is all I have. If anything you're about to do somehow gets traced back to me..."

The old man's face lost its mirth. "I'll consider it payment for your mainframe rebuild."

Chen's sudden pivot spun the conversation in his direction.

"You can't be serious." "What mainframe rebuild?"

Talia and Cindira's voices overlapped, which turned them on

each other.

"The last time you were in here competing, my entire system overloaded," Talia said. "When Authority came rushing in that night? That was because the San Francisco power grid red flagged my property. The extreme network activity beyond what we're licensed to draw was putting off enough heat to bake a building. They were positive the place was about to burst into flames."

Cindira had the good sense to cower. "Is that something I did?"

"Can't say for sure. But every time you've been in the games here, my processors feel it for days afterward."

Before the girl could respond, Warren pounded the table. "Gong gong, she owes us two thousand greens for that job!"

The grandfather sat back in his chair, picking lint off the knees of his trousers. "It's worth it."

"No, it isn't," Cindira interjected. "I wouldn't ask you to give up that much money to help me."

Warren nodded his approval. "Finally, this chick is saying something that makes sense."

The daughter of Omala Grover leaned over the table. "Miss Green, if you let us use your devices to do this, not only do I promise it will never get back to you, but I'll pay to upgrade your mainframe."

Talia raised her glass to her lips. "Seems appropriate, since you were probably the one who's caused all its damage."

"And for the next year of maintenance for your systems."

Warren's jaw dropped to the floor. "Wait a second. That's four thousand greens. If you really had that kind of money, why did you barter with us for this?"

"I don't have that kind of money. Not right this second. But I still have a one-percent interest in Plaxis that my father gave me as a twenty-first birthday present. It's really no more than a symbol; somehow he managed to set it up so that my share of company profits are donated to charity. But if I sell my one-percent, I'll have plenty of funds. It will just take me a few months to handle all the legal requirements."

"With that kind of credit, you could rent space from any jackpod in the city," Talia said. "And yet, you're here."

"True, I could head down to the Ferries and rent out the machines this second if I wanted to," Cindira admitted. "But I can't buy the kind of trust Mr. Chen has shone in you by bringing us here, or deny that it's one hell of a coincidence that you know who I am and what I can do. So few do, and for good reason. Are there those who suspect? Maybe, but I've never admitted it to anyone except my mom. I need you to keep the secret."

Talia motioned to the bar for a refill. "Excuse me for saying so, but you don't negotiate too well. You've already given us the secret. If it's really all that valuable, I could sell it for far more than you're offering me."

Cindira narrowed her gaze. "I can do other things too, Miss Green." When she spoke, her voice had lost any trace of its sweetness or innocence. "Be a shame if the next time you were jacking into your favorite beach vreal or casino platform, you ended up in the middle of an active wardome battlefield instead."

To run a successful legal business with an underground semi-legal line of income in the basement as Talia did, one had to balance a sense of fairness and compassion with the recognition of when you could turn someone's disadvantage to yours. No doubt there were many things someone with Cindira's capabilities offered, things she couldn't refuse from the sound of it. But Talia also remembered a time when someone else had come to her needing help only she could provide, and how she'd carried it through, benefiting in the long term from the consequences.

"I guess my only remaining question is for you then, Chen." Talia fixed her gaze on the old man. "I thought we swore never to go see him?"

The girl lost all her conviction in the wake of her confusion. "Him who?"

But Chen only shrugged. "That was before she found his body," he said, pointing a bony finger in Cindira's direction.

The coder's eyes widened. "Wait, you mean you know who the man I found is?"

"I do."

The pregnant pause finally gave birth to the young woman's outburst. "Who is he?"

The old man shook his head. "Sorry, Mistress, that's not my secret to share. We'll go see him, and he can decide whether you need to know. That's our deal, Miss I-know-Purusha-Prime. Take it or leave it."

SIXTEEN

THE CLEAR BLUE SKY and clean, crisp air told Cindira this was indeed a virtual world. If not for that, she never would have known.

Even the most intricate builds maintained some surreal and impossible aspect. It wasn't because the coders weren't capable of reproducing, at least visually, the smallest detail. It was because without these design flaws, the human mind found it difficult to break the cognizant boundaries between what was real and what was code. Oddly, it was the perfection that provided the flaw: even with the environment on the rebound and all indices showing improvement since the launch of Gaia, an endless view of alpine mountains rising above a verdant valley against an azure backdrop without a hint of haze was an impossible sight to behold in the real. And yet, as breath-taking as it was, this wasn't the most impressive thing about the place where Cindira stood.

What really knocked her socks off was the vegetable garden.

"They grow carrots."

If there was one thing she'd never conceived of in her wildest imagination, it was virtual horticulture. The vreal was a touchstone in timeless time, an ephemeral experience. Sure, food was part of the marketing and jacked-in experience. As one of the five senses, taste could not be ignored, and it certainly had brought pleasure as well as any born of sight, touch, or scent. But stepping back for a moment, the reason for this anomaly became clear. The man they were going to see had been jacked continuously in the vreal for years. He wasn't just visiting. He was living here. The first sign of a civilization was settlement, and the first goal of a settlement was to protect or produce a stable source of food. One of the history teachers back in her school days was fond of the phrase, "Agriculture is culture, farming is foundation."

Was this land and the medieval tower rising sixty meters above it the crux of a new civilization? The possibilities and complications of that were beyond even her thoughts.

"I know, right?"

Here in the vreal, Chen presented as a much younger version of himself. Grey, thin hair had filled in and turned black. Wrinkles had disappeared. His aged eyes remained full of wisdom, but there was a bit of whimsy peeking around the edges of his expression as well.

"I mean, you don't have to make things here like the real world. They could have made a plant that grows milkshakes. Or better, women."

Cindira ignored his jibe and took a step forward. Only then did she remember her predicament.

"What in the hell is that?" Chen pointed at the one glass slipper on her right foot. "Is that what the kids are wearing these days?"

"Nope, just me." With a few lines of Purusha Prime, she warped the shoe's shape. Low rise heels and shoes fit for dancing made sense in the palace. Here, though, a hiking boot seemed more appropriate. With another line of code, she made the so-called normal shoe on her left to match the style, if not the transparent quality of her remaining glass one. That settled, Cindira ticked her chin toward the only building on the horizon. "I suppose we should knock on the door, but there's a problem."

"We forgot to bring a present?"

This time, she did smile. A little. "There's some kind of perimeter coded around the property. I don't know if it's just a notification protocol or a forced boot from the program. All the code is inside, so I can't see it and I can't untangle it."

"What happened to 'I can think in Purusha Prime'?"

"You're not amazed that I can see code?" After all, it was invisible to the virtual eye. But Cindira had always had an ability to perceive it as a sort of second reality, like she saw the illusion and the truth all at once.

"Hey, you said you can think in code. I suppose extending that out that you can see, smell, and hear it too makes sense."

Fair enough. "It's kind of like when you're listening to someone speak a language related to one you know, but different. Like German with Dutch or Italian with Spanish. I can make out the basic gist, but there are details I'm missing, syntax I'm unable to grasp."

Chen glanced with great contemplation, humoring her. "So not Purusha Prime, then."

"More accurate to say, not only Purusha Prime. And don't ask me what. I'm not sure. All I can say is that whatever's coded around that tower, it isn't derivative, like Plus would be. It's not a subset. It's..." She squeezed her eyes, forcing the image to separate from the text and code floating that made it all possible. What she was seeing was impossible. "...iterative."

Only a handful of coders in the world had the smarts to pull off such an accomplishment. She was one, and she personally knew the two or three others who might have had a hope, if they had also had the resources only working at Plaxis could provide. Even then, none of them could have done it without her help.

She'd start with the most logical suspects and cross them off her list as she went. "I thought you said this Bas guy, the one whose death date we used to pin the pumpkin... You said he created this world, but you also said he was only a techanic. Any chance you were wrong about that?"

"Bas couldn't code a stick figure back when I knew him, but what the hell do I know?" Chen pushed fisted hands into his hips and arched his back. The young-looking elderly man batted the air. "Well, let's go."

He managed three steps before she got her hands around his arm and stopped him.

"Are you crazy? You can't just walk in there. You have no idea what that barrier will do. I don't know what it will do."

"Seems a really quick way to find out would be to go through it." Chen lifted a foot.

She pulled him back again. "Do you seriously think I could get us here with no one the wiser but this"—she gestured toward the tower—"is beyond me? I just need a moment. And I need... I need..."

"Ow!"

She pinched one of Chen's hairs between her fingers, even as he slapped a hand over the part of his scalp that she'd nicked it from. Vigorous was the rubbing and dramatic the expression, but Cindira knew it was the recreation of a sting of pain and not the actual thing.

"What was that for?"

"I need a bit of your... Well, it's not quite DNA, but let's just call it that."

The coder opened her palm, laying flat the stolen hair before reaching up to her own. She winced despite herself, the illusion no less painful. The two black, wavy strands, one long and the other barely long enough to stretch across her palm, only wavered at first. Then, as though magic, they animatedly twisted and turned. The code came together with a few wayward thoughts, and soon two tiny beetle-like masses took wing and flew away.

"You made insects?" Chen's nose wrinkled as he watched the "bugs" flitter in the castle's direction.

"Not quite. I thrashed together our hair with framing for a ladybug. The barriers don't know the difference between an ear and eyetooth. It just reads biological attribute tags."

"Oh? Oh, that's smart."

If she'd had a bit more of an ego than she did, Cindira would have agreed. And that would have made her look like an even bigger idiot a moment later. Two ladybugs reached the barrier. One of them sailed across with no problem, shrinking from sight as it flitted through the air. The other became a small cache of flame, zooming toward the ground.

"So one of us can cross." Chen's head turned at a measured pace. "But which one?"

Her wide eyes belied her teeming mind. She'd never considered there'd be a difference. "This time, one at a time."

Cindira reached for Chen's head again, only to have her hand slapped away.

"Ach, you codejockeys!" he spat. "Everything, one command after another. Systematic. Machines don't work that way. The whole system goes, or it doesn't."

"I don't think that's true. If you just—"

But there was no chance to stop him this time, not when they were so close. Chen turned, marched forward, stepping over the boundary only she could see... and was fine.

Which meant—she was the one trapped on the outside. "Well, that sucks."

"Not for me, it doesn't." Chen turned, gallivanting in the tower's direction. "Keep cool, Tieg. I'll knock on the door. I'm sure he'll want to come out and meet you."

Cindira was about to raise an objection when everything went black. Her hands shot to her head, trying to pull the bag off. No luck. In a moment, her feet swept out from under her, and in another, she was thrown over what must have been somebody's shoulder.

"Let me go! Let me down!"

She tried to piece together the code. Maybe she could turn the ground to a pit of mud or summon a wind that would knock them both over. Maybe she could try to turn the black sack over her head into a glass bowl. Each thought and its corresponding matrix of commands fleshed out in her mind, but nothing happened. The code was failing her.

And then she felt it, a buzz, a singe, like a flame had kissed her body and seared off all the hair.

Her ass hit the ground hard.

When the sack was lifted, a man snarled at her. Hazel eyes and olive skin, with hair even darker than hers. His clothes were so... was that meant to replicate a woolen jacket? He took one look at her and blinked. Blinked again. Took a step back.

"Omala?"

Cindira had been told for years by those who'd known her mother that she bore a striking resemblance, but everyone knew her mother was dead and had been for fifteen years.

She pushed herself up on the butt of her hands and shook her head. "No, my name is Cindira."

"Cindira?" His head cocked to the side. "You're her daughter."

"Yes, I am." She was surprised to find that her mouth had gone dry. "And you're Sebastian Archer."

SEVENTEEN

HE'S COMING TO TAKE the last thing I have. He's coming to rob me of what is mine. He's coming to unmake the world.

The rain did something to the city. Francisco wasn't sure if it was something good or something bad. On one hand, it refreshed plants and trees that once more were beginning to thrive. It washed away the grime and grease that coated everything on the street, and for an hour or so, made everything fresh. It also made everything about modern life so much more complicated. Traffic slowed. People going about their day, passing from here to there, did so with either hurried steps or a decreased awareness of their surroundings as they covered their eyes and sprinted.

Carlos didn't bother to knock, bursting into the office with anger more visual than audible and slamming the door behind him. Francisco kept his eyes fixed on the window and the water-colored drip of the horizon, even as his former guardian and most trusted advisor fumed at his side.

After several interim moments of being ignored, the attaché growled his words. "Well, have you anything to say?"

It was funny how everything looked darker when it was wet.

Carlos's hand lashed to the left, back in the door's direction. "Do you have any idea how difficult it was for me to get Hugo Ferrente to agree to meet with you? I promised him that what happened between your father and his uncle would stay in the past. That you were dedicated to acting in the best interests of Gaia and would treat him with courtesy and respect. And now you've gone and exiled him from the very vreal that will rely on his company to have a chance at independence?"

Francisco cracked his lips, and though he spoke, he felt disconnected from his words. "He isn't the only way to save Gaia. More than that, he isn't the right way."

Carlos balled his fists on his hips. "Oh? And just what is the 'right way'?"

That caught the prince. He felt more what he had to do than knew. What had Omala said to him? Fill the cup?

Clasping his hands behind his back, Francisco turned, searching his attaché's expression. Anger endured. For that, there was no blame. No doubt what Carlos had said was true. Hugo wouldn't have been an easy win. But what about Carlos himself? Could he be pulled over? Everything Francisco was about to do was so in conflict with his policies, his beliefs. And yet, he knew it had to be done. He was the sovereign of Gaia, not a prime minister or even a president. Liberty was the millstone of democracy, but the Kingdom wasn't a democracy. It was a platform people elected to visit. It couldn't violate their freedom to force them to enter it, could it?

"I want you to issue an edict," Francisco said. "I want everyone who attended the ball where I was kidnapped recalled into the Kingdom twenty-four hours from now. They are to stay at their residence on the platform until I've visited. For those who have no residence, they can either shelter in someone else's by invitation, or remain at the palace. Those who attended but don't appear will have their avatars immediately destroyed and be referred by Gaia to their national offices and charged with obstruction of justice."

If Francisco had asked Carlos to prepare a guillotine and a pot of tea for the executioner, it might have been met with less scrutiny. "You don't have the authority to do something like that."

"Actually, I do." Francisco's chin motioned toward his desk, where a datapad still showed the evidence. "Article Seventeen, Subsection C, Part Three: 'the ruler of Gaia has the authority to direct Plaxis to issue a virtual shelter-in-place order for a period of up to twenty-four hours in the event of a security breach.' The adoption of the charter was a decade before the founding of the Kingdom, but Plaxis never requested an amendment to that section. I just finished speaking with Kaylie Fife and our own legal department. They both confirmed that the authority extends to the Kingdom, as I was present in it at the time of the incident, based on my reading of the Charter."

He turned back to the window.

"I admit, Carlos, I had a moment where I thought I might fire you for inviting Hugo back into my life, but now I realize that I owe you. It made me remember. Hugo's family overthrew mine because they thought we were placing too much emphasis on the possibilities of Gaia. They said my father's support of Omala Grover's early work stole limited resources from the Andalusian people, all so we could stake a claim in this new vreal world. For years, I fought that idea on principle. When I won election to the throne, I swore to recall that claim, and assure that we... that I did nothing to feed those accusations. But now I see the truth."

The red bleached away from Carlos's face. "What truth?"

"That my grandfather and my father didn't go far enough." The prince pivoted, locking his attaché with sober eyes. "You spoke of independence for Gaia. I don't think that's enough. If it's to truly deliver on the promises Omala Grover made, then Gaia must have the authority it's been denied until now. We have the power. Our systems are wired into the function of every major government on the planet so that they can come to us and find solutions when they could no longer do it among themselves. We're going to reverse that flow. From now on, I want to stop the problems before they begin. At the root. But to do it, I need... her."

Carlos took a step back, one hand raised to the level of his chest. "Her, Your Highness?"

Francisco nodded. "The bandit."

EIGHTEEN

TINY HAIRS ON THE BACK of Cindira's neck tickled in a variable breeze. The scent of snow danced about her, matching with a view of distant purple mountains topped in white. The grass felt like a mat of wool beneath her feet, not the dry crisp crunch of the kind found in California. She'd had to swat a fly from her eyes at one point. A fly! Did any other vreal include insects?

"You're looking at it like you expect a dragon to jump out of the clouds."

Cindira spun on Bas, his words breaking her from her revery but not her thoughts. "Will it?"

Bas's mouth seized up. "Not unless Harper is in a very bad mood."

It was a reply but not an answer. She was getting used to it already. In the fifteen minutes since Bas had discovered her and Chen standing on the edge of his secured property, she'd bombarded him with questions. The older, handsome man—he might be thirty? Thirty-five?—did his best to address her query, but often ended a rambling attempt at explanation with a shrug and mumbled frankenword, helliffino.

Without further explanation, Bas stuck his right index finger in the air and traced a series of symbols. At first, Cindira wondered if he was doing some sort of visualization thing. She knew brilliant mathematicians and savants who "wrote" their thoughts in invisible ink as part of their process. But in a moment, the truth became plain. The code that served as a barrier between them and the tower thinned, then toned down into something resembling the type she was more used to.

"There, security field down. Luckily, I put a pot on the stove before I trudged out to see what had tripped it. Let's get you in before it rains again."

"Pot?" Chen sprang up. "No way, you have that here?"

The two younger people exchanged stitched expressions before Cindira pressed on.

"Rain?" Cindira looked up at the sky. The dragon was more likely. "It doesn't rain in Plaxis vreals."

"It never has before," Bas confirmed. "The landscape just stays perpetually green because... reasons. I pull buckets of water from the stream down the hill for the garden. If I had a real back, it would have broken six times over. Anyway... Yesterday, suddenly, deluge. Riki and Tavi had one hell of an afternoon running around in it. I don't think there was a single mud puddle left unexplored."

So he didn't live here alone. Together with Harper, that made three others now. She wondered if that meant there were three more jack mummies in some other warehouse out there.

Cindira turned her attention to studying every aspect of the structures built around her as Sebastian led them through a red door at the bottom of the tower. The kitchen, if it could be called that, pulled its design straight from medieval civilization. A well-worn wooden table stood, covered in cups, plates... drawings. Nothing technical or advanced, she saw at a quick glance as she passed. The amateur art sat in contrast to the digital renders beside them: bread frosted on top with green and pink mold spores, and cheese that had gone dry around the edges. She remembered the kitchens at the palace in the Kingdom, and how the cuisine was specifically programmed with imperfections. It was only by seeing some flaw that its beauty could be truly appreciated.

Their host pulled several mugs off a shelf tacked to a masonry wall and proceeded to pour out helpings. "Hope you don't mind tea. We tried to master coffee for years, but neither of us were fans of it out in the real, and eventually we gave up."

"I could code some, if you were interested," Cindira offered.

Bas turned, wearing a half-cocked smile. "I bet you could. Rumor has it you can do just about anything. But, no, thanks. We like our tea, and we're proud that we were able to make it ourselves."

Even the code that swirled mist above the cup was intricate, interacting with the air flowing down the chimney, from cracks in the wall, pouring through an open window... Cindira had always been fond of the fact that she was the only known person to have complete mastery over Purusha Prime, but for the first time in her life, she'd found something she couldn't decode.

She accepted the tea and took a sip. Eating and drinking in the vreal had been a mixed bag, she remembered from when she was young. At the end of the day, the taste of something was a simple matter of chemistry. Salt, sweet, umami... A machine could analyze those aspects and signal to the physical brain back in the vreal what was being consumed. Texture was a little more difficult to convey. Luckily, tea, which was basically stained water, presented itself nicely on her palate.

"So..." Cindira smacked her lips once. "What exactly is this place? Some kind of exclusive super hacker sand box or something?"

And if so, why hadn't she ever heard of it?

"It's the or something." Bas passed Chen, handing him his cup. "You really didn't tell her anything, did you?"

"I promised that I never would, didn't I?" The old man plopped a large blueberry picked out of the fruit basket in the middle of the table into his mouth. "You think I'd go back on my word?"

"The fact that you're here says something." Bas set the teapot on the stove before reaching out a hand to his former friend. "But I am glad you did. Messages sent through comques just don't hold up after a while, and it's nice to see a familiar face after so many years."

"Ha, if you saw my real face now, you wouldn't say it's familiar!" Chen grinned, each of his teeth stained blue. "I'm old and everything hurts all the time. And I'm so soft. Soft in places I don't want to be if you know what I mean. Do you know how long it's been since I've had a—"

"Chen!" Bas's sharpness wasn't without its own softness, more an admonishment than anger. "I'm sure Cindira doesn't want to hear anything about that."

True, but remembering her presence brought their focus back to her and the question she had to shape out of wet clay. "How did Chen know you'd be here when we showed up? You obviously weren't expecting us, based on how you first reacted."

Bas grimaced and cupped his stubbly chin with his hand. "He knew I'd be here because I'm always here."

"Is that metaphorical, or literal?" Cindira wrapped her hands around her cup, pulling it to her lips, leaving it there for a moment and enjoying how the steam condensed on the tip of her nose. Darjeeling, if she was correct.

"After a while you start asking yourself that." Bas palmed and rubbed the back of his neck. "I live here. I have for years. This is my home."

Only a stupid person wouldn't connect the dots, and Cindira was not a stupid person.

"You're the man in the first-gen jackpod that I found."

He didn't nod. Didn't say yes. His silence was his confirmation. Then Bas leaned across the table, pinning her with a tight glare. "How did you find me?"

She measured out just the right amount of truth to dole out. "I was assigned to work at an old Plaxis-owned warehouse when I found a hidden closet. You were there, along with a flotilla of biobotics keeping your body alive."

The young man's eyes slid left, settling on Chen. "You hid me in a Plaxis building?"

Chen stuck his index finger in the air and closed his eyes. "There's a quote from one of the old-time flickers. 'The closer we are to danger, the further we are from harm.' I figured if anyone from Plaxis ever came searching for you, the last place they'd look would be right under one of their own roofs."

"But how did you get me there, Chen?"

After a moment of stillness, his hands went up in the air. "I had a very fortunate run in one night at the Stadium. Coder who overextended his bets, couldn't pay up. We made a deal. I settled his debts. He squirreled you away somewhere no one would find you. It wasn't like you could just stay in Talia's basement forever. Sooner or later, someone was going to find you down there. Don't worry, I made them hardline you to the outside world. I've been remotely-monitoring you for years. I knew you were still alive and kicking. Or at least, alive."

Cindira folded her arms over her chest. The service tag! It had seemed strange to label something on a machine that would be easily found in its onboard service manual. "So you don't just work at the Stadium, you also play, huh? I guess that explains how you could afford that brand new building with all its modern safety designs in your neck of the woods."

"My gong gong told me the way to build real wealth was real estate." The old man shrugged. "For once, I listened. And after the shop exploded, the building was cheap. What was left of it, anyway."

"Sonnuva—" But there was a lightness in Bas's muttered curse which suggested amusement. "So how does my body look after so many years in a broom closet?"

Chen shrugged, the corners of his mouth tugging down. "You'll have to ask that one," he said, pointing at Cindira. "I didn't see you. She showed up at the store."

Which brought the attention back to her. "You're, um..." What a tough spot to be put in. "Good? I guess, given that it's been minimally supervised for so long." When neither of them objected to the vagueness or the description, she rushed through the rest of her thoughts on the matter. "The jackpod has the antigravity feature, and the biobotics have been doing their part. Whoever packed you up knew you might be unattended for a while. Still, they probably didn't think you'd be broadcasting for over twelve years."

Bas shook his head. "That ain't exactly what's going on. That jackpod is more of a... backup, I guess you could say. You see, Cindira, I'm not an avatar. This iteration of me? It's not code. Or, well, just code. I'm a living, breathing, functioning human man. That body you found? It's just the organic incubator that led to this."

Cindira reexamined the man before her anew, trying to read beneath the layers of his build. Most avatars, no matter how diverse their appearance, were the same at their core. The basic human shape had remained unchanged for millennia. All a coder need do was tweak the attributes to meet the image they wanted to present. But when she looked at Bas and attempted to pull apart the branches of his construct, nothing would separate out.

"You're not an avatar, and you're certainly not a VAPOR." Her eyebrows arched up under her bangs. "What are you, then?"

"I'm a..."

Before Bas could fill in the blank, the door to the humble kitchen at the bottom of the tower opened, and a woman dressed in deep brown and soft lavender clothing befitting a medieval aesthetic walked in. Her brown-black hair sat atop her head in a dizzying configuration of weaves and braids, complete with little white flowers pushed in at intervals. She froze in the doorway, eyes wide, her sand-hued skin bleaching at the sight before her.

"Harper!" Their host was on his feet, stomping towards the door with perhaps a little too much excitement. "We have guests."

"I see that."

Harper looked around the edges of the man between them. Her eyes settled on Cindira for a moment, the latter staying still, feeling like she was in the presence of a beautiful thing of nature who might bolt if she moved too fast. Cindira was about to step forward, to introduce herself, when she found herself struck dumb.

Behind the woman, two other sets of eyes peeked out, one brown, one blue.

One like the mother's, one like the father's.

It was as instinctive a thought as it was revolutionary. Cindira stumbled back, the table behind her the only thing saving her from a fall. A light breeze could have knocked her over. Knowledge had a force all its own.

"Children?" Her gaze traveled from the little ones to their parents. "You have children... in the vreal?"

Did her voice sound so hollow and airy that no one heard, or was it the fact that the woman across the room had turned her attention to their other guest and made a connection that kept the question from being answered?

"Chen?"

Harper sprang forward, all but jumping into the old Asian man's embrace. The energy in the room followed, riding on waves of laughs and happy cries, and an intimacy fell in the room that hadn't been there before. For the first time that she could remember, Cindira came to feel like she'd found a place in the vreal where the world didn't make sense. She was an outsider here, a stranger. She was the interloper.

Bas's hand settled on Cindira's shoulder, a little shake to wake her back to the moment. "You okay there, Cindy? Looks like you saw a ghost."

Is that what they were, ghosts? Bas was technically still alive, or so the biometers on the jackpod said. Then again, Chen had given the day he died as the metadata that had led them here. But that didn't explain who the woman was, and it certainly didn't explain how children were possible.

Pupils dilated, voice shaking, Cindira ignored the newly arrived woman and Chen exchanging pleasantries like old friends and forced out the only word she could manage. "How?"

To her surprise, Bas blushed. "Pretty much the same way it happens in the real." He let out a small chuckle. "I know, you'd think at least your mom would have made it less bloody and painful here. But no, she—"

"My mom?" All her senses plummeted off a cliff. "What about my mom?"

Bas's eyebrows knitted. "She... built this place." When she said nothing, he continued. "For us. I mean, its foundation may have just been another pumpkin, but everything it's become? All her. I thought you knew. I thought that was why you were here."

"No, I'm here because of my—" Spinning. The world was spinning. "How could my mom build this? You've only been in the jackpod for twelve years. She died three years before that, and—"

This time when Cindira looked up to see whose arm had braced her, holding her up, it was to find Harper at her side. She smelled like lilacs and something... vaguely familiar, but untraceable in her memory.

"Breathe." The command was accompanied by slow steps toward a fluid form that took on the appearance of a small bed as they approached it. "If you pass out, the jackpod you're riding in the real might think you're injured and pull you out."

Cindira shook her head, only to find her hair clinging and pulling across the moisture on her brow. "I can disable the safeties. I can—"

"You can't if you actually pass out." Harper's voice was both firm and soft, much like the mattress Cindira suddenly found herself sitting on. "You may be the daughter of a saint, but you're not one yourself. I don't expect any miracles out of you today."

Reflexively, Cindira wanted to say that she wasn't, that her mother, while the sunlight in her heart and the moonshine of her memories, hadn't been holy. But she couldn't talk. If she tried, everything would come out all at once. When you became consumed by letting everything out, you couldn't take anything new in.

In the periphery of her blurry vision, Cindira watched Harper cross the room. She leaned down to where the children played with a their surprisingly receptive guest.

"Riki, Tavi, why don't you take Mr. Chen upstairs and show him your bedrooms?"

"Can we take the weird woman too?"

The child's voice held the hint of a plea, and while Cindira suspected she was the "weird" woman they were asking about, she couldn't find it in herself to be upset.

Harper shook her head. "No, Mom and Dad need to talk to her alone." She tapped them on the shoulders. "Hurry, now. Uncle Chen and Cindira won't be able to stay much longer."

Footsteps dissolved slowly as the sound of two children pulling on their elderly "uncle" carried up the structure above. Cindira did as she'd been told, her focus on breathing in, breathing out. Breathing in, breathing out. A cool cloth dabbed at her forehead.

"After all this time, why now?"

Harper's words weren't meant for Cindira's ears. Bas, who'd hovered in the background since the trio had arrived, stepped forward.

"She says she found my body in the real," he said, taking a seat on a stool he pulled out from under the table and set before them. "We didn't get much farther than that before you came in."

Harper's teeth ground, but her voice remained even. "And I suppose you were just going to tell her everything, then."

"Couldn't see why I wouldn't." Bas shrugged. "She's Omala's daughter, Harper."

"Which means she's also Rex Tieg's daughter and Johanna Tieg's stepdaughter." Harper turned aside, fanning the cloth over the bedpost. She pulled herself forward and leaned down by the coder. "Throw out this tea and get her some water. I have a feeling Darjeeling isn't going to help us to keep her focused right now."

Cindira nodded, even as a wooden mug was placed in her hands. Then, pulling herself to the edge of the bed, she reached out, taking Harper's hands in her own. "I'm sorry. I don't usually panic like this."

"I don't doubt it for a second." Harper smoothed back the piece of hair still sticking to Cindira's cheek. "But maybe if you tell us why you're here, it will help you not to get worked up again. Take a drink, take a breath, then let us hear."

There was something so odd about this situation. If she'd been forced purely on looks, Cindira would guess Harper was about her age, if not younger. Yet this woman who appeared to be in her mid-twenties had the compassion and patience of a nana.

The coder nodded and raised the mug to her lips. Cool water hit the back of her throat, easing an ache she hadn't realized she had, bringing her pulse down. "I don't know. I found... I guess that was Bas's body? And I didn't understand, so I went to see Mr. Chen. Maybe I thought finding out how someone could survive in a jackpod for so long could help me figure out something about my dad's situation. I don't know. Mr. Chen told me he'd help me figure out what the deal with the body I found was if I could hack him into this pumpkin, and here we are."

"Your father?" Bas's voice came from the edge of the room, but the question was followed by approaching footsteps. "What about him?"

Cindira tried to find economy with her words. "He's missing. Johanna said he was kidnapped on a business trip to China a few months ago. But his avatar is lying in his bed at the Kingdom palace. It's like he's in a coma. I don't know if that means there's a glitch in the system or if he's in an actual coma, or even if... even if..."

The burn felt like it was shoved up in her cranium this time. Hot tears formed of their own volition, and she couldn't stop sniffling.

"We've never been close." Cindira didn't know if the other two were understanding her through sobs dramatic enough to please a playwright, but she had to get this out. "But he's still my dad, and I need to help him. Even Johanna says I'm the only one who can. I just don't know how."

"Of course, you don't, dear." Harper kneeled on the floor, a hand on each of Cindira's knees, squeezing. "And I bet that's something that hasn't happened to you much, not understanding something in the vreal."

"It hasn't. I can see the code. I can think about it, manipulate it. But something about my dad's condition isn't adding up." She let out a laugh. It must have made her look crazy. "When I found Bas's body, I thought it might be the opposite, like he's in a coma out the real, but living permajacked here. But for twelve years? It didn't make sense."

Harper patted her knee. "That's because he's not permajacked. He's alive, just like me. Just like our children."

"But this is the vreal. You can't be alive in the vreal." Her logic was fighting with her wishes to believe it was true. If these two could be alive inside, maybe her father was. "I get Bas. Not get it, but he has a body. Who are you? Are you stuffed in another closet somewhere in that warehouse? Somewhere else in the world?

Harper's eyes narrowed, and a v formed on her forehead. "No. I don't have a body anymore. But, what, you think that means anything? I still love my children. Most of the time, I love my husband. Just because you don't understand how it's possible, you think that negates it?"

"That wasn't what I was saying at all." Breathe. It had been an excellent suggestion, one she returned to now. Cindira closed her eyes and pulled a deep draw of air through her nose and down into her lungs. "I'm sorry. I wasn't expecting anything like this. When Mr. Chen asked me to bring him here, I didn't know I was stepping into the dark."

"You can't control what comes at you out of nowhere. But if there's one thing I have learned—" Bas put a tender hand on Harper's shoulder, squeezing. She looked up at him with emotions that no code could ever produce. "It's that you're better off dealing with what's possible once it does, rather than bother about what you hoped might happen."

"My husband's right," Harper said. "So, let's look at your situation that way. You said your father's avatar is active, but he's not in it. Have you ever seen anything like that before?"

The tears waned as Harper pulled Cindira out of her emotions and pushed her toward using her logic. Her brain went fuzzy with thought. "No, I..." But that wasn't true, was it? In fact, Cindira had seen another avatar who looked very much like that, but she hadn't connected it because the reasons behind it were already known.

"Yeah, actually, I have," she amended, pulling herself to the edge of the bed. "My mom's avatar was like that the first time I jacked into the vreal after she died."

Harper's face beamed with pride. "Good. Do you know why?"

"Yeah, of course. It's because normally when a person exits the vreal, an activation switch triggers in their avatar, and it goes into a memory file until the next time they log in. But my mom's... And mine, for that matter... They both always stayed active. We had an apartment... um, a pumpkin that vined from the Capital City in Gaia. Our avatars went there, always on. I remember asking her one time why, and she said so there'd never be records of us coming in and out. I don't know why that was important but..."

And then something snapped into place. Something that should have seemed obvious from the start. "The slippers."

Harper and Bas exchanged screwed-up expressions before the latter said, "Sorry?"

Cindira got up. She had to pace. It always helped with thinking, like moving her feet also moved her brain. "My mother had a pair of shoes made of nanobot-infused silicone. They let her slip in and out of the vreal from anywhere and at any time. That's why she needed her avatar to always be accessible, so that she could pick up from there at any moment without delay."

"Silicone?" Harper said the word like it belonged to a foreign tongue. "You mean she had literal glass slippers?"

"Silica is used in the making of glass, but technically, silicone is...." Cindira stopped, realizing rambling didn't have the habit of bringing clarity. "Not the point. Look, I know it sounds crazy."

"Unconventional, maybe. Uncomfortable, for sure." Harper stood. "But is it possible that your mother and your father, both original inventors of Gaia, have avatars that stay active no matter what?"

It made sense. Even if her parent's separation had been contentious, a fact she knew from both scattered personal memories and having read a few gossip streams archived from that time. As Users 1 and 2 in the vast log of avatars created since, it seemed logical that the builds were roughly the same.

Harper must have seen the conclusion grow in Cindira's eyes. The smile on her face broadened. She folded her hands in front of herself.

"You're reading too much into it," Harper said. "The state of your dad's avatar likely says nothing about the state of his physical being."

All the tightness that had built up around her heart uncoiled. Cindira's arms dropped to her side, and her breath whooshed out. "I can't believe I didn't see that before." She reached out a hand to Harper, who took it.

"Sometimes, when we're too busy keeping our head down, we can't see what's right in front of us." Harper let go her hand and moved toward the stairs. "I should check on Chen and the children, if you'll excuse me."

Bas stood in silence, though the loving gaze he kept on the graceful mother as she turned up the stairs answered one of Cindira's questions.

"You're jacked in here for her."

Bas's smile stayed intact as he turned to the coder. "I'm here for all of them," he corrected. "And even though I had told you before I crawled into that jackpod twelve years ago that I would be the last person to defend the vreal, it's saved me."

"So you didn't know Harper in the real?"

A little of his smile faded. "Cindira, in the real, Harper died twenty years ago."

"So she's a..." What was a kind way to put it? "An echo?"

"A simulation of a real person?" He shook his head. "No, my wife isn't a digital museum piece. Besides, you ever heard of the Mona Lisa giving birth to two children?"

"I've never heard of anybody giving birth to two children in the vreal." She let the silence permeate, refusing to poke at holes she'd hoped Bas might still fill in.

"That pod you found my body in?" he said. "It isn't just a jackpod. Back in 2128, Harper built it as a prototype. It doesn't serve as a portal for the brain to project into the vreal and the vreal back into it. It, um, copies a person."

"Whole being copying?" She remembered reading the practice discussed in her college days, and also why that discussion had been brief. "I thought that was deemed impossible."

"Yeah, well, not so much, it turns out." With two fingers, he pointed at the stairs. "It worked for Harper, but unfortunately, she died in the process. So, in terms of being alive the way you think of it? No, she isn't. And neither am I, even if you found my body. Everything that was in that noodle dome called a brain was sent here years ago." His gaze drifted back to her. "I remember reading this quote once about someone seeing a picture of himself as a child after he'd grown old. He said something like, 'He and I have nothing in common except that he is me.' Don't ask me who said it, but my ignorance doesn't make it any less true."

Cindira had heard that one before too, even if she too couldn't remember who'd uttered it. "So, your body?"

Bas shrugged. "There's a series of words that if I say them out loud, I'll download back to my flesh and bones. But between you and me, I forgot what they were years ago, and stopped caring that I had not long after that. This is my home now. The only person back in the vreal that I care about is Chen Wu, and we've found a way to keep in touch through the years."

Did that pique her curiosity? Of course it did, but she'd reached her daily limit of universal expansion.

"What about Harper?" she asked. "Doesn't she have anyone?"

"She had a brother once, but..." Bas's voice trailed off. "So, yeah, not really."

Of course. If she died so long ago, she might have no one in the real left. But that triggered another thought. "So what happens if the system goes down? All it would take for everything to disappear is for the source code to get into the wrong hands by someone motivated to destroy it, to destroy you."

"Pretty much same as the real, then. We'd die if we were in the real, too. If that happens, I guess I can't complain. Still, if there was a way to save my kids, I'd jump all over that, but as far as I know, there's not."

"You could save one of them."

Bas's head cocked to the side. "Come again?"

She pulled herself back, turning away her eyes. It was a stupid, stray thought, one she should have kept to herself. "I mean, it wouldn't be the ideal solution, but your body is still out there, aging and weak as it is from disuse, but still viable. Theoretically, if you had an escape mechanism for yourself, one of your kids could—"

So that was what it felt like to have lightning hit your brain.

Damn.

Damn.

Damn, damn, damn.

"Mr. Chen!" Cindira shot to her feet and bolted to the steps, yelling towards the second floor. "Mr. Chen, we need to go."

"You do?" The techanic turned. "What's happened?"

"I figured it out!" Details could come later. "And I also know why the people who took him want the source code. It isn't about war profiteering. It isn't even about destroying Gaia or the Kingdom. It's about upgrading it, or at least, it's about having the next best thing."

Bas rubbed the back of his neck. "You got that out of what I said?"

He sounded surprised. But that was the thing about the drop of water that broke the dam; it never understood its impact.

Cindira grimaced. "I mean, not totally, but yeah, kinda."

The solution had been so obvious, even she was surprised by it. "They assumed my father could get to the source code." It made sense. One wouldn't be blamed for assuming one of the original creators of a platform knew how it worked. But her father had only built roads and buildings and bricks out of what her mother had provided. "I mean, coincidences don't just happen like that, right? My dad goes missing, and then soon after that, the shoes show up at my door. He must have had them this whole time. And he knew what they did, but he didn't know how. But they did. They figured it out."

"Who? What? What are you talking about?" Bas threw his hands up when Cindira shot him daggers with her eyes. "I'm on your side here, but you're not making much sense."

"I know, but that's okay. Because they don't know." Cindira's mind kept on ticking up the post. "But somehow, I need to let them."

NINETEEN

WITH TWO FLICKS OF Francisco's finger, the girl advanced, making her way up the pathway leading from the home's front door to the street. Purple flowers fidgeted as the folds of her pink dress brushed past.

"Your Majesty, may I present Miss Elisabetta Ronescu, youngest daughter of Magyar Ronescu, Grand Duke of the Northern Balkan Conglomerate."

Dressed in white knickers, a long navy-blue jacket trimmed in gold cord, and a hat that looked like a three-dimensional bell curve, Carlos opened the gate and offered the young woman his hand. She bowed when she got close enough, but Francisco could see both the fear and the confusion in her eyes when she turned back to face Carlos and him. She was a girl, in spirit if not by the clock. Probably hadn't been permitted in the Kingdom more than a few months. Unlike Gaia, this more permissive platform had a minimum age for entry. That she was scared was evident in the way she seemed to second guess each movement, the way she avoided his gaze.

"Miss, if you would sit a moment?"

The prince held out his arm, indicating a puffy armchair covered in ivory fabric and tufted across the back. It had been brought from the house by the Magyar himself. The family employed a good coder. A family of means. Political influence, for certain. But would this youngest daughter of the Magyar hold the ability he'd been searching for all day?

"Thank you, Your Majesty." She blushed at the smallest sign of kindness, her alabaster checks warming. Her dress, a soft thing with frills and lace aplenty, made her look like an upside-down carnation, with a trim, tight bodice atop and a bloom of petticoats beneath. She was a bud on the edge of blooming, and suddenly, Francisco found himself questioning his resolve.

Don't be softened just because she looks young and innocent. Easy enough to say. Avatars could be misleading. Even though design guidelines in the Plaxis system forced users to have a close alignment between their real-world selves and their virtual designs, leeway was exploited with a master artist's attention to detail.

The prince waved a hand in the air vaguely. "If I could please ask you to present one of your feet, Miss?"

Her innocent eyes went wide. "Your Highness?"

When moments passed without Francisco's reprieve or clarification, Miss Ronescu complied, gingerly pulling at the bottom of her skirt, presenting two shoes that, while of an appropriate design to meet the Kingdom's esthetic requirements, were neither embellished nor suggestive of a great deal of thought. No wonder the young lady showed reluctance. All the code design funds had been spent on the dress. And the chair. There must be nothing left for the shoes. Even now, she looked up to him, as though she might fear her secret had been found out. Financial problems for the NBC's nobility. But fiscal constraints weren't what the prince was after.

He left the fire and shook his hands before him at waist-level. "Don't worry, Miss Ronescu. I don't care about what your shoes look like. But the security object I have requires me to press something against your foot. May I do that now?"

She rapidly blinked several times. "Do I have a choice?"

"Of course, I would never force you to do something against your will." The surprise in her eyes told her this was something she'd not heard on another occasion, and it made his insides hurt. "If you prefer," Francisco continued, "I can place the object in such a position that you can try stepping into it instead."

"If you do not mind, Your Majesty, I would much prefer that."

The black pouch the hid the shoe was made of velvet and cinched closed with a gray ribbon. Or at least, the coding for the bag he'd requested from his staff made it appear and be perceived as velvet here in the vreal. As before, the glass slipper had been in his desk the moment Francisco had jacked in. He'd picked it up, turned it about, even tossed it up and let it fall to the ground. The moment of worry that seized him, thinking it might break, turned out to be for nothing. Carlos had been his first unwitting test subject. The attaché could feel the bag's contents through the velvet pouch. He could test its weight in the palm of his hand. But when the old man tried to reach in and grab the shoe, he clutched only air.

Not Francisco. As long as the prince instigated action, the slipper obeyed the rules of physics that all VAPORs did inside the vreal. It had mass, dimension, weight... The slipper even made a little din as he dropped in on the stone pathway, pushing it nearly flush with the young woman's foot.

"Lift your feet about four centimeters, shift them to the left, and lower them slowly."

Her nose scrunched up. "This is a very peculiar security screening."

Gingerly, showing a great care for the instructions given, the young woman lifted her legs, moved them the implied direction, and began to lower them again with great deliberation.

A trick of the sunlight reflecting off the dress's detailed bead work fooled Francisco for a moment. In a moment, however, the truth was revealed. The dainty feet closed the distance and the shoe, as though a phantom object, allowed Miss Ronescu's foot to pass right through it, neither affected by the exchange. The moment of excitement, followed immediately by frustration, must have played out on the prince's face. Suddenly, the girl tensed up when looking at him.

"What happened? Am I in some sort of trouble? Was this some test that I have failed?"

Francisco bit his tongue and the curse that gurgled in his throat. "No, you've done nothing wrong." *But maybe I have. Maybe this was a foolish idea.*

Carlos stepped in when the prince turned away. He leaned over, taking the sack from the confused debutante. "It only means that you have complied with His Majesty's orders, and that now you may leave, my dear."

With a furrowed brow, the young woman cocked her head. "Shall I go through the exit gate in the village or shall I—"

Her words were cut off as Francisco raised his hands, dialed in the forced exit code Plaxis had prepared for him, and she promptly ceased to be present.

Somewhere in the upper Carpathians at this very moment, Elisabetta was blinking her way back into the real, no worse for wear. No doubt she'd run to her mother and five older sisters, already tested and released, to exchange notes immediately. The whole world at this point was awash with conspiracy theories about "Prince Francisco's trick VAPOR." Some suggested even that Francisco was looking for a wife, and this was the way he was screening candidates. It was only the women he seemed interested in at each house, after all. Thank goodness no one inside the vreal except a handful of VIPs, himself included, still could communicate with those on the outside while the security measures stayed up. He feared how the remaining eligible women would be presented to him if they had.

Carlos fixed Francisco with an even-eyed glare, as to say are we done with this foolishness yet?

The prince offered the pouch. "Maybe I should screen you again."

The attaché guffawed. "You know I tried. It's just something heavy, but when I put in my hand, I find only air."

"You ought to be relieved. That means I don't have to arraign you on charges of conspiracy and attempted regicide."

They turned out on to the main street, walking further up the road. When first they'd set about this endeavor, Francisco had been filled with both anticipation and nerves. Something about the bandit had haunted him for weeks, and it wasn't just the fact that she had abducted him at knifepoint. The more he thought of her, harkening back to their brief time together, the more he felt he knew this woman. Not her identity, and he'd have that once he found the person who could hold the glass slipper, but her. It was like she was a memory returning to him slowly through subtle reminders. Her mindset, her intentions, her ambition. In the logical parts of his mind, Francisco knew better. All they'd had was ten chaotic and dangerous minutes, and a brief, though admittedly flirtatious, conversation. But he had to wonder: was it possible to glimpse the true nature of a person in so short a time?

He could fill out facts and figures revolving around her later. Tonight, he wanted to meet... to meet again... her soul.

But maybe he should have given credit where credit was due. The kind of hacker who could sneak into the second most secure vreal in the world, impersonate Omala Grover, take him hostage, and escape without detection probably could have gotten out of this simple form of entrapment too. She had to know that the shoe was his key to finding her, and with its self-concealing design, must be valuable. Then again, maybe not. After all, if she was really that good of a hacker, couldn't she just make a new... glass slipper? Not quite an accurate term, but a wonderful piece of shorthand.

Francisco closed his eyes and drew in a deep breath. Detest the Kingdom as he may, the scent of it, clean air with a hint of jasmine, had always reminded him of home.

"I admit my fault in this, Carlos."

The attaché turned up a graying eyebrow. "Sir?"

"I thought this would pull her out of the woodwork. But there's only three more houses to visit, and I'm losing hope."

"There's also the palace to see to."

Indeed, there was. Francisco lifted his eyes to take in its edifice not too far in the distance, while letting go of his expectations.

"But who knows how many will be there? It might be as many as I've already seen." He ran his free hand through his thick black hair. "Are you certain that the IVs back in our bodies in the real are supplying sufficient hydration and nutrients?"

"According to the operators I spoke to, there shouldn't be any problem. When I said we may be jacked in for an exceedingly long time, they assured me that the jackpods in the Palace of Fine Arts were designed to allow the sovereign and a few others to stay connected for up to thirty days. We can't have been here for over ten hours." Carlos's eyebrow arched again. "Why do you ask?"

"Because my stomach is feeling upset."

Carlos attempted to bury a laugh in his chest. "Could that be because you're nervous about meeting your captor?"

"Her? No, I'll be thrilled to find her." The weight of the shoe in the pouch seemed heavier as he thought about it. "But what I'm not thrilled about is whose house is next."

The silence that fell between them had mass; it turned their steps heavy and their faces long.

Finally, Carlos stirred. "You did say everyone who was in attendance at the ball, Your Highness."

"No need to remind me. I just didn't pause to think who that might include."

A few more steps brought them to a new footpath, and the new footpath, to another door.

The house, built to resemble the Alhambra on a much more modest scale, sat in contrast to most of those they'd visited so far. With its alabaster walls, intricate archways and tiles, and reflecting pool in place of a front garden, it recalled a time in Francisco's country's history long since past, when an invading people had washed over the land, removing the last remnants of Rome and installing a new era of grandeur. He had to wonder if the design might not be an implication by its owner that this kingdom too would fall to him.

Carlos cleared his throat before rapping on the door. "In the name of our sovereign, Francisco Batista de la Reina, Prince of Gaia, you are hereby ordered in compliance with the edict communicated by Plax—"

"Good god, Carlos, stop droning on. I know why you're here."

It had only days since their exchange in the Capital City, and yet Francisco felt that both an eternity and no time at all had passed. The anger, a tide of crimson fury that had only washed away, foamed within. *You are the prince, and he's only here because of an edict you proclaimed.* Francisco wasn't certain if the voice in his head was his own anymore. Was he a man of passion or a man of reason? Could not both have issues with who stood before him?

Hugo grimaced his displeasure. "Now what is this all about?"

TWENTY

TALIA WAS TWO MINUTES away from throwing all caution to the wind and calling for ambulances. It was one thing to be pinned in a plot of hacking into the highly secured Kingdom. It was another to have two people, one the daughter of one of the most powerful families in the world, die in her jackpod. A murder-four conviction came with two possible sentences: ten years in prison, or five years in service in the Gaia wardomes for whatever country bought her contract. She'd been there, done that. She wasn't doing that again.

Cindira was the first to open her eyes when the jackpod's interface retracted. She went from unconscious to terrified in an instant.

"Let me out!" Her delicate fists banged the pod's transparent lid. "I have to get out of here."

Talia rushed to open the device. Not out of any sense of sympathy, but to make sure the lid wasn't cracked by Cindira yet again. Who would have thought the Mistress of Cinders would be claustrophobic?

"Calm down!" Benefactor or not, Talia didn't do comforting. "They don't make new panels for this lid anymore. You break it, you're paying to have one custom cut."

With Cindira's eyes still racing in all directions and chest heaving, Talia half-expected to hear that the coder and Chen had been chased out of Bas's property by pit bulls. Or, hell, maybe dragons. Who knew what kind of monsters and myths that man had conjured in his hidden little bubble?

"I know where my father is!" Cindira bellowed it like a forced confession. "I have to go. Please get me out of this."

Talia ignored her and pushed her back into a seated position inside the jackpod instead of helping her out. "Drink first. Then talk." She pressed a glass of water to the young woman's lips. "My biobotics kept you hydrated, but I imagine your mouth doesn't taste the best after two days down."

The physical body never failed to consume that which it truly needed. The codejockey's animal body needed water; it would take a second for her higher brain functions to follow what had been said. Talia recognized the moment the comment landed. Cindira's eyes widened; she lowered the glass, panting.

"Two..." Breath, breath. "Days?"

"Is that how long it was this time?"

In total contrast to the first-timer, Chen emerged from his pod unaided and as rejuvenated as if he'd just awoken from a pleasant afternoon nap. Regardless, Talia suspected he was no less uncomfortable. He took the glass with a gentle nod of thanks and sipped his water at an easy pace.

Cindira blinked. "This time?"

Chen's eyes tracked in her direction even as he finished his drink first. "Not my first visit. Time moves differently there. No need for it to sync with the real world if you have no connection to it, right?"

The young woman's jaw dropped. "You didn't need me to get you in there at all."

"Not really, and still, yes." Chen held out a hand, asking without words for help to rise. Jackpods were magnificent devices, but the ones in Talia's hackdome hadn't been designed for use by those with mobility issues. "I can only get in when I'm invited, but I wanted to see if you could get us there on your own."

"So you were testing me?" Cindira was calming now. Or, at least, her respiration was coming under her control. Her anger, however, was slipping from it. "Why?"

"Because I knew you'd barter something." The old man waved a hand like he was swatting flies away. "You were so desperate. And it doesn't change anything. I still expect you to pay up everything you offered to me and to Talia."

Unlike Chen, Cindira didn't need any help standing. She shot to her feet still inside the jackpod, and lashed out an accusatory finger. "You hustled me!"

"I gave you the opportunity to prove yourself." Chen tapped Talia's hand to tell her he was good. "And to earn my trust. Neither Talia nor I have ever told anyone about Bas or Harper. For all I knew, you were lying when you showed up. You could have been trying to get me to tell you where his body was."

"And what if I had nefarious intentions? You gave me everything I needed. Once I was in there, I could have destroyed everything."

"You, destroy Bas and Harper's world? Ha!" Chen threw back his head and cackled. "She'd never let you."

"Are you saying Harper is some kind of crack coder who could take me on? I doubt that very much."

"She's not who I'm talking about."

The young woman finally managed to crawl out and get her feet back on the ground, leaning against the jackpod when she realized how two days in a forced coma didn't do wonders for your sense of balance and strength. Cindira tried to walk but jerked back. The tubes that regulated her body's function pulled taut, then popped off: one, two, three... Such a first-timer, Talia thought. The woman deserved the crimson drops that formed on the surface of her skin over her abdomen. If she hadn't flown off the handle, Talia could have properly removed and treated them, placing an artificial skin patch over the insertion points to avoid bleeding and possible scarring.

Cindira looked up, her face at war with her thoughts, her eyes begging for an explanation. "Who?"

Talia went to work removing Chen's hookups. "Everyone who knows about her just calls her the fairy godmother." Before the coder could ask the obvious, Talia continued. "We don't know who she really is. In fact, we don't think she is at all. Our best guess is that she's an archaic AI system left over from when your mom was alive. Sometimes either Chen or I will get a message, saying Harper or Bas is inviting us to visit."

"The fairy godmother? Yeah, she's helped me before, too." Suddenly, Cindira's forehead scrunched up. "So you've been to that pumpkin?"

Talia shook her head. "Never said I accepted the invitations. I helped Bas back in the day. I did my part to get him there, and I don't regret it, but I'm done. Don't get me wrong. I'm not going to do anything to bring them harm, but I don't want any further involvement with them."

Talia stayed silent then, watching as Cindira's face shifted through a cascade of expressions, her hands manipulating the empty air as though she were shoving and pulling out threads of understanding. Finally, after a minute, her arms dropped to the side.

"This all makes sense somehow, except..." She looked at Chen this time. "There's no way the jackpod with Bas's body and all those biobotics have been in the building without someone in Plaxis knowing, or that pumpkin hasn't been lanced from the servers through some kind of security sweep, fairy godmother or no. Do you know who?"

Chen smirked like a little boy sharing a secret. "Believe it or not, Johanna Tieg helped make Bas and Harper's pumpkin possible, but she doesn't know about it anymore."

Cindira's eyes went wide. "Johanna did something nice?" Her forehead creased as her gaze narrowed. "Wait, what do you mean, she doesn't know anymore?"

"That's the thing about letting your brain directly flow into the vreal, isn't it?" Chen scratched his nose. "Gives the vreal the chance to do the same back."

"Are you saying someone, what, hacked into Johanna's brain? Erased any memory she had of Bas?"

"I would never say that." Chen's eyes scanned the ceiling, busily looking removed from the conversation. "You could say it, but I never would."

Which was exactly why Talia wasn't in any hurry to go see the tower for herself, or personally jack into any vreal. She'd done her time in the wardomes, and she'd seen nations and men be made and be torn down just as easily. It didn't matter that they'd only experienced it in the minds.

A fairy godmother who could bend time? Help two people to abandon their bodies and go to live in the vreal? She imagined a woman (assuming she was a woman) with those kind of abilities could do much more, if she wanted. She remembered still the words Omala Grover had quoted when the first vreal wars were fought. She'd been there that day, her first assignment, fighting on the front.

Omala had looked out at the battlefield, the virtual landscape littered with bodies, broken and bloody and some still shrieking in pain.

"This is my creation," she'd said in a tone that had made it difficult to know if she spoke with pride or with shame. Then, after a deep breath, she'd pulled herself to the top of the broken ramparts and held her arms to the sky. "Now I have become Death—the destroyer of worlds."

BY THE TIME CINDIRA managed her way back across town, the setting sun had stained the sky behind her in mottled reds and oranges with pink margins over the graphite clouds to the west. Her shadow loomed long before her, whenever she wasn't consumed by the shade of a building or the odd tree, that was.

The botic mouse scurried up the hallway the moment she entered the building. "Miss?"

"Laporte." She shuffled past it, pulling off her respirator while letting the bicycle fall haphazardly in the hall. Pedaling across the city was tough on her legs, but having breathed in so much of the air, even with things improving, could have left her dizzy and wheezing for days. Not to mention that her body was still reeling from spending two days in statis. "I know you want to know what happened, and trust me, it will have to come later. I think I've figured something out and I want to see right away."

To her surprise, the little creature, generally genteel and accommodating, scurried up her pant leg and jumped on to her arm. "Miss, no, stop. Please understand, I wanted to stop her, but I couldn't. And without my connection to the wireless grid, I had no way to warn you."

Cindira's face screwed up. "Stop who?"

But that was a silly question. There was only one other person who had access to the warehouse: Johanna.

Which is why Laporte's response was even more surprising.

"Your stepsister."

TWENTY-ONE

SHE WOULD HAVE RUN faster if she could. Two days in a jackpod and pedaling across the city as fast as possible might have taken their toll, however. When Cindira left and Kaylie was there, just outside the secured doors to the warehouse, she'd taken her stepsister's sudden appearance at face value. Kaylie had relied on exploiting Cindira's coding talents since she'd returned to the city a few years ago. Of course Kaylie would track her down, and of course it would be for the same reason it always was. Another dress, another hairstyle, another custom-built room to hold her liaisons... That was what Kaylie had always wanted from her. That was what Kaylie had always expected from her. What other reason could she possibly have to just show up?

If they don't look your way, they never see you coming.

Truer words had never been uttered.

The warehouse was a massive structure. In the few days Cindira had spent in it, she'd only just tapped the surface of its contents. Maybe in hidden rooms in other parts of the building were all kinds of secrets and lost treasures that could keep her engaged for days. Kaylie, therefore, might be anywhere and after anything. But she wasn't. Cindira knew that because she knew exactly why Kaylie was here. The lights in the storage room were already on when she stepped in, and the door to Bas's secret tomb, ajar.

Cindira hesitated. Should she just go in? Maybe if she got something heavy and snuck up she could—

"Well, Cindira, are you coming in or not?"

Kaylie. The voice was unmistakable, as was the condescension.

Reflexively, Cindira lifted her empty hands into plain view before pulling herself forward. Two men wearing both surgical masks and blasters at their hips flanked her sister, as several other people wove about the small space, working to dismantle the equipment. They must not have been here for too long; there wasn't that much in this space to fiddle with. Something must have prodded her stepsister to act. What had happened, Cindira wondered, while she was off exploring Bas and Harper's pumpkin?

"Look, boys." She grinned like the cat who got the cream. "My little sister has shown up."

Cindira cursed herself inwardly for leaving the door open, but how was she to have known that her stepsister had somehow stumbled onto the truth? "I don't know what you think you're going to do, but don't hurt this man."

"This man?" The blonde looked at the jackpod. Even if unopened, the unit still held a live, if inactive, body. "Is that why you think I'm here? To kill some ugly old guy who's been a wired vegetable for twelve years?"

Cindira blinked her confusion. "I... Um, yeah."

"Oh, honey, no." Putting on an exaggerated frown, Kaylie wrapped a pointy-fingered hand over Cindira's shoulder. "I'm just here to take all the tech. The eggplant in the freezer section? Don't care."

That part didn't surprise Cindira. What did was that her stepsister seemed to know who was in the jackpod. "I don't understand. How did you... Why did you..."

"Cindira, sweetie. You've seen one too many old flickers. Do you really think I'm going to reveal my whole evil plan to you just because you walked in on me executing one of its greatest steps?"

If your opponent is temperamental, seek to irritate him. Confronting Kaylie in any physical way would be pointless, especially if she wasn't sure what the end game was. Cindira just hoped Sun Tzu wouldn't fail her now.

"Of course not." Cindira shook her head. "I expect you'll reveal your whole evil plan to me because you're simultaneously vain and insecure. Because we both know I'm smarter than you, so I should have suspected you had something to do with my dad's disappearance, but I didn't. I think you'll want to brag about how you outwitted me and deceived your own mother."

"Don't forget the part where I set everything up so you get all the blame," Kaylie said, taking the bait. She put one hand in the air, opening and closing it as though pointing out the words flashing on a marquee. "Daughter of Plaxis's founders behind attempted coup of Gaia and conspiracy resulting in murder of Rex Tieg."

The lightning that hit Cindira's brain burned a path all the way into her heart. Stance shaky, pulse pounding in her ears, a shock of pain went up her frame when her knees hit the cement floor. "Murder?"

Kaylie examined her fingernails for defects. "Oh, don't worry. I didn't kill Rex."

As frigid as she'd gone the moment before, Cindira felt herself melt at the news. She placed a hand over her heart, as though the effort might calm its erratic beat. "Oh, thank goodness."

But no sooner had she comforted herself with the thought that her father's corporal self had faired better than his vreal avatar than Kaylie spoke again.

"I just locked him up under a castle and forgot where I put the key."

This time, the weight of truth brought her hands to the ground. Open-palmed, Cindira tried to keep herself from complete collapse. Too much. This was all too much, and none of it made sense.

"All for what, Kaylie? For power? For money? Isn't the obscene amount of each you already have enough for you?" The words came out through Cindira's teeth as her terror turned to anger. "Or did you just want to crush him the way you crush me?"

"Oh, come on. You I just torment for fun. And, well, yeah, I might be a little jealous at times. But no, Rex had to die because obviously, he was going to get in the way of my plans." Kaylie rolled her eyes at the sky before she let out a series of giggles.

"All this time, did you really think I was playing a dumb blonde and letting my mom use me as a pincushion for whatever prick she needed beguiled or cajoled, just so I could aspire to be the Senior VP of Coding at Plaxis? Please, bitch, I'm going to be queen. Not just of the Kingdom, not just of Gaia, but pretty much of everywhere, vreal and real world."

"You're insane." Later, there would be time for tears, if they were due. At the moment, there was only space for fury. "Queen of the Kingdom? Easy. But Gaia isn't yours to have. It belongs to the world."

"It belongs to Plaxis," Kaylie shot back. "And as soon as I kill Francisco and profit from the chaos to seize his throne and ' uphold Omala Grover's sacred vision'"—these words she said with feigned reverence—"then I'll seize that throne too. And then, everything will be mine."

"Gaia is a democracy. Its sovereign is elected to his office. Do you really think you'll just be able to overturn the freewill of billions of people? Just because you're in the vreal doesn't give you de facto control over the human mind. Free will isn't something you can just program and control."

"Fear controls people." Kaylie crossed her arms over her chest. "It doesn't matter that your mommy moved war online. Everything it wins in the wardomes is still material and every nation on earth, everyone, now depends on the systems Plaxis provides. That means that whosoever rules the vreal rules the world."

"The hackers of the world won't let that happen."

"With the source code under my power and the ability to upstream a kill command back into their scrawny, scraggly meat? Ha!"

At last, Cindira had led Kaylie to the flaw in her plan. Her mouth brimmed into a smile, her voice flattened into a matter-of-fact tone. "But you don't have access to the source code."

"Don't I?" Presenting both her hands, Kaylie stuck up her index fingers before pivoting them in the jackpod's direction. "It's right there."

Cindira had been so sure until now. Any argument that Kaylie could have presented, she knew how to outmaneuver. Every one except this.

"Oh, so you're going to act surprised?" Kaylie asked. "See, when Rex found out what I was after, he said the same thing as you. 'I don't have access to it, Kaylie. No one does.'" She mimicked Rex Tieg's smooth-bastard way of talking. "'If I did, I'd give it to you.' Even after I threatened to destroy Plaxis from the inside out, found coders willing to help me bomb Gaia's infrastructure, he refused. But I knew he was lying."

Cindira was tempted to flow with the assumption that Kaylie's arrogance might be her undoing. But something about the way she'd said it triggered Cindira's instincts. "How did you know?"

"Because I found it." She bent over, her hands on her knees, to whisper in her stepsister's face. "I think we both know what I'm talking about, right?" Her eyes slid to the side.

She knew about the code in Bas's pumpkin. Of course, Cindira thought, that must have been what led her here. Somehow, Kaylie must have found out about Bas and Harper from her mother and realized what it meant. If she had coders good enough to bomb down to the source code in Gaia, they might be capable of erasing Johanna's memory like Talia and Chen had said.

Cindira's breaths came deep and hot, even as her mouth went dry. "Please, Kaylie, don't. Whatever you're planning to do, don't."

"I'm sorry, little sis. It's too late."

As though her techanics had merely been waiting for their queue, the monitor on the jackpod that had hosted Bas's body for over a decade went dead.

Don't panic. It was almost like another voice was saying it in her ear. The pod wasn't what was keeping him alive. His body will be weak, but there's no reason to think he's just going to suddenly pass away. No, but it would likely take a few minutes for the brain to reset and realize it was no longer under the aegis of the machine. Would it be long enough, though?

One techanic presented himself to Kaylie as though reporting to a military superior. "Ma'am, we've located the transmission line and severed it, as well as the temporary one that was put up in the room across the building. All the data in this unit is intact. Once we have it repowered and networked, you should be able to use it to jack in and have all the programming in the machine accessible."

"Data?" Cindira's confusions wasn't just for play. "What data?"

"The 2.5 petabyte transfer that arrived to this unit three months ago, of course." Condescension dripped from every word. "Don't look so surprised, Cindira. My mother tried to hide it from me, but I knew about it all along. Well, at least I knew it had been sent. And when she trusted you enough to tell you where it was received, I knew that part, too."

The scrunched-up look on Cindira's face must have signaled her confusion.

"I guess I should have mentioned that I made sure the equipment in Rex's last known address was just slightly broken, didn't I?" Kaylie continued. "Your dad always bragged that he never got enough credit for his work in building Plaxis. He hated how everyone praised your mom's code but never talked about how his hardware let it function. Turns out he wasn't lying. A few days alone, and he had all the machines running again. I knew he'd try to hide anything he really didn't want me to find, and wouldn't you know it? The first chance he got, he tried to stash the source code here."

That's what Kaylie thought the data dump had been? Cindira fought every urge in her body to reveal the truth, but it was the only advantage she still had.

"Ma'am?" The head techanic begged attention again. "We've finished collecting what we need. We'll load it on the transport now. What shall we do with the rider?"

"What, that old thing?" Kaylie pointed at the pod, and at the body that two of her henchmen were attempting to pull up to a sit, pulling out the biobotic's feeder and drain lines as they worked. "Leave it here with her."

"Leave it with me?" Cindira's confusion manifested for a moment until she realized what the intention must be. "Another body to add to my murder count?"

"We're not taking any of the biobotics." Kaylie made a motion in their general direction. "Looking at their supplies, there's probably enough there to keep one of you going for another ten years. You know, assuming one of you is in a comatose state. If you want that to be him instead of you, tag him out."

"You're going to leave me here to die." Cindira's face fell. Between what Kaylie had said and Johanna telling her that no one had been in the facility for years, she was beginning to understand Kaylie's plan. "And no one will even know I'm dead."

"If you die, I have to be all sad and conflicted about it." Kaylie said. "But if you only go missing, you become a phantom I can invoke at every inconvenient hiccup. The threat you'd represent in the eyes of the masses can keep people running to me for years for protection. I'm tired of pretending that I care about you and your mother's legacy, and your ghost will open up a path for me to taint it. So, no, I don't want you found."

"And what about him?" Cindira jerked her head to the side to indicate the body the henchmen were lowering to the ground. "What if someone else knows about him? What if someone else comes looking for him?

Kaylie sneered in the body's direction. "Doubtful. If he was anyone important, he wouldn't have been left in this carcass of a building."

Was that Kaylie's way of telling Cindra she thought as much of her own stepsister?

The three workers piled a few boxes of equipment they'd gathered and placed it inside the jackpod, itself mounted on a pop-up cart base.

"We'll be on the transport as soon as you're able to go," one said.

One of the armed goons nodded. "We should go then, Miss Fife. The prince will expect you at the palace within the hour."

"The prince?" Cindira asked as her eyes followed the techanics' exit, leaving behind only Kaylie's two armed guards.

Her sister made her way to the door before stopping in the door frame. "Oh, yes, you don't know, do you? I downloaded this so I could show you. It just made me so happy because I couldn't have planned it better myself."

At two taps on her comque, a video image projected, levitating right above Kaylie's wrist. She swiped the image left to right, pivoting its access, giving Cindira a clear view of Johanna, the Plaxis logo floating to the left of her face.

"This is Johanna Tieg, vice president of customer relations," Johanna began, her words slow and precise. "If you have received this message, you were active in the Kingdom at the time a security event occurred two weeks ago. When you established your Kingdom membership, you cosigned yourself to obey Article Seventeen, Subsection C, Part Three of the Gaian charter, which allows the Sovereign of Gaia to order a lockdown and recall of all identified users for a period not to exceed twenty-four hours. At the request of His Majesty, and to support the investigation, you are required to jack into the system by noon Hague time today, after which time all inbound jacks will be frozen until the security event concludes. Those with residences on the platform should wait there to be screened by security personnel. Tier-two users without a residence, or who were present using special event passes, will report to the palace instead. Once security has met with you and assessed your profiles, you will be forcibly jacked out immediately. The Kingdom will be closed to all other users during this time and will credit all affected accounts with a fifteen percent refund in the next billing cycle. If you do not comply, the one hundred sixteen member states countersigned to the Gaian charter have agreed to issue immediate temporary seizures of all cyber assets, including crypto, of any user who fails to report as instructed. In addition, they are subject to real-world custody holding and forced jacking."

Kaylie grinned as the video cut out and she lowered her wrist. "As you can see, I have a date with the prince, then."

Francisco? She wouldn't. She couldn't. "Kaylie, no, you—"

"Ta-ta, Cindira." Kaylie shook her hand with aplomb. "Pleasant, slow death!"

They left, and it took every fiber Cindira had not to follow. She looked down at the body, listening to the wheels of the cart and the sound of footfalls as Kaylie and her goons made their way up the hall. His chest rose in fell in a steady, slow rhythm, but without struggle. Soon the effects of the machine that kept one unconscious would wear off, and eyes that had remained closed for over a decade would open.

But what would she do then? Without the wireless grid to get into the building, even Cindira's comque was useless. Now even the hardline that had fed Bas's jackpod was dead. They were here, both trapped. Cindira shifted, crawling her way over to the body, taking the hand, skin dry but undamaged, into hers.

The door at the entryway sealed, the sound of air compressing as the locks slid in place echoing up the corridor.

Laporte scrambled alongside her, taking turns at looking between Cindira and the man on the floor. Cindira heard the mouse—could not help but to hear it, yet the voice sounded miles away. "Miss, perhaps I can find a way of getting outside and calling for help, if you think it wise?"

"Not until we have a plan, and not until he wakes up." She swallowed. "I can't believe he did this. Francisco, what were you thinking? You're playing right into Kaylie's plans."

"Sorry, miss?"

"He's abusing the limits of his power. He's doing it to find me. And now Kaylie can twist that into a reason to kill him. And with that kind of coup at hand, how can Gaia survive?"

"Miss, right now I'm more concerned about your survival."

"I'm fine. If you need to think about anything, try to think of a way I can save the prince. It doesn't have to include me getting out of here."

The body stirred, a gentle unwinding of muscles as his head fell to the side, and he looked up at her face. Blink, blink, blink. A deep breath.

He opened his mouth. The voice was weak, airy, but audible. "Cindira?"

She smiled, pulling the hand to her mouth and kissing his knuckles before pressing it against the side of her face.

"Hi, Dad."

TWENTY-TWO

HER FATHER'S WEAK VOICE struggled to clear Bas's throat. His hand on her face flexed ever so slightly, a tiny difference of pressure that made tears come to her eyes.

It was odd how it could be another man's face, and yet still be her father's smile. "You found me. You figured out it was me, my smart girl."

"Smarter you for escaping." She stroked the side of his head, lecturing herself to see the man within, not the body beneath her. "How, Dad?"

"A man married to your mother for five years would pick up a thing or two." His hand dropped, and when his fingers only lifted slightly, Cindira suspected Rex was trying to wave dismissively. "They stuck me somewhere that the equipment was... Let's say, conveniently and slightly dysfunctional. I knew it was a setup. They thought I'd fix it and use it to hide the source code, since that's what they asked in exchange for letting me go. Instead, I sent myself."

"Instead?" She didn't miss his choice of word. "Dad, do you have access to the source code?"

The shaking of his head was so slight it was almost imperceptible. "Once upon a time, but no, not anymore."

That both relieved and upset her. As happy as she was to find her father, Cindira still knew what kind of man he was. If there had been an easier way of getting free, he would have taken it. Luckily, her mother had known who she married too. Thank goodness for that. Kaylie might find a way to have herself crowned Queen of the Vreal in name. Unless she had not only access to the source code but control over it, there was no way it would go anywhere.

But to even make the attempt, she'd need to kill the prince. The thought quickened Cindira's heart. She needed to get out of here, needed to get into the vreal. Without understanding the events that had led to now, however, she might not do either.

"Dad, what happened?"

He struggled to sit up, and she rushed to aid him in the effort. Biobotics may have been keeping Bas's body alive and functioning, but that didn't mean it was by any means thriving. The loss of muscle mass, body fat, even bone density that must have occurred over the years... The mind might endure, but the mortal coil aged rapidly through disuse. If her father survived the transition, and if the neurological consequences of existing in another person's head didn't doom him, he was in for a long and painful physical recovery.

"I was in Beijing. Standard meeting, nothing special. I got on our company transport to come home and someone..." His fingers splayed over his forehead. "Hit me, I think. Or maybe injected me with something? Anyway, the next thing I knew, I woke up in a lab your mother and I used when you were little."

"Here in the city?" She looked around.

He shook his head. "It was beneath the palace of Omala's biggest benefactor, over in Europe."

"And Kaylie was there?"

"Not in the flesh, no," Rex said. "But there was someone else there, a man with a foreign accent of some sort."

International relations and awareness had never been her father's strong suit.

"He showed me to a jackpod and forced me to jack into a limited platform inside a generic avatar," Rex continued. "Kaylie was in that vreal, waiting for me. I made sure it really was her, not some NPC fueled by AI knowledge. I asked things only Kaylie would know. She told me I had a week to give her access to the Plaxis source code or else."

"Or else what?"

He tried to shrug, but it looked more like a tremor. "I don't think she thought that far ahead. Or maybe I don't remember. I think...

I know some of my memories have gone missing. I'm not sure if that happened there, or when I transferred myself. Honestly, I'm amazed I managed to do it at all. Your mother only hinted at how it worked, and even she said it was more theoretical than applicable."

Cindira bit her tongue. There would be time to tell her dad about Harper and Bas later. Only, that brought up a question.

"How did you know Bas's body was here for you to transfer into?"

Her father's face screwed up. "Who?"

"Bas. Sebastian Archer," she clarified. "This is his body you're in."

"I thought it felt off." Her father examined his new-to-him body as best he could. "I have no idea who Sebastian Archer is, or how I ended up here. I was aiming for one of the bodies at St. Dymphna's."

Cindira tried to think beyond the implications. Not understanding how whole mind-copying worked, she didn't know how to tell if something had gone wrong or how to deduce if it had. What her father had done, downloading back into the vreal, into someone else's body no less, was far beyond anything she could comprehend. She took a deep breath through her nose, resolving to stay focused. For the moment, at least. For now, her father was found. He was safe, and no one else knew it. It was an advantage, one she wasn't sure how long would be hers.

"You're not at St. Dymphna's."

"No, we're not." Rex looked around, but the eyes, so long closed, must have lacked focus. "Where are we then?"

"In a warehouse down in the industrial part of the city. Johanna said it was Gaia Lab's first location," Cindira said. She laid a hand on her father's bony shoulder. "And we're trapped in here. Kaylie sealed us in."

His eyes went wild, taking her in as best he could. "Oh, no. Did she hurt you? Are you okay?"

"Don't worry about it, Dad. I'm fine." I'm always fine. Without you, I learned to survive. "She thought the download here was the source code, and she thought it was stored in the machine. And now, she's on her way to the vreal to kill Francisco. Prince Francisco," she amended, her cheeks blushing at the casual mention of his name.

If she hoped to hide any truth from her father, it didn't work. Rex's face blossomed into a knowing grin. "Just Francisco, is it?"

"Dad, focus. Yes, I've met him." She left unsaid: when I kidnapped him and held him at knifepoint, but I swear, it was only to save him. "But there's nothing going on between us."

"That's a shame. I always liked Paco."

Cindira blinked. "Who?"

"Paco," Rex repeated. "You did say prince, as in Prince Francisco Batista de le Reina, didn't you? Your mother and I knew him when he was young. But what has he done? Why would Kaylie be trying to kill him?"

"The same reason anyone assassinates royalty, I'd imagine. To gain power and overthrow their government. But it's more than that, Dad. She wants to integrate the ability of the Kingdom to inflict harm to the body outside the vreal into Gaia. She wants to use it to force the member nations to recognize her as their leader."

"Of all the conceited, selfish bitches..." Rex's face went white, and for a body already pale because of years with only artificial sunlight provided by a biobotics, that was saying something. "Other than you, Gaia is the only good thing I'm leaving this world. If Kaylie destabilizes the peace, war will come back to the real, and none of us are going to survive if it does. You can't let that happen, Cindira. I know you haven't been in the vreal since your mother died, but you have to jack in. Stop her."

"Actually, I've hacked in a few times recently. And I am going to stop her. Except..." She lifted her head and looked around. "Like I said, Kaylie sealed us in this building. Not only that, but she took the only jackpod I've found in it and cut the data connection to the outside world. I don't know how to get into the vreal from here to do anything."

"Do you have the shoes with you?"

She started, sitting up straighter than a post. "What?"

"Your mother's silicone slippers," her father said, his eyes narrowed. "I left them in the care of one of my most trusted assistants with instructions that, if ever I disappeared, she was to send them to you. She didn't know what they were, of course. I don't even completely understand them. I know your mother could use them to be in the vreal and real, but I have to admit I don't know how. I can only hope you figured it out."

"I..." Her face tensed up. "Wait, you mean all these years you knew about the shoes?"

"Not the entire time, no," he said. "After she died, the shoes were sent to me by the executor of her estate, along with a letter that said I was only to give them to you when you were ready."

"Ready?" It didn't make sense to be mad at a woman who'd been dead for fifteen years. Even so, heat drew to her face. "Just what does that mean?"

"I think Omala understood you better than I did. No, I know she did. You were always so dreamy as a child, always living in your imagination. Don't get me wrong, Cind, we loved that about you. You were more focused on your dreams of what might be possible than what was. But I think she also knew that meant you were... disconnected. You didn't mind when people took advantage of you or treated you mean. You'd just close your eyes and imagine yourself some place safe, let yourself be overlooked. Over the years, you got used to letting others determine your fate and your choices. I'm sorry to say, but I think I've been one of those people."

Tears threatened. Not because her father was wrong. Not even because he was right. No, it was because for the first time her father admitted to any mistakes in raising her.

"Anyway," he continued. "I was supposed to give you the shoes when I saw you change and stand up for yourself."

Cindira shifted, bringing her feet from underneath her. She

pulled down the top of her sock, revealing the silicone lining underneath. Her father must have realized the implication, even if his borrowed eyes were weary.

His head fell back against the floor. "Thank god."

Cindira let go the sock and leaned back on her heels once more. "Don't thank him yet. In the Kingdom, I only have one. Francisco has the other."

"You gave the Prince of Gaia one of the silicone slippers?"

She shook her head. "I didn't mean to do it. It was an accident."

"What were you doing with him that you were taking off pieces of clothing?" Even in a weak state, she could read the suspicion etched in her father's features. Luckily, before she was forced to answer in what surely would have been too eager a denial, Rex pressed on. "Of all the people to end up with one of the silicone slippers, it would be him, wouldn't it?"

Now it was her face that was marred by suspicion. "Why, Dad? What's so special about Francisco?"

"Nothing that matters now." His hand shook as he reached for hers. "Cindira, stop Kaylie. If she kills the prince, everything your mother and I did will be for nothing."

"I know, Dad, but like I said, we're sealed in this building." She lifted her head, looking around as if to remind him. "The wireless grid is scrambled by devices built into the structure. There's no hardwire line out; Kaylie's goons cut it. She also changed the passkey for the main door. We're trapped."

Laporte decided to make itself known. The mouse jumped up on Rex's stomach, using the old man's borrowed body as a stage from which to address his mistress. "I think I might have a solution."

"Laporte!?" Rex positively gleamed. "My heavens, you're still alive. How wonderful."

The little botic's nose twitched as it rotated. "As you know, sir, I am not, nor have I ever been, alive. Nevertheless, I am glad to see that you are."

Rex glanced down at his hijacked body. "I hope it sticks."

Cindira was curious what her father knew of the mouse (it was likely she'd told him about Laporte herself when she was a child, if Laporte was to be believed), but now was not the time. "Laporte, what are you talking about? You know another way out of the building?"

It spun again. "Not for you, miss. Not per se. But although the ingresses and egresses to the building are all hermetically sealed, both for the sake of security and to preserve the inside environment, there are several paths that connect to the outside world which might be navigable for someone or something much smaller. Something closer to my size, say."

"Path to the outside world?" Cindira's face scrunched up as she searched her memory for a window or even an air vent without mesh gridding from the street. "I don't remember any."

"He's talking about the plumbing," Rex said. "Brilliant, Laporte! You always were such a clever little bot."

"I'm not a bot, sir. I'm an advanced robotic AI entity capable of superhuman thought and with unlimited access to the vast resources of all data and vreal systems simultaneously. That I could postulate a viable alternative to reaching the outside world is, dare I say, beneath me?"

Was the mouse making a pun?

"But what good does that do us?" Cindira asked. "How would we get out?"

"I'm fairly certain I could crack the new code, miss. It is a closed loop digital system, but I did see an interface on it when first we entered."

She hadn't, but the mouse's eyes (or at least, the hardware that served as its eyes) were far more powerful than anything biologically created, and hardware interface ports tended to be tiny and tucked out of the way.

Still, Cindira frowned. "I'm not sure you could type it into the keypad with your tiny feet after you figured it out, not to mention there's no way you'd be able to spin that huge captain's wheel."

"You're right, miss. I would need some help. Luckily, I also think

I could find some. If I were to use your comque and call Miss MacAvoy—"

"No." Cindira slashed a hand through the air. "I'm not getting Scotia involved with this. The work she does is too important, and I won't endanger her career that way."

"In all fairness, miss, you already have."

The accusation cut into her gut, twisting her insides. For one moment, Cindira lifted her pointing hand and readied her counterargument. She most certainly had not done that to her best friend. Only then did she realize what Laporte meant.

Rex, however, did not. "What is he talking about? Scotia who? Oh, wait, is that the pretty little redhead you're always going around with?"

Cindira grimaced. Yes, Rex was her father, and she was thrilled she'd found him alive and well (or at least, well enough). At the same time, Rex was Rex.

"That's the one." She kept her tone as flat as possible, but she had a feeling the eyeroll was still implied. "And Laporte's right. I got her involved. I used her invitation credential to get into the palace during the ball."

Rex narrowed his gaze. "Why would you do that? You have complete access to all things in the Kingdom. You always have. It's your right as my daughter. More than that, it's your legacy as your mother's daughter."

"Well, your wife might disagree with that, because I don't. But, no, Dad. That wasn't why I did it. I was trying to find you, and Johanna refused to tell me anything about where you were. I decided to sneak in and look around, but I didn't want any record of it. That's why I used Scotia's invitation." Which begged the question: "Did she know? Dad, do you have reason to think Johanna was part of Kaylie's conspiracy?"

"My sweet Jo? No, she'd never do anything to harm me. Although there are very few people who knew about the Andalusia lab under its palace, so maybe."

"Andalusia?"

Wasn't that the real kingdom Francisco was from? But, no, his family had been ousted from power years ago, right as the tiny former Spanish state was becoming the European leader of vreal technology. Plaxis's principal rival, insofar as it had one, was based there. In fact, didn't a close relative of the current monarch own it? Hugo....? Ferrente! She'd met with him once after graduating college when he tried to lure her to Tagentry instead of working for her own father's company. She almost took his offer.

Suddenly, it all clicked. Kaylie was ambitious, and that had driven her to achieve far more in life than Cindira might have otherwise supposed. But her stepsister wasn't the kind of coder or leader who could pull off something like a virtual coup on her own. She'd need help. She'd need technological backing, not to mention a good deal of crypto not chainblocked to her directly. Hugo Ferrente was the King of Andalusia's nephew. Surely that would allow him access to a lab beneath the old palace, and he would have jumped at a chance to level the vreal playing field by working with Kaylie.

Rex's eyes closed as he shook his head, only to slowly, slowly open them a moment later. The ordeal he'd gone through to get here must be catching up with him. Although her father's spirit was strong, he was now trapped in a body unused for years. He needed rest. Even Kaylie had recognized that the biobotics would keep him going for some time, meaning Rex would be safe here for now. She, however, needed to get to the Kingdom.

Cindira turned eyes on the mouse. "It's a good thing you don't have to breathe."

Laporte bobbed its head. "Even better, I have no sense of smell."

TWENTY-THREE

HUGO BURIED BULKY FISTS into his hips. "Well, let's get on with it. And I hope this security-screening farce you've concocted finally convinces you I don't have it out for you."

For a moment, Francisco hesitated. The pouch in his hands felt heavier as its implications grew. Did he want Hugo to pass the screening or fail it? If, like everyone else so far today, his former friend and lifelong rival reached into the bag and grasped empty air, it merely meant that he had not been the bandit. If, however, he could handle the shoe, pull it into his grasp, Hugo at the same time would twist Francisco's belief in not only who his former friend truly was, but who was Francisco himself.

Neither, however, would mean that the person who had actually wanted to kill him at the ball wasn't Hugo, a thought that had never occurred to him until now. He'd been so focused on finding his savior, Francisco had forgotten all about what he'd been saved from.

Francisco lifted the pouch, gazing at it, and opened his mouth to let the first thought at the top of his concerns bubble out. "Was your offer to Gaia sincere?"

The query surprised both the questioned and the questioner. Hugo gaped, his hands dropping to his side, all the tension in his face melting. "Of course it was."

"And what would you... What would Tagentry gain from it? I know it can't just be money; you have plenty of it, thanks to your uncle seizing the throne from my father."

"Come now, Francisco. You may have been a few years behind me in school, but you used to be smarter than me. You've had to figure out by now what was really going on back then."

"It's never eluded me. Your uncle killed my father in front of my eyes, led a band of mercenaries and an angry mob into our palace, and made me at once an orphan and a commoner." Francisco cocked his head to the side. "Yes, I'm smarter than you, but even you understand what a coup d'état is."

Hugo turned his head into his shoulder, trying to hide a laugh.

"What's so funny about that?"

The smile on the other man's face flattened. "Yes, I know what it is, but do you really remember? You seem oblivious to the one going on right in front of you."

Triumph broadened the prince's expression. "So, you admit you're trying to overthrow Gaia?"

"Me, overthrow the best hope humanity has for survival?" Hugo shook his head. "This time, hermanito, I am trying to save your throne."

And just like that, the crimson tide rose anew. This time, however, Francisco funneled it not into words, but into action, punching out with the pouch, hitting Hugo with it just below the ribs.

Ferrente stumbled, clutching the bag, wincing in surprise. "You must have forgotten that pain blockers are disabled in this vreal."

"I didn't, but thanks for bringing a smile to my face by reminding me." Francisco jerked his head towards the pouch. "Open it and pull out anything you find inside."

"What is it? Something meant to kill me. Fenatheral? I'm sure you and all your royal resources could develop a VR version of it. Or would you go with something much simpler? A scorpion, perhaps?" Hugo cinched open the pouch, peering into it from above with one eye closed. "I don't see anything in there."

The words, the command, came from the seat of Francisco's soul, the anchor of his years without family, without means, without power. "As your prince, I command you!"

The act rendered the two men strangers. Hugo blinked. Then, without words, a sadness came into his gaze. His shoulders drooped. With the satin pouch in his left hand, Hugo reached in with his right. For several moments, he explored the space, and when Francisco saw the muscles of his forearm flex as though something heavy demanded their use, the prince's heart cried out in despair. He could not owe this man his life. It would turn his world upside down. There could be no amends for what he lost.

Hugo's eyebrow arched. He turned his arm over and pulled it out with deliberate care. The heel of his hand crested the bag, and Francisco raced to think of what words to say next.

But then, there was nothing.

No shoe.

No revelation.

No need to harvest old memories and eat at their withered grain.

Francisco exhaled his relief. And his disappointment. Could part of him have wished that Hugo saved him? Why? Instead of stumble for conversations, or perhaps undertake a new barrage for verbal jests, the prince seized back the pouch, eyes downcast, turning to go.

"Is that all between us, my old friend?"

The word sent a chill down Francisco's spine. He stopped where he stood, several steps up the path leading to the road, and turned his head halfway over his shoulder. "What more could there be?"

"Forgiveness," Hugo suggested. When that brought nothing, he continued. "Okay, how about self-sacrifice?"

The prince snorted. "Ironic, seeing as your family sacrificed mine."

Even in his occluded view, Francisco saw Hugo take a step forward. "You think I don't grieve for your loss?"

"When it brought your family everything it has now and set you up for fame, fortune, love...? No, I don't."

"What was I supposed to do, renounce circumstances not of my own making? I doubt you would have done that, if the coup had never happened. I just played the cards I was given just like you did."

"The cards you were given?" Francisco saw red, spun, marched up the path. "Why don't you understand? My father molded me to be our people's servant, to work towards their benefit and welfare. I existed to live up to his vision, both of me and for them. Then your uncle took it from me. See, you didn't just deny me my crown. You denied me my destiny." The prince turned back toward the road. "Now I have a new kingdom to serve and protect, and I'm not going to let you or Tagentry anywhere near it."

Three more steps brought Hugo to Francisco's back, and he placed a hand on the prince's shoulder. "And I pray it understands how lucky they are to have you as its ruler, and I know our people suffer because you are not."

The hook landed in his heart, the lump hardened in his throat. Francisco almost let himself be pulled and choked at the same time. Luckily, his tongue remained under his control. "Your uncle has no children. That makes you next in line for the throne."

"That's not my fate, Francisco." Hugo took back his hand. "Haven't you ever wondered why, with all the wealth and power my family stole from yours, I used it to create a vreal design and hosting firm?"

"It was the '30s, everyone was creating vreals."

Kingdom knock-offs and Gaia wannabees, most of which came and went under Plaxis's sharp eye.

"They were, but I didn't create a vreal. I created a low-cost and robust opensource platform. Yeah, it's not Purusha, but it's something everyone with minimum skill can do and afford. Because that was our vision once, or don't you remember?" Hugo laughed under his breath. "Dios mío, Paco. Some of the times you hacked into the heart of the Kingdom and tried to corrupt it? I knew way back then you were either going to rule Gaia or be sentenced to back-to-back life terms."

"And I never did thank you for bailing me out when the Plaxis lawyers tried way back when. And for convincing the judge in the case to seal my juvenile records."

Was this it: his great accommodation? Francisco found

sympathy for his enemy, but could that erase everything else? He managed three steps when Hugo said the only thing that could stop him.

"I never needed thanks. I just wanted my best friend back, and I wanted a chance to tell him that I regret every moment before now where I haven't owned up to what he lost, or how I benefited from it."

His fingers tightened into fists so hard, Francisco's palms would have been bleeding if this was the real. Even now, the pain bit deep. Regret. If Hugo had merely said sorry or even offered his sympathies, the prince would have acknowledged the gesture but moved on. But Hugo had said regret.

"You take responsibility for the crimes against my family?"

Any hope was quickly dashed away when Hugo shook his head, but he rushed to add, "I can't and I won't apologize for what my uncle did. His actions were not mine. But I regret that the benefits they brought me were at the cost of your.... Well, your everything."

Jaw clenching, Francisco nodded. And then... he stood. And stood.

And stood.

A momentum had built between them, but there was only so far he'd let himself be carried. He could never again embrace Hugo as his brother or friend. Could Francisco forgive him enough to work with him in partnership and build a better future for all of humanity?

Gaia can save the world. He remembered Omala's words. But only if it remains true to its own intentions. Yes, we will bring our conflict there, and settle them with as little damage to the planet and each other as possible, but it can only serve in this way if the losses and destruction done by conflicts before it is abandoned. Nothing can heal that which is forever scarred.

"You said that I'm blind to the coup going on right before me." Francisco turned. "What did you mean?"

At first, Hugo looked confused. Brow furrowed, he rubbed his chin. "You know the first part. The night of the ball, someone intended to kill you."

"And do you know who?"

Hugo shook his head. "But I can tell you, they came to me first, wanting me to help. That's why I was there. I was watching over you."

"You knew there was a plot against me?" The ember not yet cooled flared. "And you didn't bring this to anyone's attention?"

"If I exposed the plot, the plotter would have slipped through my fingers." Instead of sheepishness, this time Hugo brought as much heat into his voice as Francisco had. "I have no idea who they were. They showed up in one of Tagentry's vreal disguised as a little old woman selling apples in the public square, but we could never trace their origin or true identity. It was from outside our system. And who would believe I would do anything to aid Gaia or you? Everyone knows the bad blood between us. Not to mention my company is Plaxis's only viable rival. Besides the truth that I had no reason to want you dead, there's also the fact that if something damaged you or Plaxis is such a bold way, I'd be suspect number one."

"But keeping it secret makes you look complicit."

"Keeping it secret has been what's let me keep you from getting killed!"

The brute force of Hugo's words hit him as well as a punch. Francisco reached back, trying to find mooring on a fence he could have sworn was there. Hard ground told him it wasn't.

"Your Highness!" Carlos rushed in from the street and set to work trying to right the prince.

Francisco waved a finger and hefty breaths, wide eyes searching the old man's face. "He...He says he knows... someone was trying to kill me."

Instead of a reflection, Carlos's whipped his head in Hugo's direction. "You told him?"

No sooner had Francisco risen than he fell back again. Just a few moments ago, he'd had a man he despised at his front and one he wholly trusted at his back. Had they reversed themselves? Had they switched avatars?

"You knew." Francisco's voice cracked, and he wasn't certain if he was saying it as a fact or an accusation.

A straight-faced Carlos jerked his head once. "Hugo came to me last week and told me the truth. Why do you think I invited him into the advisory committee, even knowing what he did to your family?"

"But why didn't you... Why did you not just tell me?"

Carlos played the role of father, kneeling beside the prince and running a hand over his royal brow. "Would you have believed me, niño?"

No, probably not. And more, the sense of betrayal would have blinded Francisco to any argument. But now... Now his eyes and his ears were opening.

"Did your suggestion that we part ways with Plaxis come before or after this talk?"

Rather than answer, Carlos swung his gaze up to Hugo. Some truth had come to the fore, but there was more of its body hiding in the shadows.

Hugo huffed and bent down, forcing the prince to his feet. "Tell me, Your Highness, what does Johanna Tieg say about where Rex has been all these months? What is her explanation for his long absence, both here and in the real?"

Confusion pushed lines into his forehead. "She hasn't said anything. I've heard rumors. The last confirmed sighting of him my people can validate was months ago in Beijing."

"That seems a little suspicious, doesn't it? And I won't even mention the fact that she was also the last person to see Omala Grover alive." Hugo crossed his arms. "Whoever hacked into my vreal and got away without so much as a trace must have had tremendous resources to do it. Resources that Johanna has complete, unfettered access to. You know she's always been cold on the viability of Gaia."

"She outright told me she detests it." Was this the truth,

Francisco wondered? Had he been playing tit-for-tat with his potential murderer the whole time and not realized it?

His memory went back to the night of the ball, and the way that Johanna had look so flustered and frustrated when the bandit had put the knife to Francisco's throat. At the moment, the prince took Johanna's reaction at face value; a world leader was under threat in her platform, and Johanna could do nothing about it. What if the bandit had known all along, and that's why she did what she did? She'd gotten him away from danger. She'd gotten him away from Johanna Tieg.

Francisco turned his gaze, catching the towers of the palace rising high above the enchanted valley. One stop left to go, and she's there. I could face her, but she might see this as an opportunity to do what she couldn't do at the ball.

Something she'd hate to do in front of the owner of her biggest competitor.

"Hugo—"

Francisco cleared his throat, unable to believe what he was about to say.

"Yes, Your Highness?"

He wasn't sure if Hugo's use of his title was meant in sincerity or jest, but the offer was earnest enough.

Francisco extended his hand toward the road. "Accompany me to the palace. I'm going to need a witness."

TWENTY-FOUR

THE HOUR BETWEEN LAPORTE disappearing down a toilet with Cindira's comque in its teeth and the front door of the warehouse opening was one of the longest of her life. It had, however, given her time to prepare what she hoped would be a brief but sufficient explanation for Scotia as to what was going on. But when the door locks decompressed and a whirring sound brought news that someone was opening the hatch, it wasn't her redheaded friend on the other side.

"Warren? Mr. Chen?" Cindira blinked at her own surprise. "How did you—?"

"Blame Grandpa's ghost friends," Warren said. "They sent him a message saying you might be in trouble, but don't ask me how they knew. They asked us to come over here and help." Warren pointed down just in time for Laporte to scurry between the teenager's foot, its faux fur slightly worse off for the wear. "By the way, your botic both smells and looks like a piece of shit. I almost kicked it into a wall when it snuck up on us outside."

They came inside without being asked. Chen shuffling with his trusty walking stick beside him. Warren looping him while Laporte scrambled to keep up.

"I'm sorry. I'm sure it meant well." She pushed the hatch door, leaving it just open enough for the latches not to catch and the locks not to engage. "Laporte, you were supposed to call Scotia."

"Miss MacAvoy was unavailable in the real."

"What, she's in the vreal right now?" The thought filled her with dread. "Please tell me she's not in a Plaxis platform."

"I regret that I cannot. Recall, miss, that it was her invite you used when attending the ball. Thus, as have all users jacked into the Kingdom at that time, she's been obliged to heed the edict. She's in the palace, awaiting screening by the prince."

Cindira's face screwed up. "You mean Francisco himself is conducting the screenings? That's going to make things even easier for Kaylie."

"Luckily, Miss MacAvoy is just one of many at the palace queuing. While comque communication in or out has been disabled, I was able to relay a message to her personally when others weren't paying attention. I asked her to make her meeting with the prince take as long as possible without arousing suspicion."

Thank goodness for that. A tiny fraction of the tension in her body eased.

"In any event," Laporte continued, "I arrived back here, intending to sneak my way in through the sewer lines and allow us to work out something else, when I saw Mr. Chen and Mr. Wu at the door, trying to figure out a way in."

"Jesus, your rat talks a lot." Mr. Chen swatted his hands in the air. "I'm only here for Bas's body. It went offline. I want to make sure the jackpod is still in good order first, and then we'll working on getting that line fixed. Warren can do that, and then we can reconfigure it to allow you to jack in from here."

Cindira froze. "Um, Mr. Chen?"

He stopped, pivoting slowly. "What?"

"Bas's body is here." Pinching her finger and thumbs together, she fidgeted. "But my stepsister Kaylie took the jackpod."

One of his eyebrows became more sloped than the San Francisco streets outside. "Why? She must have a hell of a lot better jackpods at Plaxis."

"Oh, she does. Way better ones." Then, realizing that sounded like an insult, Cindira hastened to add, "but she took it because she thought a 2.5 petabyte download that came through it a few months ago was my dad hiding the source code in it. But it wasn't. It was actually my dad hiding... well, himself, in Bas's body."

Now one half of Chen's mouth mirrored his eyebrow. "Your dad, Rex Tieg, downloaded himself to Bas?"

"I know, I was surprised too."

Chen turned and hobbled up the hall again. "Not as surprised as

Bas is going to be."

The biobotics hadn't waited for anyone to give them permission. When they turned into the small secret room, it was to find the machines reasserting their care protocols. Rex lay flat and straight, with some kind of improvised bolster under his head and knees to give his hijacked body support. A quick query reported Rex as diminished due to extending jacking, but otherwise healthy and stable, which meant that it was time she went. Who knew how long she could count on Scotia's diversions to keep Kaylie from Francisco?

"You could go to the Stadium," Warren suggested as they discussed her course of action. "You already hacked into Plaxis systems from there once without getting detected. You should be able to do it again."

"No. I've already endangered Talia Greene enough, and the illegality of what I'm about to do is ten times worse." Cindira shook her head. "Besides, I need to be as close to Kaylie's physical body as I can be."

"Why?" Mr. Chen kept his eyes fixed on Bas's body.

"Same reason I wanted to be by yours at the Stadium. It will help me be able to do... certain things with code, things for which even the smallest lag time could be the biggest difference."

Cindira left unsaid that it was also a backup plan. If she managed to get to Kaylie in the vreal and pull her avatar apart as she intended, all her stepsister would have to do to escape would be to quit the platform. If she were close then too, Cindira might head her off in the real. True, that would leave her own body exposed, but it was a risk she was going to have to take.

"I only wish there was a way for me to know where she is. My best guess is back in my family's compound. There are guards around the main house, and it's on its own network, one that only we can access using a DNA key."

Warren sorted through a box of miscellaneous tech scraps he'd found in the main lab they'd passed through to get into the secret chamber. His eyes had gone wide the moment they walked in, and the oath he uttered made it perfectly clear the items stocked in the warehouse were choice finds. "She's at Plaxis."

She swung on him at a dizzying speed. "What? How do you know that?"

The teen turned out his comque to face her. "It has our tracking monitor on it, remember? Your creepy little mouse friend here asked if we could ping it. Took a hot minute; it didn't have any power, right? But as soon as it was hooked up again, it told me its new location. Luckily, right before my comque's signal went dead around this building." He tapped at the device on his wrist, as though doublechecking the last data download before continuing. "She's at Plaxis HQ, nineteenth floor, room fifty."

Laporte and Cindira exchanged a knowing glance. "The Kitchens?"

Warren stopped long enough to give her a double take. "You know it just like that?"

"Yeah, it's where I work. Where I worked." The correction held a drop of bitterness. If not for the fact that Johanna had fired her, she could have gotten in as easy as pie. "That complicates things."

"How?" Warren asked.

"I was fired. For show, or at least that's what Johanna—oh, that's my stepmother—that's what she told me. But maybe she's been working with Kaylie this whole time, and she was just trying to get me out of the way. In any case, I don't have access to the building anymore, and the Kitchens was one of the most secure rooms inside the tower. The people who work there make the Kingdom what it is, the crème de la crème of the coding world."

"You're shitting me. Someone who can hack into the most secure vreal platforms ever, and you can't break into a building?"

Cindira gave a noncommittal shrug. "In the vreal, I can turn switches on and off with my mind. Out here in the real world, though, a secured door is always a secured door, and no amount of Purusha Plus is going to let me push it out of the way."

"Yeah, but it's hardware. And in case you've forgotten, you have the crème de la crème of techanics sitting right here with you."

Cindira cast her eyes on Mr. Chen, who looked to be smoothing down Bas/Rex's hair with a great deal of tenderness. "Your grandpa?"

"My grandpa? Seriously, woman?" Warren shot to his feet. "If you and your rat—"

"Mouse."

"—can handle overriding the security software, I can get you through any door. As long as it isn't one of those ancient ones that uses manual locks, that is."

"A manual lock door at Plaxis? I don't think there's a single one of those anywhere in the entire building. But the problem isn't getting into the building, it's getting past all the people in it."

Closing her eyes, Cindira visualized the layout of the company her father had built, and all the security measures they'd have to cross. She knew where the cargo elevators were, and how to get in through the loading docks. She'd always appreciated slipping in unnoticed. There were camera nodes, of course, as well as several places where employees or contractors were supposed to scan their comques for ID verification. Taking the cameras down for a few minutes wouldn't be a problem. What was was the comque check. That was hardware that would have to be changed, and that was where her skills fell flat.

"Warren," Cindira said, "how long would it take you to alter a comque and make it read as someone else, assuming I can patch alternate profiles to the unit?"

He shook his head. "I see what you're thinking, but that's not going to work. I can jailbreak a comque in a few minutes but setting it up as someone else requires a DNA sample to be grafted on a chip inside of it, and then it scans the DNA of the person wearing it, and then that's bounced against the national registry for verification. If ID theft with a comque was easy, it'd happen all the time. That's why they're such damned good devices. You can only be you."

She thought about using Scotia's, which would certainly get her into the building, but Plaxis would know she was in the vreal.

If she suddenly scanned in downstairs at the loading dock, the security bots' algorithms would know something was up. But who else could she patch whose profile had a high enough clearance to get them all the way to the Kitchens?

For not the first time that day, Cindira looked at Laporte and thought about how much easier all this would be if she were as small and as tiny as it was. People might be upset at the sight of a mouse in their midst, but they'd never for a second assume the threat that tiny little botic held or how much power it had in the vreal. They only looked at it as a rodent, something to be processed and done away with. Hadn't it even said something to her to that effect once? If they don't look your way, they never see you coming?

She was the CEO's daughter, the progeny of a woman held in esteem by many. She'd tried to keep her head down, to escape their gazes. Sneaking into Plaxis was a no-go. She could fool cameras, but she couldn't walk through the doors and past employees as anyone else but herself.

But... maybe she didn't have to?

Cindira jumped to her feet. "Warren, how would you like to be a techanic contractor at Plaxis?"

He coughed a laugh. "Sure, just tell me who I have to bribe."

Mr. Chen looked up at last. "They don't contract outside the company. Everyone knows that. You'd have to swear on your firstborn to get a job there."

"Not with highly specialized equipment," Cindira countered. "I remember last year there was a problem with our Kitchen Sink." Both of their faces screwed up. "It's a small walk-in unit that lets us periscope into the vreal and interact with it while still in the real, but that's not important. What is important is that, because there's so few of them, there are only a handful of techanics in the world able to service them. We have to fly someone in from Seoul twice a year just for the maintenance. If we can't change a comque and I can't trick a building of people to look the other way while we pass, maybe you can."

For the first time in their brief acquaintance, the boy dared to look overwhelmed. "Not sure how you think that's going to work."

"I can hack into the personnel records and hire you as a contractor," she said, passing through into the main lab, leaving Mr. Chen behind. She had a feeling he'd stay in vigil with his friend's body, even if it wasn't his friend's mind in it. "Do you have any late model jackpod at your shop? Especially one that doesn't have a clear faceplate that lets you see I someone is in it?"

"Of course, I do." He followed as best he could, both his train of thought and his feet. "It's the older units that break down, right? I have tons of third and fourth generations, and the 4Gs really embraced the concept of a closed coffin set up."

"Perfect!" She reached down and pressed the power button on her own comque. Better safe than sorry on that count. "Laporte, come on! I'm going to need your help on this, too."

TWENTY-FIVE

THE REDHEADED WOMAN Carlos showed into the library was vaguely familiar. That meant little; most of the users of the Kingdom held lofty or luminary posts that had forced his acquaintance on more than one occasion. If she was truly important, Francisco would have known her on sight. Still, there was... a memory there, somewhere. Could she be the one? Hope remained, but with no success in finding someone whose touch the shoe recognized, it was quickly fading.

Carlos closed the library door and motioned to a tufted wingback chair placed in the center of the room. "Please have a seat, miss. State your name, your Kingdom membership information, and why you were at the ball."

The woman, dressed in a simple gray gown with limited embellishments, didn't look like the typical Kingdom goer. She was underplayed, and her face hadn't lit up the way the other young women's preceding "Red" had. Implications and even invitations had been laid at his feet when Francisco asked some women to lift their skirts and reveal their feet. Leave it to the social debutantes and virtual plaything class to think this entire operation was concocted as some way for Francisco to get a peep, and maybe a little more.

The woman before him now didn't smile. She scowled.

"Scotia McAvoy. I don't have a Kingdom membership. I was invited to the ball by a member of the ruling family."

Her voice held the faintest suggestion of Northern Britannia where the surviving Scots scratched out a rough living. Francisco drew his eyes away from the rolling flames dancing in the fireplace to examine Scotia with more care. There was a tightness in her jaw, a defiant glare, and if he wasn't wrong, a slight tremor in her posture.

"I assume by ruling family you mean the Tiegs and Fifes." He swiveled his hand. "And just why did one of them want you there?"

"Officially? Because I'm the spoonful of sugar that helps the medicine go down." Scotia sat back in the chair, her arms resting at her sides. "Or the bleach that helps clean the gutter if you prefer. I'm sure you can sympathize with that, Your Majesty. For all the good Gaia does, how much bad comes from the Kingdom? What, with all the insider trading, illegal human trafficking, and price fixing that goes on in these"—she pulled her shoulders in and hugged herself—"hallowed halls."

Carlos took a step towards the young woman's chair. "Just facts please, miss. Answer the prince's question, this time without embellishment."

"Fine." Her voice became suddenly sharp as she sat up on the end of the chair. "I head several outreach and care programs in the Vreal Addiction Community Services office at Plaxis."

For most of the time, Hugo had tried to hide in the background, serving the post of silent witness he'd been drafted to take. Now, however, something alerted him. "You're the chipshrink that's running that charity thing next month."

It turned out to be of significant benefit to have the head of another vreal corporation present. These people weren't Francisco's people. He didn't love the vreal for vreal's sake as they did, didn't treat it as a playground where he could get cheap thrills at a low risk and an even better price. For Francisco, the vreal was a garden, one planted a generation ago and which he could now tend and gather fruit. Kingdom clients could see him for what he was. Hugo, however, inspired their trust. The prince had a feeling that tongues had been looser through this process because of it.

Francisco turned to his once friend. "Is that important?"

"It does raise a question." Hugo held up two fingers in Scotia's direction. "Why would someone like her be invited to a royal ball?"

The prince wasn't sure why Hugo might question it, unless by "someone like her" he meant someone so clearly not a member of the elite. "It's obvious: because it's where the money and influence were. The ball was a perfect place for someone looking to raise funds for charity."

"Said like a man who's spent very little time in the Kingdom. A royal ball at the palace is the last place Plaxis would want to remind their VIPs of the seedy side of their favorite pastime." Hugo pushed himself away from the wall and leaned down, putting himself just an arm's length from Scotia's face. "Tell me, Miss, are you often asked to attend Kingdom functions to drum up support or at least, provide some illusion of charity?"

"Hugo, don't badger the poor—"

Hugo put up a hand, stopping Francisco's plea in its tracks. "Well?" he said after a moment of silence.

Suddenly, the redhead's eyes were on a swivel, left to Francisco, right to Hugo, and back again. Her answer was as sharp as her tone. "No."

Francisco folded into a chair across from the girl, the sack still in his grasp. "And yet... you did."

There was something heavy in the air between the four of them, but Francisco couldn't figure out just what it was. Cleary, this woman had what used to be called "beef" with one of them. He hadn't dated much since his school days, and even then, only a handful of women, but was that why she was familiar? Was this some ex of his resigned to the pages of forgotten memory?

Francisco pulled the velvet pouch up and rested it on the chair beside him. "Miss MacAvoy, was it?"

"It was."

He swiped a fingertip across the tip of his nose. "You're clearly very upset. Can I ask why? Is it just the inconvenience of this interview, or something more?"

Scotia unfolded herself. "I know what you're up to." She gave Francisco an accusatory glare. "Call it a hunch."

"And just what am I up to?"

Why was gaining every answer like pulling teeth with this woman? Francisco leaned back in his chair, wrapping his right hand around his chin. "Not sure I follow."

"This is some kind of power barter. What your aim is, I don't know, but there's bigger dynamics here than looking for a kidnapper." For the first time since she'd arrived, Scotia looked uncertain of herself. She adjusted her position, settling on the edge of the chair. "Seriously, you've got Hugo Ferrente here while you're interrogating members of the Kingdom—a violation of our rights, by the way—"

Carlos cleared his throat. "It isn't. Clients who open Kingdom memberships agree to be subject to certain international jurisprudence as it shares servers—borders, if you will—with Gaia."

The lady's head spun. "Do I look like a member?" She motioned down to her simplistic garb. "Does it look like I paid some high-end codejockey to drip me in diamonds, make my clothes easy to take on and off in case I find a hidden alcove, and bump up my humble B-cups to Ds?" She turned back to the prince. "But I'm here. Correction: I was forced to be here. On top of that, you have the next biggest power broker of the vreal next to the Tiegs here to lick your boots. I would say someone is trying to throw his jurisprudence around."

"And to think, there was a time earlier today when I was jealous that you were prince." Hugo took a step out of the corner. "Paco, you may have found your kidnapper. At the very least, I can picture this woman wanting to hold you at knifepoint. Then again, not sure I can picture her letting you live."

Francisco lifted two fingers, asking for space, as he worked through the situation. At the surface, something about MacAvoy's behavior made sense. A chipshrink would have a whole building full of problems with a sovereign of the vreal. St. Dymphna's Hospital was such a building. But this much hostility? There was only one thing he could think of.

Francisco sat back at a deliberate pace, hoping to disguise the pounding of his heart, the fervor of his thoughts. "Miss MacAvoy, it occurs to me you'd have ample reason to have been there to kill me that night."

Suddenly, the color drained from the woman's face, a remarkable feat given her natural paleness. "What are you talking about? Wait... You mean you think that—" Her mouth closed on a dime. "I'm not saying a word more without representation."

Carlos grinned. The old man did love flexing rules and regulation, especially when to his own advantage. "Miss MacAvoy, as the office of the regent of Gaia includes the clause to assume that authority, it also means you have no de facto right to outside representation. Now, please, answer any question His Majesty asks."

Scotia snapped out of her temporary meekness. "I'm not a Kingdom user. I'm an employee of Plaxis." She put the prince at the pointy end of her glare. "I was invited that night because Cade Fife invited me. He said he wanted me there in case anyone wanted to discuss our Addict Outreach programs and our upcoming charity event, the same one that Tagentry is cosponsoring. You see? Official business. And since I was on the clock at the time of the ball, I may defer this matter to Human Resources."

A ring of red lined the edges of Carlos's face. "I don't believe that's accurate, and it's obvious even to me your bluster is an attempt to cover up something else, so answer the question."

Scotia pointed to the prince but kept her eyes on Carlos. "He didn't ask one."

With a long exhalation, Francisco leaned forward, pinching the bridge of his nose. "Carlos, Hugo... Can I please have a moment with Miss MacAvoy alone?"

"What?" Hugo said at the same time that Carlos, eyes to the floor, said, "Sire, I don't think that's wise."

The prince's hands fell into his lap. "Please, gentleman, I know what I'm doing. The only thing she can threaten is my patience."

The redhead settled back into her chair, tapping the arms in a one-two pattern. "Really? Because fifteen seconds ago, you accused me of attempted murder."

"I didn't. I said you'd have cause to want me dead," Francisco amended. "If my attaché and Mr. Ferrente would wait in the hall, I'll let them know when I'm ready to continue."

Carlos and Hugo exchanged a look. Then, the former shrugging and the latter rolling his eyes, they did as requested, closing the door to the parlor behind them. Francisco waited to hear the click, then reached down to the chair beside him, picking up the velvet pouch.

"Is it okay if I call you Scotia?" he began. "Miss MacAvoy is such a mouthful."

"Your Highness doesn't roll off the tongue either. But then again, neither does Mr. Batista de le Reina."

He placed the pouch in his lap and smiled through a laugh. "You can call me Frank. And now that we're chums, I'd like to tell you something."

She feigned intense interest, leaning forward and resting her chin on a balled-up fist. "I'm all ears."

If Scotia had been the first person that he'd screened instead of one of the last, Francisco might have called out the award-worthy dramatic performance he was witnessing. He might even think it was evidence of guilt or distraction. But the prince prided himself on his ability to pay close attention to people and hear what they were really saying, particularly by paying close attention to what they weren't saying.

Sometimes it was the blank spaces that brought color to the picture.

He pulled out the shoe and braced it in his two hands, holding it level with his chest. "This belonged to the woman who kidnapped me that night."

"Okay." For the first time since she'd walked in, Francisco saw confusion write itself into Scotia's expression. "And that has what to do with me?"

"Nothing, directly. Except, the funny thing about this shoe is that no one can handle it except me. And I've been trying to find the bandit by making all the women of the Kingdom present at the ball try it on. Whoever can actually wear the shoe... that's her. You're the first woman tonight for whom I'm not even going to make the effort, and do you know why?"

"Other than the fact that I'm not the bandit?"

Francisco chortled. "Well, yes, there is that. But the reason I know it won't fit is because you weren't there that night."

She'd claimed there was a power play going on. That hadn't been true until now when suddenly, Francisco felt the room shift. Scotia blanched, her mouth gaped. She stumbled for a response, but the prince wasn't quite ready to let her talk just yet.

"I pay attention to the words people use, Scotia, and yours have been carefully chosen. You were invited. That's what you said. You didn't say you attended. But your credentials were used by someone, and given this extreme drama over simple questions, I have a feeling you were complicit with their... or should I say, her efforts?" He swallowed, hoping with every fiber of his being that this was the right path. "You should know, she's not in trouble. The Gaian charter allows me to override Plaxis's legal department in pursuing criminal charges in some cases. I'm going to tell them in no uncertain terms this is one, since I was the intended victim. I just need to find her. If you tell me who she is, I promise I'll do everything in my power to see that you aren't charged with any crimes either."

"Crimes?" Scotia's fingers danced at her throat. She was doing her best to keep up her righteous rage profile, but the cracks in her voice belied her determination. "What crimes?"

"Many, actually." The prince stood, pivoting to watch the fireplace once more. "Aiding and abetting a hacker, avatar fraud, accessory to a kidnapping, maybe even an attempted murder charge... I'm sure in your role as a social worker, you've heard about Authority's new v-prisons. They're more humane than those old brick-and-mortar kind, in my opinion, but still..."

Francisco had seen that look on the faces of countless politicians and senior staffers many a time: the one through which he was being analyzed, seeing if truth could be found in the glint of his eye or the twitch of his smile. Finally, after a long moment, the redhead spoke.

"Why do you need to find her?"

"I need her to access the source code."

Scotia laughed without time to stop herself, pulled it back to silence, then let out one more guffaw.

"Okay, now I know you're bluffing," she said. "There's no way that Saah—… That she has access to the source code. No one does; it's one of the worst-kept secrets at Plaxis that if the underpinnings of the world corrupt, we have no way to repair it."

"I know everyone claims that's true. Hell, even Johanna Tieg told me the same thing. But here's the thing, Scotia." Francisco sat on a low table in front of the woman in question, setting the shoe next to him. He sucked in a breath through his teeth. "I have two theories. Either your friend whose name starts with Sahh can manipulate the vreal to a degree that could only happen if she has access to the source code, and-or it was all an inside job and your friend was hired to cover up someone else's lies. Now I'm going to ask you again… Who is she?"

Scotia bit her bottom lip. "Why do you need to access the source code?"

"Yeah, you want to make sure I have just reasons, I get that." Francisco looked around, trying to think of the best way to say what should be obvious until he struck on it. "This—" He held up a hand to indicate the room at large. "This posh, exaggerated, elitist plaything reality… This wasn't Omala Grover's vision. Gaia was, and it's under threat. Someone is trying to destroy it, and what they're doing is leaving damage that could only be repaired if we had the code. You see, if they destroy enough of it, whoever does have access is going to have a very tough decision to make if they're not willing to step up. Either they can let the source code become public so others can repair the damage and save Gaia in the process, or they can let everything that Omala built be destroyed."

"But what if they're only trying to damage it enough so that someone releases the code? Once it's exposed, every platform built on Purusha Plus would be endangered. At this point, it's been leased out to thousands of companies. Hell, even St. Dymphna's machines run a light version of it. That's a significant threat to… Well, the world."

Scotia was obviously an intelligent woman, the way she pieced together the next step in his line of thinking so effortlessly.

"Not to mention what it would do to the wardomes," Francisco said. "Imagine if war itself could be hacked. It would no longer be one side winning, it would be one side causing the other to lose. I know that sounds like the same thing, but you and I both understand the difference."

Through a slow nod, she agreed. "If they can't fight on equal ground inside the vreal, they'll take war back into the real."

The prince leaned in, like a child whispering secrets in class. "And let's be honest, Gaia's existence hinges right now on whoever runs Plaxis. Rex Tieg has always had its back, but he's God-knows-where, and I'm not sure Johanna's going to be eager to keep it going. Then what does that do to the real when war leaves it again? I need to secure our assets in case it becomes necessary for us to go it on our own."

Her eyes widened. Did she understand the implication he'd chosen to share with her?

"You're talking about independence."

"I'm talking about sovereignty, and you are one of only six people who are aware that I'm even considering it, so your confidence would be much appreciated."

Suddenly, something in his memory tripped. "You gave a talk in Congressional Hall last year," Francisco said in time with his remembrance. "The conference on vreal addiction."

Scotia's eyes went wide. "I didn't think you'd remember me, or that you heard my talk."

"I didn't, but I read a brief on your paper afterward." Francisco sat erect, his eyes going to the far wall. "Scotia, you're obviously a person who cares a lot about consequences. Please, I'm only trying to find the bandit because I know how dire the consequences would be if I fail at this." He left unsaid that a living upload of Omala Grover had told him as much. "I can tell you're trying to protect her, and I respect that. Just, please, tell me who she is."

The redhead bit her bottom lip and cycled through a deep breath. For a moment, Francisco expected the next thing out of Scotia's mouth to be a name. Instead, when her body relaxed and her shoulders folded in, it was only to say, "I'm sorry, I can't."

He nodded through his disappointment. "I understand."

"But I can tell you this."

His head jerked up.

"She asked me to stall," Scotia said plainly. "I'm the last one at the palace to be cleared, right? Because I was the last one to arrive before everything went down. Or at least, she was."

Francisco nearly fell off his chair. No, Scotia wasn't the last to be cleared—there were three others still unscreened. Now that he knew the bandit was definitely female, one of them had been dropped from his list of possible subjects.

But that wasn't what had caught his attention. "You spoke with her? Recently?"

Scotia hesitated, her mouth agape. "I... got a message from her. She told me you might be in danger, and to take up your time."

"Danger?" He looked around, as if expecting to see an enemy that had appeared in the shadows. The security measures in place should be able to keep anyone not already in the world at the lockdown point from entering, but if the bandit could find a way around it (and he had no doubt she could), so could whoever was coming for him. "From what? Or is it a who?"

"She didn't say." Scotia's huffed a laugh. "She knows me, and she knows that I wouldn't be able to not go after the guilty if she'd told me. But I can tell you that, if you've seen the things that she's able to do, you would know you don't need to wor—"

Scotia cut off when the door to the parlor opened.

Francisco stood, ready to tell either Carlos or Hugo that he needed just a moment more. He couldn't blame them for their impatience; they had to be curious what the prince was discussing with some random Plaxis employee.

Only the two faces he saw in the doorway before bodies followed into the room weren't his two countrymen.

Johanna Tieg, hands on her hip and a scowl on her face, paraded through the door. "Your Highness, I'm sorry, but this has really gone on for far too long. Every moment the platform is closed is costing me a fortune. Whatever protocol you dredged up to identify your bandit has failed. Besides, there's no one left for you to screen."

Francisco looked around the huffing VP to the infamous blonde bombshell behind her.

Click.

"Actually, Miss MacAvoy and I just concluded our conversation." The prince grabbed the shoe and made his way toward the door. "And actually, Johanna, you're perfectly on time."

TWENTY-SIX

SHE'D SPENT HER LIFE limiting trust and acting on data, but Cindira had come to a place where faith was her only option.

The jut-jut-jut of the rickety cart was enough to send her pulse to astronomical levels. Warren insisted that even though the wheels squeaked and one of them pulled to the left, it wouldn't collapse under the weight of the ancient jackpod he'd loaded onto it before loading her into it in the back of Mr. Chen's business van.

"One problem with it."

Cindira, not one to be particular for the sake of fashion or other's opinions, had looked at the device with due apprehension. "It smells bad?"

"Well, yeah, of course. It's old, who knows how many people have ridden in this thing or, you know, what they were doing in the vreal with it." Warren's expression momentarily soured to match hers, but he'd quickly shaken it away. "Problem is, I haven't had time to repair it yet. It's a dead coffin, but it's the only one I had in the shop that didn't have a transparent faceplate."

A nonfunctional jackpod wouldn't be much help to get into the vreal, but they couldn't even think about that unless she got to the Kitchens first. Cindira had never bought into the idea that her mother was a saint, but even the dispassionate realist would bow to prayer in such a crisis.

She had forced down the sick inching up her throat and crawled in.

That had been eight minutes ago, when the van had self-parked near the service docks. She slid down the body tray as Warren escorted the loaded cart off the ramp. When he got to Plaxis's loading dock, the pitch reversed, forcing her to glide headfirst into the neural array and hitting her head. The first sigh of relief came when, after a pause during which she imagined Warren sweating photons, the wheels started turning and they were moving again. Her freshly forged vendor records and work order must have passed inspection.

Was it the smell or the rickety way the cart bounced that was turning her stomach? Was it the fact that she might be too late, and Kaylie may have executed her plan and the Gaian sovereign along with it? Or was it that she worried more about saving Francisco than saving the prince, and how that didn't make any sense since they were the same person?

The service elevators at the backside of the building moved with all the urgency of a tree growing leaves, but at least they made it that far. The high-pitched tone that played with the passing of each floor permeated the cavity of the jackpod, echoing in her head. Cindira counted in time with the musical accompaniment. Thirteen, fifteen, seventeen... Then finally, a ding like a clarion bell, and the cart was rolling again.

It worked. This harebrained scheme actually had worked.

Assuming they could get into the Kitchens, which was no small feat. Especially since who knew if Kaylie still had her goons with her, or which staffers had been trusted with staying on.

From the cargo elevators, Cindira estimated it would take Warren three minutes to get them across the grid of the nineteenth floor. Which was why her stomach dropped when they stopped moving after thirty seconds and the jackpod cracked open.

Warren leaned down, one hand on the lid, holding it up. "Something's weird here."

That, being the obvious statement of the year. Luckily, he went on unprompted.

"There's nobody on this floor."

She blinked, trying to realize the significance of the statement. "It's the middle of the day. Most people would be in their offices—"

"I said nobody, and I meant nobody, Cinders. I can see in the offices through their glass walls. This place is a ghost town."

She tried to sit up, wanting visual confirmation herself, but Warren pushed her back down.

"You crazy? I got you positioned so the camera node overhead can't see in, but that won't do much good if the weasel goes pop."

Cindira assumed she was the weasel. "Kaylie must have ordered everyone off this floor. She wouldn't want anyone witnessing her coming and going from her office at the same time the prince was killed."

With that, he let the lid slide open all the way. "That means these cameras wouldn't be on either." But as he helped Cindira pull her body up and out, lowering her on the floor, the little teenage techanic presented another query. "But then why would security give me a pass to get up here? If she's cleared the deck, the last thing she's going to let us do is take the plate."

"I don't really get your analogy, but I think I understand the meaning."

She looked at the camera node, its tiny status light blinking blue instead of the typical red. Warren was right, it was off. And he was also right that something felt wrong about that. Kaylie was arrogant; it was possible she'd just assumed the only person who could know about her plan and have a reason to stop her was still trapped in a warehouse across town. That presumption wouldn't stick, however. Conceited as she may be, she wasn't stupid. She might have gotten her position in the company because of who her mother was, but she performed her duties well enough. The worst mistake Cindira could make today would be underestimating her stepsister for a second time.

"She must have opted for a shield instead of a wall."

Warren's face went blank. "You're right, it sucks not understanding the analogy."

"It's something I learned in the hackdomes when I was competing," she clarified. "Some people try to stay safe and avoid getting hit by hiding behind walls. Thing is, you can't control, change, or move a wall. You're only as strong as its weakest point.

But if you use a shield instead, being the master of diverting a blow, you have much more defensive strength and a greater opportunity to attack."

"Meaning?"

The optical lines that connected the camera nodes ran through the ceiling, as did the lines that powered the data-hungry Kitchens. "If we go into the Kitchens through the door, her shield—her goons — will be waiting there, ready to kill us. Probably with blasters. Which means, the only way for me to get in is by bringing down a wall."

For not the first time in their brief history, Warren looked at the coder like she was, in fact, insane. "I'm a techanic, not an engineer. And don't take this the wrong way, but I don't look at you and think, now, there's a woman who could really bust through a wall."

"Not by myself, no." She pulled him in close and walked towards one of the empty offices. "Here's what we're going to do."

THE LENGTH OF THE JAW drop would be measured in feet, not inches.

"They're going to recognize you."

Warren looked down at the disguise she'd been able to throw together from what they'd found rummaging through a few offices, which luckily included a hoodie that covered her hair and looked, for lack of a better word, industrial.

She shook her head, burying her eyes and positioning herself, Warren's techanic toolbox in hand, behind the teenager who luckily had had his growing spurt earlier rather than later. "They think I'm trapped in the warehouse, and most of them didn't look at me too much while they were there. Never overestimate the blindness arrogance causes."

"Oh, I don't. Remember, I'm a low-level service worker from the wrong side of town. I know what it feels like to have people look at you at not see you."

"If they never look your way, they never see you coming."

Or so she hoped. Everything they'd done made sense. Once Warren shared with her the block-c API for his grandfather's remote monitor installed on the machine, uploading error codes had been as simple as breathing for her. After all, it was an old machine, and they were known for being glitchy without proper maintenance. This one had sat in a warehouse tended only by botics for twelve years. Would it be a great stretch of the imagination to suppose that with being moved and having a new user, something would break?

Cindira only hoped Kaylie's goons had an imagination, or else a driving desire to save their own asses when the jackpod their boss was riding in suddenly started busting out abort codes.

They buzzed the doorbell.

The goon who opened the door had been holding the same blaster at the warehouse. She respected consistency. He squinted at them, as though he doubted what he was seeing. What he was hearing couldn't be denied. A good thing that Kaylie had cleared this part of the building, or everyone would have come running to see what was making such a god-awful racket.

Warren cleared his throat, clutching the handle of his toolbox so hard his knuckles went white. "A machine at this location requested service. I happened to be nearby, so the boss asked me to stop in and take a look."

The goon's expression eased a modicum and he leaned out, looking up and down the hall to make sure they were alone. It gave the two of them a chance to see inside. The halo of stations were manned by two coders Cindira didn't recognize, not Plaxis staffers who'd she'd worked side-by-side with for the last few years. Thank goodness for that; she didn't want to make any of the people she considered her friends choose between appeasing Kaylie and helping her commit a half dozen cybercrimes. The jackpod itself had been squeezed into the open floor space in the middle of the room, butted up against the edge of the Sink.

"You're a techanic?" The goon drew back and looked Warren up and down, a task that from his height was more down that up. "Aren't you a little young to be handling such ancient equipment?"

"Funny, your mother said the same thing to me last night."

The kid had chutzpah; she'd give him that.

Neither of the men with weapons responded to the jest, and Warren pressed on. "If you want someone with a few more years under their belt, I can call the office and ask them to send out a more senior tech, but my feed here"—Warren held up his comque—"says there's an active rider on this unit. She tries to jack out with the machine in this error state, it will be like passing her subconscious mind through a potato grater. So if she's going to be awhile and you don't mind the sounds of a toucan being murdered by a tuba, no prob. If not—"

"Greg!" the second goon deeper in the Kitchens called, followed by footsteps. "That monitor is going crazy, and ain't nothing neither of them two dipshits seem able to do about it. Better let them in or our meal ticket might run out on us."

Cindira also expected their freedom too, but that was going to be true no matter how this turned out. Didn't they realize Kaylie would need a scapegoat? She could picture her stepsister now, batting her fake eyelashes and putting on her pouty face. *I didn't want to kill the prince, but they held me at blaster point and forced me into that ancient jackpod. It was so disgusting. And they were watching me through the Sink the whole time to make sure I'd do what I was told.*

The Sink! Cindira had been so focused on keeping quiet she hadn't dared to look, but now she couldn't resist. Deep breath, eyes up, see, eyes down. It was only a moment, but it confirmed her suspicions. She could tell from the aesthetic that the vreal was the Kingdom, even though the view suggested Kaylie, Johanna, and Cade weren't at Alsace. She knew every inch of her family's vreal home well enough to make the determination. Which meant, they must be at the palace. Why? The trio walked up a hall towards one of the private parlors not far from the ballroom. It must be where Francisco was.

She was running out of time. He was running out of time.

Warren's laugh brought her back to the moment. "Let me guess," he was saying, "you got a couple of code jockeys poking at that ancient jackpod." He clicked his tongue. "There's a reason they do all their work in the land of make believe, you know? Give them something that requires them to use their hands, and they're as useless as a one-ball monkey."

He's just playing a role.

"We get a feed of all the diagnostics so I know exactly what's wrong with it." The techanic tapped his box. "Also have some outdated parts that these old machines use, and my assistant here who knows how to help me put them on. I'm sure I can have it fixed up in no time. Or you can leave that rider in there and just... let things happen. But you should know, there's a reason the old machines earned the nickname 'coffin.'"

"Greg!"

This time, when his colleague snapped, Greg heeled. He brought the blaster into an at-ease position at his side with one arm and used the other to pull Warren forward by the sleeve of his khaki uniform. Luckily, he made no objection to nor took any great interest in Cindira scooting along in their wake.

"Fix it and quick."

Warren harrumphed and doubled over the top of the jackpod as Greg flung him forward. For a moment, Cindira worried that the scowl on Warren's face forecasted the teen losing his temper and fighting back. From the moment they'd met, it was obvious the young techanic wasn't the type to let himself be pushed around. Instead, he just huffed and pushed himself up and off the machine.

"I'm going to charge extra for hazard pay if you're going to be a dick." He nodded at Cindira, answering her unanswered question about his condition. Without hesitation, he circled the machine and tapped in a series of commands, turning off the piercing pitches, before launching into the script they'd just improvised out in the hall. "These errors aren't anything uncommon for this type of machine. I can have it fixed in about fifteen."

Greg's master smoothed down a brown tie hanging from his neck. "You can't do it any faster than that?"

"Faster?" Warren swallowed, but otherwise didn't break character. If they survived this, Cindira was going to owe him big. "You want me to rush through a delicate repair like this with someone actively jacked in? Sure, 'cause that's always a good idea."

Goon Senior's eyes drifted to the Sink, taking Cindira's along for the ride. The Fife children and their horrid mother were at the door now, and Cindira was surprised to see something very unexpected on her stepmother's face: desperation, and the look was aimed at Kaylie. Could it be that Johanna hadn't been in on the scheme? To her surprise, Cindira hoped for once that her stepmother was an even worse person than she already knew her to be. If she was innocent in this, Johanna was just as much a victim as Cindira was. Which meant... Cindira had to save her.

But first the prince.

Big Good took a mental inventory. "You get her fixed up in six minutes, you can name your price, kid."

Pulse spiking, Cindira realized they'd just been given a ticking clock. In the next six minutes, Kaylie would find her way to the prince, murder him, and escape. Perfectly safe at that, since there wasn't anything really wrong with the jackpod. Stopping her in the vreal was something the coder knew she could handle. If the confrontation happened here in the real, however, both she and Warren were going to get an intimate knowledge of those blasters' capabilities.

Warren lifted the lid to the service bay of the jackpod. "Six minutes? Do you think we can do that?"

Cindira met his gaze, wishing there was a way for them to have a minute, even ten seconds, of privacy. There'd be none of that now. No way for her to tell Warren that Kaylie's jackpod was in the way, and she couldn't do what she'd hoped to.

Her original plan had been to claim that the Sink was causing a feedback loop with the unit, that she needed to get into it to do the repair. Once inside, she could ask Pele to open the interface. Assuming the others didn't get wise about what she was up to, she could at least interact with VAPORs in the vreal, even if no one there would be able to see her. Doubtful that the hired guns had any tech skills; they probably thought of the Sink as some fancy periscope. Would the coders know she was bluffing? Neither was likely to know about the intricacies of how the Sink operated or what its parameters were. The devices were extremely rare.

Ignorance was a fertile ground for deceit.

She needed another plan, something quicker. Something that was guaranteed to take her less than six minutes.

Warren leaned over the machine, repeating the words in crisp tones. "I said, do you think we can do that?"

"Something wrong with your assistant there?" Greg's suspicious tone was hard to ignore.

Warren turned over his shoulder. "She's just a little slow, is all."

"I'm thinking," she huffed, then, to dissuade any further doubt, she added, "you know how hard that is for me."

For once, though, it was proving true.

Cindira bit her knuckle and racked her brain. What options were there? She'd spoken to the prince through the Sink back in the warehouse, and all she'd had to do was touch it. There was no way to do that now. Kaylie's people might not be the brightest, but they'd be able to see what was playing out in real time. Besides, she wasn't completely sure how that had happened to begin with, so recreating the phenomenon would be impossible. Perhaps her body only needed to have a single point of contact with some portal into the vreal? The shoes allowed for that, but only if she were wearing them both in the real and vreal at the same time. In the vreal now, her avatar still had one.

And in the Sink, she could see Francisco had the other. Her heart leaped to see Scotia being rushed from the room by Cade as Francisco pointed at the sofa in the parlor. His mouth moved, but on this side, no one present had turned on the audio fee. The only thing Cindira could see clearly was that he was talking to Kaylie and Johanna while Cade puttered in the background. So that's what it was. Francisco was trying to reveal her identity by forcing every woman to try on the shoe. Only, without the connection in the real to the shoes with the embedded nanites, they couldn't hold it.

But if that were true, how was he holding it?

Warren followed her gaze and seemed to understand at least part of the puzzle at the same time she did. "Oh, that's the prince's top-secret security litmus test, huh? Got himself a barometer on the chick who tried to steal him away?"

Greg and Big Goon pivoted in time, taking in the sight the Sink allowed, while Warren mouthed a silent but fierce, "What the hell are you doing?"

She wasn't sure. Going on instinct, maybe. In any event, there wasn't a way for her to tell the helpful techanic anything that made sense. Instead, Cindira cautiously opened the lid of the jackpod, one of Warren's tools in her left hand to give her a cover story and something shiny for the others to focus on if they turned.

Kaylie's power heels slipped off easily enough, and Cindira put her mother's shoes on in their place. Then, she too lifted her head, watching the vreal play out. Francisco took a knee in front of Johanna, who deigned to lift her dress and reveal a foot adorned in a jeweled shoe monstrosity. The silicone slipper performed as expected, passing right through her stepmother's foot.

Cindira buried her head into the stiff, pilfered shirt, where Laporte was probably very thankful it neither required air nor had a sense of smell. The whisper was as low as it was dangerous. "Get ready to run the commands. You're going to port me in, on my count."

"But, miss, without the shoe, how will you…."

"Oh, yeah, looks like." Big Goon laughed, pointing a finger and a grin at the Sink. "Just like that fairy tale. What was it called, Greg?"

"Red Riding Hood."

Big Goon was as dumb as Greg looked. "Yeah, that's the one."

The prince leaned in front of Kaylie this time. Cindira cleared her mind, focusing on the task at hand. She'd have moments if this only barely worked, and probably not much more than that if it didn't. Kaylie's ankle was soft, her skin supple. Cindira's hand wrapped around it and squeezed.

"Warren, don't take her offline."

The techanic wore an are-you-screwing-with-me expression. "But I thought that was the whole plan?"

"Laporte, on three."

In the Sink, the prince paused, evaluating Kaylie with an amused, reverent glee. He must have thought he'd found his savior — though how Francisco thought Kaylie had been the one to kidnap him from the ball while already standing at his side, who could say? Then again, the one who'd saved him turned out to look just like Omala Grover, so maybe he just thought it had been a night for the mysterious.

"One..."

"Hey, what you doing?" Big Goon finally had caught on that something was afoot. He bolted out of his seat and started his way into the pit where the jackpod lay.

"Um..." Warren pulled the word out like taffy. "It's a special kind of... parallel soul jack popular in Asia?"

Greg's face screwed up for a minute. He checked back with his partner, then turned to the coder at the user bay. Cindira felt their fate balance on the programmer's ignorance. Finally, after a moment where the tension cut off her ability to breath, the man behind the terminal shrugged.

"Hell if I know. They do all kinds of weird techno-spiritualism things there."

Warren deflated, and Cindira hastened.

Come on, Francisco, stop dillydallying.

As if the prince heard her, he lifted the hem of Kaylie's skirt and pulled her foot to rest on his knee. He removed her ivory dancing heel with extreme care, placing it on the floor while collecting the silicone slipper from where he'd left it momentarily.

"Two...."

Greg scrambled behind his boss, and moments before they got to her, a blur of black hair and righteous intent screamed between them. No one would have thought Warren had it in him, which is probably why they were both knocked down.

Cindira caught his eye just long enough to smile her thanks before looking up again — to see Kaylie reaching into the waistline of her dress. What had appeared to be belting rotated, and where there had been fabric, now there was something long and shiny.

Francisco pushed her foot into the slipper.

Kaylie lifted her weapon.

Cindira closed her eyes.

"Three!"

TWENTY-SEVEN

FOR ONE BRIEF BUT BRILLIANT moment, his quest had ended. The shoe fit Kaylie. Never mind that it didn't make sense. What couldn't a talented hacker do? The shoe fit Kaylie.

And then she'd stabbed him.

Blinding pain tore through his body. Across the room, the doors that led to the hall shook. Animalistic voices shouted and fists pounded. Carlos and Hugo. They must have heard the commotion, but why wouldn't they just come in? Didn't they know he needed help? Didn't they know he needed them?

Francisco pressed a hand to his stomach before pulling it to his eyes. Red fingertips. No, he hadn't imagined it. He had been stabbed, and without the safety protocols engaged, the injury could be more than virtual. A filter in Gaia rewrote the code on its way back to the brain to protect the mind from anything deemed injurious, but not here. Here, he may be in mortal danger.

His legs gave out from under him. He fell to his knees.

"Francisco, are you okay?" Johanna's eyes were wide, her face, pale, as she kneeled down beside him.

"I'm..." He swallowed his words and tasted blood. "Kaylie stabbed me."

"I know. Let me see how badly you're hurt."

Let her see? What about Kaylie? Why wasn't she going after her, trying to disarm her daughter?

Because the knife was still in his gullet. His fingertips reached down, confirmed it. Francisco slammed his eyes shut, wishing it away. Whatever he'd done to make an umbrella, unmaking a knife couldn't be that different. The lines of code refused to line up in his mind, however. Like his thoughts, they flew in every direction.

As Johanna started to pull and push the fabric of his constrictive period clothing, Francisco became aware of the struggle going on across the room. Two women. One was Kaylie, grunting more than screaming, trying to throw off the other, who had her locked from behind. The second woman was... who? Maybe a member of his security team who'd detected the commotion had jacked in to assist? If so, he wasn't going to let that effort be in vain.

Francisco lifted his bloody hand. "Help me stand. I can perform the emergency exit procedure."

It was good to be prince and have such options. He'd be fine once he got back to the real. In pain, maybe, but not dead.

Johanna ignored him, instead grabbing his vest and aggressively exploring the area where the blade had pierced him. "Where is it?"

"Where is what?"

"The knife, you fool! Where is the knife?"

"It's right there. It's—"

This time his hand reached down only to find rent flesh. As Francisco pushed fingers around the wound in his stomach, hot liquid oozing in time with his heartbeat, he found nothing. It was like it had just... disappeared.

He'd thought it. He'd hoped for it. But had it actually come to pass just because he wished for the knife to be gone?

"Mother!" Kaylie's sudden outburst stole away Johanna's attention. "Stab him through the heart!"

Johanna shook her hands in midair. "The knife is gone!"

"What?" Kaylie thrashed, heaved, trying every maneuver to rid herself of the bondage in which she found herself. "Then find another way, or else!"

"No! Think of the consequences. If you kill the Prince, Gaia will be chaos."

It was the other woman speaking. Her voice, as strained as it was from her efforts, was smooth, familiar. Although Francisco couldn't see her face hidden behind Kaylie's head, he knew that voice. He knew that voice.

And suddenly, it clicked. It was her.

No sooner had his heart leapt to his chest than terror struck at him. Kaylie threw herself off balance, and it made the bandit go flying over her shoulder, a spin wheel of blue skirts, white petticoats, and gold thread. Free, Kaylie reached into the waistline of her clothing and dug into what must be a hidden pocket. When her hand came out again, she held not a knife this time. She held a pistol.

Francisco somehow managed his feet, reeling with each movement. "Guns in the Kingdom? I thought they were contraband."

"So is regicide, but I'm willing to make an exception." Kaylie wore a cocky grin. "And when you're dead, I'll release the source code. I'll say that you were the one holding it back, that Gaia was trying to use it to hold the vreal world at its mercy. And I'll offer it to all, and they'll make me their queen. Sorry, Frank." She said his name like an insult. "But this is where I tell you that I don't think our relationship has much of a future."

Her arm was steady, her aim, readied. Kaylie cocked back the hammer, squeezed the trigger, and—

A hummingbird shot out.

It flew from the end of the barrel, up to the ceiling, and then, to the edge of the room, taking their eyes and all their words along with it.

"What?" Kaylie pulled back the gun, made the mistake of looking into it, just in time for a second bird to fly out. She blinked her confusion and stood erect. The hummingbird buzzed as it stared her in the eye, back and forth, side to side, forward, then backward.

And then it dove into the folds of her hair, sending her shrieking and clawing at her skull.

"Oh, my baby." Johanna touched one finger to her lip before bolting across the room, trying to calm her daughter enough to get her hands on the tiny bird.

Francisco wasted no time. He lunged, biting back the agony, and pulled the bandit to her feet. Who knew how long they'd survive on wishes. Francisco wasn't a medic, but he'd read enough reports from the wardomes to know that a wound to the lower abdomen might take a longer time to kill its victim, but it killed them all the same. He had opportunity. He should perform the five moves and speak the four words that would trigger the source code command to exit him from the platform. But something had sparked within him: a need to save her. He didn't know her name or how she'd gotten past the dense security protocols, but he needed to help her.

"Are you okay?" Francisco understood what the gurgle in his voice signaled.

"I am, but you won't be if we don't get you out of here." She turned him, pushed him gently. "Run. I'll unlock the doors."

"What?" How had she locked them to begin with? He found the strength to plant his feet. "No, I won't leave you behind and defenseless."

Her smile seemed to be at his expense. "I just deleted the knife from the system and turned bullets into hummingbirds. I'll be fine."

Francisco blinked. "I thought I did that."

"No offense, Your Highness, but how would you do those things?"

The mocking, tender smile she had made him feel fuzzy inside. Or maybe that was the blood loss. "I don't know. I thought if I wished it…" His voice tapered off. Francisco shook his head, coming back to the moment. "Who are you?"

She swallowed down breathless pants. "I'm the woman from the ball who kidnapped you."

"I guessed that." Despite everything else going on, he couldn't help but smile. "But who are you?"

"Oh." She blushed. "Sorry. Yeah, my name is—"

But then, she was gone.

WARREN'S BACK WAS TO hers, and in the reflection of a nearby monitor, she could see his profile in reverse: blaster up, ready to strike.

Cindira blinked, trying to get her bearings. Was she back in the real? "Warren?"

The techanic didn't turn, but she felt his body shake behind hers, his voice barely audible over the whooping. "Shit, Cindira, what happened? You zoned out, and we're in a pinch."

No doubt. She let go of Kaylie long enough to risk taking in the scene. On the floor beside the jackpod, a horizontal Big Goon blinked his eyes in a slow and measured way. A patch of black material, muscled sinew, and blood was all that was left of his right thigh. Meanwhile, both the jackpod operator at one of the code banks and Greg had their hands up. Overhead, the fire alarm whooped. Either the blast had triggered it, or one machine was actually overloading. Here in the Kitchens, with so many powerful machines and all the heat they produced, the sensors blared with the smallest whiff of anything incendiary. Either way, it meant the same thing. Building security and firefighters would come, and soon. When they did, they'd fire on Warren first and ask questions later.

In the Sink, Johanna dashed around the room, no doubt looking for her daughter. Francisco, meanwhile, continued to bleed.

Cindira swallowed her nerves. "Laporte, where is Kaylie?"

"I quarantined her when I pulled you out, miss."

She shook her head. While that would make saving the prince easier, it wouldn't get her back the shoe. Who knew if she'd ever have this chance again? "No, I need her there. Put Kaylie and me back in on my mark. Warren, I—"

"I shot a guy."

All the tough talk, and at the first sign of violence, the techanic learned that the reality of aggression cut both ways. He'd need help, both emotionally and financially. If they survived, she'd make sure he'd get it. Surely she could divert a little of her savings from Asla to the Chens. For the moment, she needed him to focus. The injury Big Good had could be healed in an emergency medical lab, but if the prince died in the vreal, there was nothing science could do to bring him back.

"As long as he doesn't bleed out, he'll survive. But don't worry about that right now. I need you to listen to me carefully, and don't ask questions I don't have time to answer. Keep an eye on the Sink. If I get that glass shoe off Kaylie's foot in the vreal, move the silicone slippers here in the real to my feet and then power down this machine."

"Shoes? At a time like this, you're worried about getting your shoes back?" The unusual request snapped him out of his loop. "Why don't I just overload this machine's circuits. I'll fry her brain."

"Because that would be murder." Cindira grabbed Kaylie's wrist and this time, instead of just standing next to the jackpod, she wedged herself in. It was a tight fit, even leaning on her side, but it meant that if something failed in the vreal and both were ejected, at least she'd be able to take on Kaylie physically. "She didn't do this alone. No time to explain. Laporte, in three, two, one...mark!"

"We have to get out of here."

Across the room, Johanna Tieg was a wild woman. Fist clenched, she pounded the door that led from the parlor into the hall at the same time Hugo and Carlos did so from the other side.

"She's going to kill him. She's going to kill Rex."

Francisco managed his feet, even if the room was spinning and the carpet stained red. What did it matter? This was the vreal. A few lines of repair code, and poof! It would return to ivory just like that. He could code it himself if he wasn't struggling to stay alive.

"Johanna?"

"I can't believe it!" Trapped in a reverie, Johanna yanked at her usually-coiffured hair, talking to no one in particular. "My child. My own child!"

"Johanna!"

The woman snapped to attention. Whirling, she glared at the prince. "Order this door open!"

"Not until you and I have a word." Downward pressure on his wound helped to staunch the pain. "Where is Kaylie?"

"You tell me. One moment she was here, and the next, Cindira shows up and they just... vanish."

Cindira? Was that the bandit's name? Why did that sound so familiar? He must have known a Cindira once. A memory danced at the edge of recollection, but at the moment, Francisco had no place in his thoughts for nostalgia.

"You said she's going to kill Rex?" The room went fuzzy. Was that his eyes, or was there something wrong with the vreal? "How?"

"Rex's avatar has been trapped in stasis here in the vreal for months, while he's who-knows-where out in the real. I've been protecting his avatar here in the palace, but I never dreamed my own daughter would be behind it all. If I don't help to kill you, they'll kill Rex."

The prince doubted that. Kaylie couldn't be that heartless, could she? She'd said it herself, Rex was the only father she'd ever really had. That didn't mean she couldn't threaten, however. "Do you know what she's after?"

"Isn't it obvious?" She spread her hands out wide. "All of it. She wants control of Plaxis, to use it to rule the vreal through Gaia, and manipulate the source code to exploit and dominant the real."

No one ever accused a Fife of a lack of ambition. Only, it was then Francisco realized something. Part of that plan sounded very familiar. Holy hell, he himself had laid the groundwork for it. A free Gaia, he'd thought. One unshackled from the restraints of its corporate hosts. One that had the autonomy to take bold new steps into the world as its own master, to make the nations of the world recognize and treat it as an equal. But was this what it took to win that independence? Francisco hadn't thought beyond the victory to complete the burden of the victorious. He trusted himself to be a just ruler. He hadn't thought about what the power of his throne could do if someone with more self-serving intentions sat on it.

Kaylie intended to rule the world. With Plaxis at her back, with the loyalty and fealty of most of the countries whose leaders and patriarchs she'd spent years charming and gathering secrets on, engaged in the treaties that bound them in war, commerce, and sovereignty to what went on inside Gaia, she could do it. But that war couldn't possibly stay on the platform. It would break out into the real, and with it, the planet might be lost to its consequences still. Yes, Francisco was prince, but he was a ruler ordained by consensus and placed in power by the elective process. Kaylie would be a tyrant.

How had he let his fantasies and his policies become so intertwined? Only, the genesis of the idea hadn't been his. It had been...

Before Francisco could come to grips with what the realization implied, there was a crash. The prince spun, the effort taxing his strength. He fell to the ground the moment Kaylie Fife and Cindira reappeared.

LIPS PULLED BACK IN a snarl, Kaylie lunged, her hands encircling Cindira's neck.

"Where is it?" the blonde shrieked. "The source code was supposed to be in the jackpod, but I can't control anything. Where is it?"

How she expected an answer while blocking Cindira's windpipe, the coder wasn't sure. Luckily, with all her efforts focused on attempted murder, Kaylie hadn't noticed the shoe had slipped off her foot. Cindira's eyes went hazy, even as she looked for the forsaken footwear. Instead, she found Francisco, hands covered in blood, on his knees.

The prince's eyes met hers as the edges of his face went slack. "She has Rex."

The words were for her. Of that, Cindira had no doubt. But what Francisco intended for her to do with that information, she didn't know. It didn't matter, though. It wasn't true. Was there enough air in her lungs to make it known? The edges of her vision darkened.

"No, Dad... is..."

"Shut up!"

Kaylie let go, turning her rage to a weapon. A fist, a slap, a hit. It all came raining down on in a wave of pain. Cindira didn't know if she let her knees give on purpose or if it was just a result of the attack. Either way, the pressure around her throat slackened. The gasp was as loud as it was deep. Cindira drank the air, even as the attack raged about her. Some survival instinct told her to cover her head. Her arms caged about her skull, but that left her torso open. This time when Cindira fell, she did it completely, collapsing to the floor, curling into a ball.

And then, just like it had started, it stopped. There was silence. And then something around her feet shifted. One foot still held the glass slipper she'd arrived with, and the other was bare. Until, that was, her left foot welcomed the missing shoe back.

She dared look out from her hovel to see at her feet none other than the prince, his eyes shining, his skin pale.

"It was you. Cindira..."

Cindira bit back cries of pain as she turned over on her stomach and spun, her hands dragging her body over the carpet. She reached for his hands as soon as her eyes were facing his. One bloody hand stretched out to accept.

"Hold on, Your Majesty. I'm going to save you."

Francisco's smile faltered. "It's too late. I've lost too much blood, and I—"

"No." Cindira refused to let him accept that this world was more powerful than his ability to know his own mind. "This isn't the real. Don't let the platform convince your mind otherwise. Fight it. Control it. Undo what's been done to you."

As if she was one to talk. Yes, she had the shoes on here, but unless Warren could see in the Sink back at Plaxis and unless he was still enough in control to move the real-world shoes in tangent, she'd still be powerless to do anything to defeat Kaylie.

Speaking of Kaylie....

It was a good thing she was on the floor. When Cindira looked to see what had finally ended her stepsister's onslaught, she found Johanna with her arms around her only daughter, holding her back. Something had happened to Kaylie's voice. Open-mouthed and harried, the would-be usurper appeared to scream, yell, shout, but there was no sound. She could wail until her face turned blue, but a mouse wouldn't hear.

A mouse!

"Laporte?"

Luckily, he arrived not as a rodent, but in the human form she'd seen him take the last time she'd been in the Palace. He looked to be an East Asian man of perhaps thirty years. A thin mustache tickled his top lip. Dressed in a tan long coat, peasant blouse, and white pantaloons, he could be mistaken for a VAPOR, if not for the lack of the distinguishing glowing bhindi.

He bowed in the prince's direction. "Your Majesty," before snapping up, focusing on where Cindira lay on her stomach on the floor with no apparent deference to the fact. "Miss Tieg, how may I be of service?"

"Override the emergency settings and reactivate the safety protocol. Then force exit Francisco from the vreal before it's too late. Don't let his body in the real internalize the damage."

Laporte grimaced. "I'm afraid I don't have the authority to do that, miss."

That didn't make any sense. Laporte could do practically anything. Who was he to defer to whoever was the current monarch of Gaia? Was there something she wasn't aware of, some kind of override built into the code that forced even Laporte to obey? Cindira had cleaned the code for years and had been writing Purusha practically since the time she could manage an interface. Yes, the sovereign had certain privileges, but they weren't absolute.

She swallowed. "Okay, who does have authority?"

"Other than himself?"

Why did botics ask such closed-ended, needless sentences? "Of course, other than himself."

"The only other person who can save the prince is you, miss, and even then, you'd need his permission. Or at the very least, his acquiescence. All you need to do is release the source code. Then Francisco will be empowered to rewrite himself in the vreal, just as you've always been."

"You?" Weak, weary, and with a voice broken by his pain, Francisco shook his head. "You have access to the source code?"

Cindira bit her bottom lip, looking up at her stepmother as she did so. Johanna's inscrutable expression hung on a hair. This was it: the precipice. All Cindira had to do was deny it, and she could continue to live her life in her quiet little corner of the world, out of the limelight and safe in the shadows. But even in the dark, Francisco's blood would always be on her hands if she made that selfish decision. He'd take the fate of Gaia with him if he died. Not right away, perhaps. But the last few weeks had shown the cracks in the foundation. Without her, without what she could do, she was dooming this part of the vreal.

She let her lungs empty in a slow and steady stream through pursed lips, before speaking. "I do."

Johanna... faltered. Reaching out, her stepmother steadied herself on the back of the sofa.

But Cindira wasn't done. She'd understood the implications of what Laporte had said. And somehow, though she couldn't be sure how, she'd felt, looking back, that she'd always known the truth. Even though Francisco grimaced, she leaned over pushing her hand to the sanguineous patch of fabric just below his ribcage and covered it with her hand. She couldn't heal the wound for him, but she could stop the bleeding.

"And so do you, Francisco."

Miracles weren't passive things. They demanded a certain amount of performance, a smidgen of spectacle, and no small amount of hope. It didn't need to be a show, but it did need to be something. The string of code came together in her thoughts, the command rendered in real time. The blood only flowed because of code. He only bled because of protocol.

Cindira rewrote them both.

Francisco's eyes watered. He looked down at her working, took in with awe the way the blood bleached itself before becoming dust and floating away on an unfelt breeze. His hand reached up to her cheek.

"Please, stop," he said. "I was on the same path as Kaylie. I would have destroyed this world. I'm not worthy of ruling."

She tightened her grip on the prince's hand and pulled his body into her lap. "The very fact that you've realized you're not worthy is the first step to making yourself the king Gaia needs."

"King? But I'm only a..."

"Shhh."

Cindira pressed her fingers against Francisco's lips to silence him. He smiled, bringing his hand to hers, pulling it to his lips and pushing a kiss into her palm. For a moment, experience told her to pull back. Every romantic advance she'd received in her life had been more about who her mother had been or her family was. When the potential suitor found out that the relationships only ran name-deep, they ran. But Francisco knew her not as Omala's daughter or the only child of Plaxis's CEO. He knew her. He was kissing her. And, somehow, she felt she knew him.

Francisco's eyes shone as her hand curved around his chin and her fingertips settled on the apple of his cheek. Then, he asked the very same question that she was thinking. "Now what?"

Cindira let her giddy smile fade. She lifted her eyes to where Kaylie had at last realized that she was only screaming into a vacuum. She'd grown still, but not complacent. Murder was in her eyes. Cindira didn't doubt for a moment that it was also in her stepsister's heart.

The banging at the door, silent for a small space, resumed again.

"Your Majesty!" The voice was unfamiliar to her ears, but it held both age and the same accented English as Francisco's.

"Francisco, are you okay? Whoever you are, you'll pay for this. Harm one hair on his head and you'll pay—"

In a single instant, Cindira gathered herself to her feet, closed her eyes, and tried to form the code. Before, she had only ever changed small things. Suspended gravity in a tiny bubble, made something change color, opened a locked door... But now there were so many things to alter, so much she wanted to do all at once. She wanted to not only remake this vreal; she wanted to merge it. She needed to bring it all together.

"It's... too... much."

Her stilted words bore evidence of the strain of it all. So much work, and she was just one little person. She felt a warm hand wrap around hers, and opened one eye enough to see Laporte beside her, the sincerity of his smile so uncustomary for a botic.

"You're not alone. I'm here for you. Let me take some of the burden."

"How?"

"Like I said..." His hand tightened. "Release the code."

Could it be that simple? Had everything that been happening to Gaia—the bombings and the damage that couldn't be healed— because she'd grown so protective of her mother's treasured programming language? Was she holding it back from everyone by holding it back from herself?

Cindira turned to the prince and offered him her free hand. "Help me."

"But I'm weak."

"No, you're not." She pulled out the threads of the world and rewove them, and in time, the prince's injuries—not just the visual representation of them—lifted. "This is our world, Francisco. No one can hurt you here without your permission. The only weapons they have are the ones you allow to exist, and the only injury the one you choose to carry with you all on your own."

Francisco's tensions eased, as though he was settling back into his own being and reassessing its parameters. But while the body might be strong, the mind still clung to torment. He rose, inspecting himself with quickening movements and dwindling doubt.

"You... you healed me."

"No, the code healed you, just like it hurt you." She shook her hand again. "Please, Francisco, my body in the real is in a very dangerous place. I could be knocked out of her at any moment... or worse."

She wished she knew if the shoes were on her feet, or if she was still just riding Kaylie's jack. Her stepsister, of course, was connected with the jackpod; losing the shoes in the real or the vreal wouldn't have any effect on her.

With a nod and lopsided grin, Francisco placed his hand into hers.

And something changed.

Not just code, even though she felt it flow into her and around her before pouring out into the vreal. Not just an ease in her heart, as she felt the connection to the vreal strengthen. There was something else, something... familiar. And it was all from Francisco's touch.

And though Cindira didn't quite understand how, she knew he was like her. Francisco could see the underpinnings of the vreal. He could call to them. That meant he could change them too.

All around, furniture became flowers, walls became air, and the massive palace that had defined the Kingdom's landscape dissolved. They were left then, the seven of them, standing in a field of long green grass. In the distance, the sun hugged the horizon. Was it rising or setting? Neither. Both. This world didn't need to conform to the ways of time. Perhaps inside of an arc over the sky, in this new world they'd make, the sun would revolve around the rim of creation. Whether it was coming or going would be for each person to decide.

And then, as suddenly as it settled, everything went red.

Cindira fell to her knees as pain shot through every fiber of her being. Francisco's hand slipped from hers. In the distance, the landscape blurred, as did the people dotting it. Johanna was the first to disappear, followed a moment later by Kaylie. Across what had been the richly appointed parlor, now nothing more than a field of swaying grasses and purple flowers remained, two Andalusian men looked on with screwed-up expressions before they, too, blinked out of being. Nearer, Laporte kept his clarity, but what had been a smile turned into a frown. Then, he too vanished.

Francisco remained.

"Cindira, what's wrong?"

Everything. She wanted to tell him. The pain encompassed every molecule, as though she'd been plugged into an electric socket like some kind of botic that needed charging. Her mouth clenched, blocking any attempt at speaking. This time when Francisco put his hand to her cheek, his mouth moved, but her ears heard nothing. She closed her eyes, trying to block the pain. It didn't work.

It was getting worse.

She was fading.

She was gone.

TWENTY-EIGHT

SEVENTY BEATS PER MINUTE, give or take. The data stream pulled it, twisted it, measured it. Blood pressure? Regular. Need for alarm? No. Suggested treatment? Further rest and a steady jack stream. She would wake up, though. If she chose to.

The voices grew quiet.

The room grew warm.

It wasn't if she was in a hospital; it was which one. But all it took was a few fingers to the forehead to tell her. St. Dymphna's, the hospice for the virtual-world addicted. And she was jacked in. Or at least, she was hooked up to one of their modified jackpods-slash-beds.

But as Cindira sat up, doing her best to fight an underlying sense of disorientation, she saw she was, in fact, not. White sheets, barren floors, and a framed print on the opposite wall showing a little blonde girl leaning seated on the ground, eating an apple and leaning against the trunk of a mighty tree. A monitor at the bedside displayed a list of her vitals, but she'd never had a gift for the medical arts and had no idea what any of it meant. All the text was green or blue, which she took to mean nothing bad. It would be red otherwise, wouldn't it?

A lone guest chair stood in the corner of the room, and in it, a man had twisted himself into an odd arrangement of arms and legs while attempting to sleep. With black hair, a handsome face, and his white suit visible wrinkled, he still presented a lovely sight. Cindira hated to rouse him, but surely the Prince of Gaia wasn't sleeping in her hospital room just to give her something pleasant to look at.

"Your Majesty?"

Francisco didn't budge, didn't twitch. He did snore once, which flexed her heart in a way that was difficult to understand.

"Your Highness?" She spoke a little louder this time, pushing fisted palms into the mattress and pushing herself up to a seated position. One thing became clear: Cindira wasn't in any pain. Whatever had happened to her after she'd passed out back in Gaia, she hadn't been injured.

Across the room, the door to the hall opened. The slender nurse wearing a starched white uniform pushed a cart with a squeaky wheel. A medical instrument, Cindira thought, until the cart came to a rest next to her bed, revealing that its contents consisted of three tea cups with saucers, a sugar and creamer set, and a petite pot of tea.

"I knew St. Dymphna's was about comforting, but I didn't know that included Darjeeling."

The nurse kept her face down as she grabbed one of the saucers and cups. "How do you know it's Darjeeling, mera pyaar?"

"I recognize the scent. My mother always—" She stopped, her hand suspended in the air as she reached out to take the cup. "What did you call me?"

"I called you mera pyaar. Or have you forgotten that after all these years?"

It was a good thing she hadn't taken the tea. If she had, she would have dropped it on the ground.

"Mother?"

The lines of Omala Grover's face had not deepened an inch in fifteen years. Still the serious black eyes. Still the long, lustrous black hair, even if now it was coiled into a severe bun. Still the slightest hint of a smirk that even the Mona Lisa would commend. The VAPOR was the spitting image of the woman who had kissed Cindira as she laid down to bed before later slipping under the waves. It was the same night that the Kingdom was announced to the world.

But if this was the vreal—and Cindira was very much beginning to suspect that it was—then it didn't mean it was her mother. Her mother was dead. This impostor could be anyone, and she knew that from experience. Not a month ago, Cindira herself had taken a shot at being Omala, walking around the Kingdom in her avatar. This was just someone doing the same thing. Maybe it was even a figment of her own imagination. Yes, that had to be it! Cindira had released the code, and without constraint, her subconscious mind must have manifested a VAPOR to play the part.

"You are probably upset with me that I didn't reveal myself to you before now," Omala began, setting the tea back down on the cart. "But believe me, I have been watching, and where I could, I have helped."

"You're not real."

It was presented as truth, not an accusation.

The sideways grin Omala had seldom worn evened out. "No, but I am vreal. And I hope you can accept me for what I am now, and what I am not. Just as I must learn to accept you not as my child, but as... well, something you have yet to figure out."

Another possibility opened up in her thoughts. One that should scare her, but for some reason, didn't. "Am I dead?"

"Only if you choose to be."

Well, that wasn't the answer she was expecting, and it certainly wasn't one she knew how to respond to. Cindira whipped back her blanket and took to her feet, rounding the foot of the bed and coming face to face with... whatever this was.

"What about Francisco?" She pointed to where the prince slept through the conversation. "Is he dead?"

"Oh, no, Paco is very much alive. Thanks to you, of course. But he might change his mind on that, depending on what you decide."

"I've never been a fan of riddles. I like data and numbers and facts, so how about you tell me plainly who you are and what in the hell you're talking about?"

"Language, Cindira!"

She jerked back at the tone. A VAPOR could look like her mother. Someone who knew her might even mimic Omala's mannerisms. But no one—no one—could recreate what a young Cindira had thought of as "the look of my impending doom."

Suddenly, she felt all of thirteen again and just as certain and as clueless about the world she lived in. "You really are my mother."

Rather than smile, which would have been welcome, Omala grimaced. "I see you haven't outgrown your stubbornness." She crossed her arms over her chest and huffed. "You get that from your father."

"I think I get a bit of it from you. Especially since most people who die, stay dead." Was this really what they were going to talk about? "No, this can't be. I kissed your cheek at the funeral. I watched them put your body on the pyre. I visit your ashes over at your memorial in Berkeley every year on your birthday. And, you're, what..." She hesitated. Putting it forward might be the fastest way to cut down her hopes. "You're alive?"

Cindira pushed fingers into her temples as though that would stabilize the room and stop it from spinning too. Suddenly, her knees turned to jelly, her stomach sank into her toes. For half her life, she'd been alone. An orphan in every way that mattered. A dead mother, an absent father who had moved on to his newer, ready-to-wear, picture-perfect family. Comfort came only from the arms of a nanny and the affection of a few close friends. It had always been enough to survive, but she'd always longed for the one person who'd allowed her to thrive. Now she was here, but it all seemed too good to be true.

"I don't understand what's going on."

"Then I will explain to you. No riddles, only facts." Her mother patted the edge of the hospital bed. "You can stand if you wish, but I really wouldn't suggest it."

In the corner, the prince let out a boisterous snore before shifting in his seat, arranging himself in another impressive position. On some plane, they must have occupied the same space. Nonetheless, Francisco slept on, oblivious to the miracle beside him.

Cindira turned her attention back to her mother, who again held out the cup. This time, the temptation for its comfort won out. Cindira took the tea, and settled on the edge of the bed, noting as she drank that her mother no longer wore the stiff, clinical nurse uniform, but her more traditional faded jeans and purple crushed cotton top.

"This"—Omala ran a hand from her face, down the length of her body—" is a copy of what I was. I am your mother, but I am not the woman who died. I am the version of her that was uploaded a few days before I drowned."

"You're like Bas and Harper."

Omala nodded. "Very much like them. The machine Kaylie used to get here, the one whose connection you so intelligently hijacked and rode into the vreal on... That was based on Harper's invention, and it's what allowed me and later Bas and I to upload our full consciousnesses into the vreal. In fact, leading up to my death, I backed up myself every week. So while I do not have the memories of my last few days on Earth, I have every moment before it, and I have every moment that I've spent here in the vreal since."

"So, you've been here the whole time. You..."

Heated tears stung, but not as much as the truth. Cindira pressed a finger to the corner of her eye, swiping away the evidence. When she choked down a gulp of air, she felt the pain burn inside.

"Why didn't you tell me? I had a comque, an inbox... Hell, if you're embedded in the Plaxis servers, you could have pushed a message directly to my terminal in the Kitchens. Why didn't you try to reach out to me?"

"When you were young, it was because I couldn't yet entrust you with the secret of how it came to be. When you got older, it was because I was waiting to tell you in person."

"In person?" How would that be possible? Only then, Cindira understood what her mother meant, and why it hadn't happened. "Meaning, in the vreal. But I didn't jack into the vreal after you died until last month."

A slow single nod, after which Omala kept her chin down. "I could never be certain others wouldn't see. In here, I can pull and push code in every direction. I've even continued to develop it in the safety of Harper and Bas's pumpkin. But no matter my power in the vreal, the real still comes with a thousand eyes and ears over which I'm powerless."

"But when I showed up at our old apartment on the edge of Gaia, you just laid there and did nothing. If you had been waiting for me so desperately, why didn't you talk to me?"

"That was my avatar, a shell for my mind when I still existed only in the real. But I was there, watching."

The silence grew heavy between them until Cindira couldn't take it. "And?"

"And..." For the first time since arriving, her mother's words held a hesitant, uncertain tone. Cindira wasn't sure if what followed was an explanation, or Omala rationalizing to herself. "If I had made myself known in that moment, you never would have gone to the palace. You never would have found out the truth about your father or saved the prince."

Cindira balanced her forehead on the fingertips of one hand and sighed. "When I was trying to get away from the ball that night, someone or something helped me. Laporte called it my fairy godmother. Bas and Mr. Chen talked about the same thing. Was that you?"

"Yes." No qualifications, no explanations. Instead, Omala continued, rushing forward, laying a hand on her daughter's arm. "I never would have let any permanent harm come to you, but I also couldn't keep you from making mistakes and running in the wrong direction. Without the struggle, the victory is meaningless. Without the journey, the destination holds no value."

"St. Dymphna's isn't exactly the destination I was after." Cindira looked around once, thought, then stated the obvious truth: "But this isn't St. Dymphna's."

"It is a very accurate recreation of it, really quite an amazing feat of spontaneous coding, but no, it isn't."

Cindira laughed once at herself. "So this is what my subconscious mind came up with, huh? A chiphead hospital."

In her mind's eye, she could imagine Scotia chastising her. Vreal Addictive Disorder. But Scotia wasn't here wherever here truly was. And frankly, wherever she truly was. Who knew what had happened to her body?

"Actually, you didn't make this." Omala pointed across the way to where a bead of saliva was running down the sleeping Francisco's chin from his gaping mouth. "He did."

"Francisco... made this?"

Cindira put the tea back on the tray and got to her feet, crossing the room to stand beside the prince. She examined him with new eyes, from top to bottom, and found something very curious she hadn't noticed before. The prince had a new pair of shoes.

Or, more appropriately, glass slippers.

Suddenly, she became aware of her own feet, and that they were bare. "I lost them... to Francisco? After all that work to get them back, he took them from me?"

"Only because I told him to. He wanted a way he could be here when you awoke. Mind, I have decided to dull his ears for a few moments." Her mother looked on dotingly. "Besides, pyar beti, you won't need the slippers anymore."

And that's when she remembered one of the cryptic things her mother had said.

Am I dead?

Only if you choose to be.

And the truth became obvious to her. "I'm not me. This is a copy of me, made by that modified jackpod, talking to a copy of you. We're two souls together, but twice removed."

Omala clicked her tongue. "What a silly thing to say. Of course you are you," she rebuked. "You are more you than you have been in a very long time." Then, her eyes turned to the floor, she added, "If that's what you wish to be."

Cindira bit her bottom lip and nodded. "After all that, and I died."

"Not died. You're in a coma. One, I think, you're in by choice," Omala said. "You saved the prince and helped Francisco to realize that his own guardian and attaché was plotting his murder. And you revealed that Kaylie Fife kidnapped and tortured your father, and then left him to die. They're now reaping the punishment of their actions, being brought up on charges in both realms. But you had to step into the light to allow that. You're still the woman who hacked into a secured system, kidnapped the monarch at knifepoint, and brought the Plaxis empire to its knees. If you return, there will be consequences to face, and every spotlight will be on you. I think on a subconscious level, you're taking refuge here."

Cindira took in the shape of Francisco's face from her vantage. He was nice to look at, it was a face she could grow accustomed to. "Francisco might issue me a pardon."

"He might, for the actions taken against him and in the vreal, but he doesn't have the authority to pardon the crimes allegedly committed in the real."

"And what is it you're proposing, then?" She had a feeling she already knew, but she wanted to hear her mother say it.

"You can live on here in the vreal alone."

Alone. Cindira bit her bottom lip. She knew what Omala meant, and it wasn't any allusion to solitude. But that's what it would amount to. Oh, sure, she'd have her mother. She might even grow to be friends with Bas and Harper and their... was it three children or two? But that would be true even if she did return to the real. The vreal would always be there, a jackpod or a pair of silicone slippers away. But unless she had Scotia and Warren and Talia and... and, yes, Francisco, what was the point?

Then again, what was the point of returning and living the rest of her days in a jail cell?

Unless, that was, she wouldn't. There was still one card she had left to play, but she'd need help to play it.

If they never look your way, they never see you coming.

Cindira spun, heading for the door. "I've worked too hard to get here, and I'm not going to let it be taken away from me for having done the right thing. But I'll be back soon. And when I am, you and I will have a lot of catching up to do. I hope you understand, Mom, that I have to do this."

Omala grinned. "You wouldn't be my girl if you didn't."

TWENTY-NINE

THE PRINCE AWOKE WITH a start to find an empty hospital bed and a cup full of tea at the ready.

Blinking away his confusion, Francisco took what Omala offered, including the sideways grin.

"I was sleeping." A statement of fact, but one that still perplexed him. "I thought losing consciousness for any reason was an automatic jack-out action. How does one sleep in the vreal?"

"Paco, you're about to learn that there are many things you'll be able to do in the vreal that you couldn't do before. Sleep is, perhaps, the least interesting of them." Omala sat down on the edge of the hospital bed. "You have the shoes on and you're sleeping in the real."

The shoes, the ones that they'd found on Cindira Tieg's body when his security people, aided by Authority, had stormed the Kitchens of Plaxis HQ. To his surprise, and for reasons he couldn't really explain, he'd slipped them on when he was back at the Palace of Fine Arts. Maybe because they had been hers. Maybe because they were the only connection he had with a woman who had saved his life twice and whose life now hung in the balance. The soft silicone shell wrapped easily around his foot. No sooner had he thought about what their purpose may be than he blinked... and found himself sitting on a bench in Gaia's Capital City. Only, where the city gates had stood, the cybercosntruct the edge of the vreal, now there were fields, hills, mountains... In the distance, he swore he even saw a tower rising against the backdrop of a setting sun.

The prince tried to grasp the situation. "So I'm dreaming?"

"In a manner, yes. And yet, no."

He shook off her half-answer. He had a feeling asking Omala to elaborate would only leave him more confused. Instead, he took a sip of the tea. The flavor hit the back of his palate like a memory. A cool night in the palace, the chill as much in his bones as in the air, and his father bringing a steaming mug to him. It had smelled of flowers and honey and tasted like comfort. Manzanilla, his father had said, like your mother used to make when you were little and had a touch of something.

"And Cindira?" Worried eyes chased to the empty hospital bed on which Omala sat. "Is she..."

"Here?" Omala sounded somewhat disappointed. "She was, and she will be. For now, I think she's gone to seek out Johanna."

Was she crazy? Johanna Tieg was a monster. He'd always thought she was a... well, there was no polite term for it. But now that it seemed she'd joined the conspiracy against his throne, even if there was still the question of whether she did so willingly or if she'd been coerced. Cindira was brilliant, but she wasn't the kind of person who could deal with a snake like Johanna and come out unscathed.

"I have to go to her. I have to help."

"Why, Paco?"

He stopped himself halfway out of the chair. "Sorry?"

"I said why," Omala repeated. "Why do you have to help?"

"Because I love her."

The words came out so easily, so plainly, and yet even he was surprised by them. It didn't make any sense. He barely knew the woman. He'd only met her twice. As an adult, anyway. He didn't know what her favorite book was, what food she liked to eat, what position she took when she slept. He didn't even know if she looked in the real like she had in the vreal, until he'd helped lift her comatose body out of the jackpod in the Plaxis Kitchen and confirmed it. But something deep within him, something almost primal, told him she was the one.

Even so, he didn't want to sound—or more importantly, be—crazy. "At least, I feel like I might grow to love her."

"There are reasons I have tried to bring the two of you together, not the least of which is because I suspected this might be true."

Omala smirked in a self-satisfied way. "I may have wasted my time in life developing vreal technologies. Perhaps I should have been a matchmaker. Harper and Bas seem very happy."

The prince lowered himself back into the chair. "Who?"

Omala cleared her expression and batted the air with an open hand. "Never mind. You'll likely meet them, eventually."

Never one to miss an implication, Francisco turned back to the other part of her comments. "Are there other reasons you brought us together?"

"Of course, because you and she both carried the nanites in your blood that would allow you to use the shoes and, more importantly, access the source code. Years ago, when your family hosted Rex and me, that was the research we were undertaking. We were looking for a way to not only allow the mind to travel to the vreal, but for the consciousness to transport there permanently. When your palace was run over, I pulled you aside and gave you an inoculation. Do you remember that? I told you in case the enemy had any biological weapons, but it was the nanites. In case we didn't get away, I wanted my technology to live on with someone else."

The prince pressed his hand against the meat of his upper arm. "I'd forgotten about that."

"The shoes in the real are necessary to ground you to the outside world, but the nanites

themselves are what do the trick," she went on unprompted. "That's why you could pick up the shoes. It's also why Cindira could generate inside the vreal without an avatar to host her. The two of you don't so much jack into the vreal as simultaneously exist in it. It's always been that way since you were children. This"—she motioned vaguely around them—"has always been here for you. For years, she didn't want it, and for even longer, you didn't understand it. Now, though, I think you both have the perspective to make it work."

"Make what work?" He pulled himself to the edge of the chair. "Are you talking about Gaia? The Kingdom? Our love affair?"

"Yes."

Like they were all-in-one the same thing.

A million thoughts ran through his head, none of them in the same direction. He felt somehow bamboozled, like his life had not been his own after all. Larger forces had set him on a path not entirely of his own making. But if Cindira was on that path beside him... It didn't make any sense, how intense the feelings were, but that didn't mean they should be ignored.

He got to his feet and marched toward the hospital room door. "I will be there for her, in whatever way she needs me, but I can't let her take on Johanna Tieg alone."

"And I will always be here for the two of you." Omala herself appeared at the door and held it open. "All you need to do is jack in."

THIRTY

NOT SO LONG AGO, CINDIRA had stood in the same spot, feeling like a mouse on her way to confront a lioness. That day, her stepmother had given her a veiled ultimatum: help find her father and free the source code or lose them both. Cindira had agreed on the surface but kept faith that she'd achieve her goal without giving Johanna reign over the consequences.

"Cindira?" Surprise colored Johanna's tone, reenforced by a lifted eyebrow and stiff limbs. "I thought you were…"

"Arrested? Gone? No longer a problem?"

Johanna took a step back. "In a coma."

The coder took a seat across the desk and relaxed back into the chair. "I decided to get over it."

"Oh, well, good. I'm glad you're feeling better." Johanna Tieg was a woman known for her composure. She had intimidated kings and critics alike. Now she was the one shaking. "I hear you're in some legal trouble. Plaxis can't defend you, of course, but I'm sure your father would have wanted me to offer you the services of our family lawyer. If you want to swing by the house tonight, we can discuss it. But for the moment, I'll have to ask you to leave. In case you forgot, you were fired."

"No, I haven't forgotten." But she did now admire the tactic, even if she'd been the victim. Not only was orchestrating a public firing a couth way to get Cindira off the radar and let her work in the shadows, it had also provided Johanna with a convenient method to keep her out of the picture once the task was done and Rex found. "I've come to express my sympathies."

"I suppose you expect me to do the same. But we both know you didn't really care for your father, did you? If you had, you would have found him alive."

"I'm not the one who killed him. And of course I care for my father. I've always loved him, even when he forgot I existed. But I'm not talking about him. I'm talking about Kaylie and Cade."

Johanna sat back in her own chair, tapping a fingernail on the glass desk. "Kaylie and Cade aren't dead. They've just been arrested. Cade insists he didn't have anything to do with it. Maybe he's telling the truth. Maybe not. I'm waited to see what Authority's investigation turns up. I hear that attaché of Francisco's was indicted."

Cindira softened her features. "And as I've said, I'm sorry for your loss."

Johanna's eyes shot daggers. "Somehow I don't think that's true."

"Of course, it's true. Wouldn't I, of all people, know what it's like to lose someone you love so dearly?" She gathered herself to the front of her chair and laid a gloved hand on the edge of the glass table. "Whether that's because they lost their lives or you just lost the idea of who they really were, your suffering must be overwhelming."

"Then, I suppose..." Emotions danced in Johanna's eyes, even as she kept her face neutral. Finally, she picked up her datapad and attempted to get back to work. "Thank you for your visit, but I have to manage the fallout from the last few days. The Kingdom is barely functional. Gaia's in disarray. Pumpkins are growing new vines with no one programming them. This company stands on the precipice of its own destruction thanks to what you did in there, so if you'd please leave, I need to fix it."

Cindira let the silence linger for a moment. "Actually, Johanna, I'm going to stay, and I'm going to fix it."

The datapad lowered as wide eyes looked up. "Excuse me?"

"Gaia." Cindira motioned around the room. "The Kingdom. I'm going to fix them. In fact, I'm the only one who can."

"Is that supposed to be a threat?" Johanna's mouth dropped open as if to speak, before closing with a manufactured smirk. "Don't play this game, little girl. You released the code. It's out there. My people are indexing Purusha Prime as quickly as they can. Now, you might be the best coder of your generation. You may even be the best who's ever lived. But this isn't the vreal, and you can't recode the truth out here. Rex is dead. They found his body right where Kaylie confessed to it being. Which means Plaxis now belongs solely to me. And as the owner, I'm telling you to get out."

"And I'm saying no. Because you owe me."

"I owe you?" Johanna slammed the datapad down. With a ferocious crick, the table spiderwebbed. "I just lost my husband and my daughter, at least in any way that really matters. I may also lose my son before all of this is done. After all I've done for you for the last fifteen years, do you really have so little compassion for me?"

"More than you know. Certainly more than you deserve."

Johanna shot to her feet and pressed the button on her call box. "Willa, get security in here." Then, without giving Cindira a chance to rise on her own, the blonde matriarch rounded the desk and pulled up her unwanted guest by the jacket sleeve. "If you want to come to your father's memorial service next week, I won't object. But if you ever enter this building or come anywhere near me again, I will make sure you end up in a very tiny cell with the smallest degree of sunlight. I have enough logs of your illegal hacking to put you away for ten years easily. Now get out."

Cindira freed herself from Johanna's grip. She took a leisurely stroll in silence across the room, stopping at Johanna's desk and fixing her eyes out on the horizon. Her voice was as serene as the bay waters off in the distance. "I have proof that you murdered my mother."

"Oh, really?" Johanna guffawed, marching to where Cindira stood and confronting her. "You've always had quite an imagination, but you've really gone above and beyond this time. Cindira, your mother slipped off a pier and drowned. It was tragic, but that's what happened."

She lifted a knowing smile and pushed a finger on the edge

of Johanna's table. "Only, she didn't just slip off, did she?" The cracks creaked, they stretched out across the length and width of the desktop. "She was pushed, just in time for the very boat that was coming to pick her up to hit her and knock her out."

"An interesting story, and the last one you'll ever have the chance to tell, if you don't shut up."

Cindira slid around the desk, placing herself behind it. "But you confessed to it.."

Blood vessels in Johanna's bulging eyes made her a fearsome sight. She raised one hand, her hair flaring as her head jerked in time with her boiling words. "What are you talking about? Confessed to what?!"

And thus, the cracks begin to show. "So you didn't admit to the bandit that you killed Omala Grover?"

Johanna's hand dropped to her side. She stumbled back.

"I thought you might have forgotten about that." Push a little harder. "And since you now know I was the one disguised as my mother that night, you must now realize that you admitted it to me."

"And so what?" Johanna took a moment to clear her throat before speaking confident words with a cracking voice. "There's no proof of it. No evidence. You couldn't even have a recording of my confession if you had known I was going to make it. We don't allow audio or video archiving of anything that happens inside the Kingdom, so it would just be your word against mine."

At the back of the room, the door opened. The three men and one woman dressed in black suits and wearing ear pieces aligned themselves, hands folded in front of them, soldiers presenting. They awaited orders with practiced patience.

Johanna motioned them forward. "Ah, there you are," she said. "Please escort this trespasser from the building and make sure the lobby staff knows she's to never enter any Plaxis property again. Farewell, Cindira. Go in peace but do fucking go."

Security didn't move.

Johanna blinked her fiercest, most threatening glare. "Didn't you hear me? I said remove her."

Finally, one of the beefy men took a step forward. "Ms. Tieg, would you like this woman removed from your office?"

"Yes, I—" "If you wouldn't mind, Clarence."

The two women exchanged glances after talking over each other.

Johanna had no words. She stood there for a moment, mouth gaping, closing, gaping, as she took turns wheeling on Cindira then the security staff.

"Yes, I want her gone, Clarence," she said in a tone that made it clear the name was a revelation to her. "Now do you goddamned job and take Cindira out of here."

Clarence leaned to the side, speaking around Johanna. "Ms. Tieg?"

"But I'm Ms. Tieg. I'm in charge of this—"

Cindira grinned at her stepmother. "Kaylie and you both thought my father sent the source code into that warehouse. He didn't. But one thing he managed to do before his body stopped functioning in the lab your daughter locked him in was to amend his will."

She didn't mention the part about her father's survival. Turned out Rex wasn't so eager to see his "Sweet Jo" after discovering she'd murdered his ex.

"Did you know you can do that in Andalusia without a witness?" Cindira continued. "I didn't. Dad didn't, but... let's just say he had a fairy godmother helping him out with some details of his situation. And, well..." Cindira gave one last jab at the desk. "Plaxis is mine."

And with a shatter, the table cascaded across the floor in a thousand tiny, sharp pieces.

REPORTS WERE THAT JOHANNA kicked and screamed the entire elevator ride down, and even tried to bite off the ear of the brave security agent who stuffed her into the transport to take her home. Cindira's lawyer had advised her that as the sole beneficiary of her father's estate, she could easily purchase the Tieg mansion a thousand times over and send Johanna packing. Cindira wouldn't hear of it. She knew what it was like to live a life never knowing the feeling of home, and a house without love was more of a prison. There was no one there now. Asla was safe in Scotland. The rest of the household staff, officially employees of Plaxis, were reassigned to other properties. Who knew if Kaylie would ever see the outside of a prison cell.

Cade had disappeared. No was certain why, but it was a mystery no one seemed eager to solve either.

Learning the truth, Rex had taken advantage of his anonymity and pursued a humbler path, one in which he didn't live with a murderer and the two children who'd conspired to kill him. Mr. Chen offered to keep him busy until he figured out his next steps. It was honest work. Most of the time, anyway. In any event, no longer running one of the world's biggest companies, he might finally have time to get to know the daughter he'd never allowed himself to grow too close to.

A knock on the door brought Cindira's eyes away from the custodial crew, sweeping up the last shards of glass from the floor. They wheeled their carts out just as she turned and found the very confused and weary expression of one Francisco Batista.

She mimicked a bow. "Your Majesty."

"You don't have to do that." Francisco put his hands up, crossing the office as the cleaning staff took their leave, shutting the door behind them as they did so. "I'm not royalty out here in the real. With all the stuff happening in the last two days, I may not be royalty anywhere for much longer. There were rumors running all around Gaia yesterday that there was to be a vote of no confidence in my reign after my vagrant overreach of power."

Her eyes went wide. "But you literally just saved Gaia from

being overthrown."

He laughed into his shoulder. "Except that I didn't. You did."

Cindira had never been reluctant to claim credit for her talents, even if others did their best to overlook them. She also believed, however, in giving others their due recognition. "No, I saved you. You saved Gaia."

"Don't you get it, Cindira? It's the same thing?" He kicked the floor under foot, his eyes turning to the ground. "I mean, I'm not that important. Not in the grand scheme of things. But the idea of Gaia is. If Kaylie and Carlos had been successful in killing me and taking over the vreal, then all the good your mother's creation has done would be destroyed. If war came back to the real, I don't think we could have rescued the planet from the edge of ruin a second time. What you did? It was about a lot more than Gaia."

She beamed. "Yesterday I was an unemployed coder. Today, Plaxis is mine and the prince is telling me I saved the world."

"I'm not sure about the world, but you saved me. And I'm not here as the prince."

The words died away as Francisco reached up, taking one of Cindira's hands in his and laying her right palm flat over his chest. The touch was so soft, the hands of a man who'd never known labor or long hours manipulating hardware. He ran tender fingertips over the calluses at the end of hers and sent a flicker of heat rushing through her body. Suddenly, the dynamic of the room had tipped, and it took her clarity with it. There was a buzz beneath her skin and a flutter in her chest.

He grinned in a way that confirmed he understood. Also, that it wasn't one-sided. But she wasn't ready to rush down that path blindly.

"What I feel for you," Cindira said, her voice shaky. "It doesn't make sense. How do I know it's real, or if it's just the nanites manipulating my biochemistry because, you know, an organism's primary mission is to seek other viable potential mates it thinks might have compatible and advantageous traits to pass on to their offspring?"

His face cracked into a smile. Francisco leaned forward, letting his forehead rest against hers. "I'm not asking for you to pass along traits to any offspring, Cindira. All I'm asking for is a chance to spend some time with you. I propose..." His palms slid into hers as he laced their fingers together. "... a ball. A show of strength and cohesion between Plaxis and Gaia, this time, without the part at the end where you hold a knife to my throat and kidnap me."

"Have you forgotten the kind of people who attend those balls? You'd be begging me to drag you out of there by the end of the night, knife or no."

He pulled back just enough for Cindira to see one eyebrow arch. "Would the queen of the Kingdom be so cruel to the prince of Gaia?"

She, the queen? In a certain way, Cindira supposed that was true now. Only, she wanted to be very clear about the way she intended to hold her position and approach her powers. "No, the princess of the Kingdom would not," she said. "Fine, I promise to restrain myself, but I can't make any guarantees on my mother's behalf. You know how Indian parents are about marrying off their daughters. She might go to extremes." She grinned. "Francisco, are you wearing the silicone slippers still?"

"I am." The prince laughed, his mouth so close to hers that Cindira could feel it as well as hear it. "Do you want to go to the vreal now? I heard you have the ability to ride someone else's jack just through touch?"

Well, didn't that open up a world of possibilities?

"Where to?" he continued. "Renaissance Florence or a Hawaiian beach or, hell, riding on the back of a camel crossing the Sahara?" He twisted her hand, using the hold to pull her closer. "Name the place, princesa, and I will take you there."

Cindira shook her head. "The only place I want to be right now is here with you."

She pressed her lips to his, savoring an experience so encompassing of every sensation, Cindira knew it was utterly and undeniably...

Real.

MEEKSOLOGY

RED CHRONICLES

Requited

Reluctant

Relinquished

Ravening

Rebellious

Righteous

RED ORIGINS

Beauty & the Betrayer

The Wolf & the Watcher

Red & the Restorer

ENTER THE KINGDOM

Court of Discontent

Freebird: An Enter the Kingdom side story novella

Mistress of Cinders

Isle of After

VAMPIRE SOVEREIGNS

Venice Dusk